3—

Seven Days in June

Howard Fast's Revolutionary War Novels

April Morning

*The Call of Fife and Drum: Three Novels
of the American Revolution*
The Unvanquished
Conceived in Liberty
The Proud and the Free
(published by Carol Publishing Group)

Citizen Tom Paine

The Crossing

The Hessian

Seven Days in June

Two Valleys

Seven Days in June

A Novel of the American Revolution

Howard Fast

A BIRCH LANE PRESS BOOK
Published by Carol Publishing Group

A Birch Lane Press Book
Published by Carol Publishing Group
Birch Lane Press is a registered trademark of Carol Communications, Inc.
Editorial Offices: 600 Madison Avenue, New York, N. Y. 10022
Sales and Distribution Offices: 120 Enterprise Avenue, Secaucus, N. J. 07094
In Canada: Canadian Manda Group, P. O. Box 920, Station U, Toronto, Ontario
    M8Z 5P9
Queries regarding rights and permissions should be addressed to Carol Publishing Group, 600
Madison Avenue, New York, N. Y. 10022

Carol Publishing Group books are available at special discounts for bulk
purchases, sale promotions, fund-raising, or educational purposes. Special
editions can be created to specifications. For details, contact Special
Sales Department, Carol Publishing Group, 120 Enterprise Avenue, Secaucus, N. J. 07094

Manufactured in the United States of America
10 9 8 7 6 5 4 3 2 1

Library of Congress Cataloging-in-Publication Data

Fast, Howard, 1914–
    Seven days in June : a novel of the American Revolution / by
Howard Fast.
        p.   cm.
    "A Birch Lane Press book."
    ISBN 1-55972-256-8
    1. United States—History—Revolution, 1775–1783—Fiction.
I. Title.
PS3511.A784S45   1994
813'.52—dc20
                                      94-20163
                                         CIP

For my wonderful wife
Bette Fast

On April 19, 1775, the first military encounter of the American Revolution took place on the village green at Lexington, Massachusetts, where a group of armed farmers contested the right of passage of British troops. The British regulars were on their way to Concord, a few miles distant, to destroy military supplies the Americans had stored there. A second battle took place at Concord, followed by a running fight as the British retreated to Boston, which they had occupied. For the next six weeks, American armed civilians and militiamen crowded the roads to Boston, until presently a loosely organized army of about fourteen thousand men held Boston under close siege.

The Major Characters

The American Officers
General Israel Putnam, commander of the Connecticut militia.
Colonel William Prescott, in command at Breed's Hill.
Major Thomas Knowlton, commanding the center at Breed's Hill.
Colonel John Stark, frontiersman, hero of the French and Indian War,
    commander of the New Hampshire Riflemen, in command of the
    left flank at Breed's Hill.
Major General Richard Gridley, engineer, in command of the redoubt.
Captain Abel Nutting, forward post at Breed's Hill.
Colonel Moses Little, in command of the Ipswich volunteers.

The American physicians
Dr. Joseph Warren
Dr. Albert Bones
Dr. Joseph Gonzales
Dr. Evan Feversham

The British officers
General Thomas Gage, nominally in command of the British forces in
Boston,
    but in fact superseded by William Howe.
General Sir William Howe, darling of the British Crown, asserting
command
    over Thomas Gage.
Major General Sir Henry Clinton
Major General John Burgoyne
Admiral Thomas Graves
Major John Pitcairn
Brigadier General Robert Pigot
Captain Joshua Loring
Major Leeroy Atkins

The Ladies
Prudence Hallsbury
Elizabeth Loring, wife of Joshua Loring.

For those readers who may express surprise at the coarse language used in some of the dialogue, may I explain that the expressions used here were common in the 18th century, and are to be found in any number of letters and manuscripts I have examined. I use them to heighten the reality of what has been bowdlerized in most writing of the time.

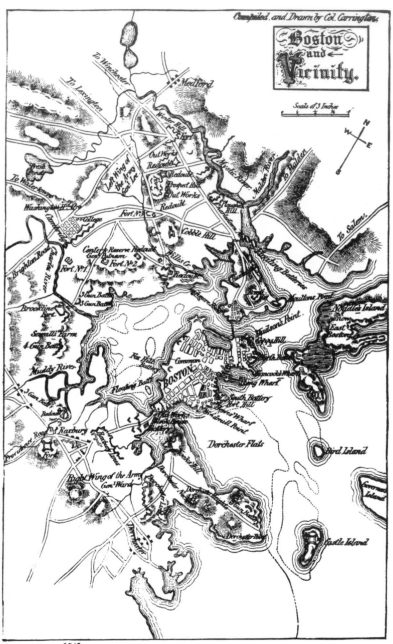

Compiled and Drawn by Col. Carrington.

Boston
and
Vicinity.

Scale of 3 Inches

THE
BATTLE OF BREEDS HILL,
OR
BUNKER HILL.

Compiled and Drawn by Col. Carrington.

▄▄▄▄ *British*
☐☐☐ *American*

Scale of 20 Rods.
20   40   60   80

Seven Days in June

June 12

Merton knew the rat; the rat knew Merton. For five months they had lived together in the stinking hold of the frigate, and during those five months they had measured and developed a healthy respect for each other. Merton had a commendable and profound knowledge of rats. They had shared living space with him since his memory began, on land as well as at sea. And the rat had also developed a commendable knowledge of Merton. The rat was very large, and Merton was small, only five feet two inches in height; they were both intelligent, ingenious, and agile. Merton simply had the advantage in being a man. As a man, he was determined to kill the rat. The rat, being a rat, was only determined to remain alive.

The rat was gray, with a white face and white paws, which identified him specifically and was finally his undoing, since it turned Merton's animosity against all rats into a single direction. Merton devised traps, poisoned bait, laid ambushes, and all of it failed. Finally, on the twelfth of June, in the year 1775, luck and the mysterious workings of doom coincided. The rat ventured onto the gun deck. Merton happened to have a marlinspike in his hand. He let go with the spike and caught the rat squarely and stunned him, which gave Merton a change to bash in the rat's head.

Dancing a small dance of victory, Merton held up the enormous rat for his shipmates to see. "Now if this ain't the biggest bleeding son of a bitch that ever lived, then I am a dick's udder! I said I'd get the bastard, and I got him!"

"You bloody well got him," they agreed.

"Weighs three pounds if he weighs an ounce."

"And what are you going to do with the little bastard, Merton?"

Merton smirked and stared from face to face at his grinning shipmates. "Now what am I going to do with him? And wouldn't you like to know?" Out with his knife. He gutted the animal, tore out its entrails, and flung them over the side into the water of Boston Harbor. Then, quickly and expertly, disregarding the pool of blood at his feet, he beheaded the rat and skinned it.

"Looks like a bleeding hare, don't it?"

"Looks like a rat to me."

"Cook it up and eat it, Merton. It'll taste better than rotten salt pork."

Merton wiped his knife on his pants and grinned.

"And get a bucket of water and wash down the deck," said the bosun.

"Ah, that I will, bosun. That I will."

His mates lost interest and wandered away. After he had washed down the deck, Merton took the rat's body into the galley. The cooks were at the bow fishing, the galley was empty except for a scullery boy, and Merton told him to keep a still tongue in his head. Grinning and chuckling, the scullery boy watched Merton butcher the rat and drop it into a pot of soup that was simmering for the officers' mess.

Few enough liked Merton. He had a mean, tortured, shrunken soul, and he lived a mean, tortured, shrunken life. The scullery boy hated him, and the captain's coxswain hated him, but since the scullery boy hated the captain as well, he waited until after the captain's dinner before he informed the coxswain of Merton's addition to the soup pot.

The coxswain communicated the news to the first officer, and Merton was duly reprimanded. He was bound to a mast to receive fifty lashes across his skinny back.

June 13

*T*he party of four men and two women had lunched with the captain of *Somerset,* a splendid frigate of sixty-four guns, and now they were on their way to the boat that would row them back to Boston when they paused to note the preparations for Merton's flogging. The first officer, bidding farewells for the captain, who was engaged elsewhere, would have hurried them by; but the tallest of the four, Sir William Howe, stayed him and remarked that this was the business of the rat—was it not?

"Case of one rat being punished for another rat—nothing the ladies should see."

"We ate rats in Germany," Sir Henry Clinton said, and one of the ladies, Patience Carter, a pretty widow of thirty or so, squealed with horror. Miss Ambleton, her companion, a plump, dull young lady, reacted not at all. "Not bad, either, done properly," Clinton went on. He knew he was being nasty and that it emerged out of his petulance with the two ladies. Childish behavior for a man of forty-five who was wretchedly lonely and wanted to be in love or what went for love or at least a pretense of love that would allow him to be amorous with a modicum of passion. The two ladies were dull and stupid and unattractive.

"Nothing the ladies should see," the first officer repeated.

A watch of twenty-two seamen was drawn up on the deck of the frigate to observe. There were two drummer boys and a piper. A large, fat, and brawny seaman, stripped to the waist, fondled a heavy bull-hide whip, and bound to the mast was Seaman Merton, no bigger than a child and as skinny as a plucked chicken. And over all, the warm and gentle June sun and a sky of pure blue.

Gen. Thomas Gage, fifty-four, by one year the eldest of the party of four and nominally the commander of the British forces in the port of Boston, served as host to the ladies and was also somewhat embarrassed by the situation. He was a rather simple-minded man slow in his perceptions, yet he felt that fifty lashes on the back of a skinny, undersized British seaman was not a sight and a tale that should be carried back to the town.

"Suppose we go now, gentlemen," he said to the others.

"Curious situation," Sir William observed. "Rat stew."

"Soup, sir," said the first officer.

"Tell you what," said the fourth man in the party, Gen. John Burgoyne—Gentleman Johnny, as they knew him—tall, slender, handsome, meticulously attired, a man who lived secretively inside himself, well hidden by his reputation as the gayest of blades, the most gallant gambler. He would bet on anything, and you make the odds. "Tell you what," he said—"a fiver says he can't live through fifty lashes. What about it, Clinton?"

Clinton frowned in distaste. Sir William Howe said, "Give me ten to five."

"Little faith in His Majesty's seaman."

"For heaven's sake," General Gage said, beginning a protest. Then he shook his head and asked the first officer to see the ladies to shore. Clinton noticed that they went reluctantly. He would have gone with them, but he could stand their company no longer. Anyway, he was curious.

"All right, Sir William," Burgoyne agreed. "A tenner to your five. Trouble is your bloody army background. If your brother were here, he would stand up for the guts and tenacity of an old seadog."

"Old seadog," Clinton muttered. "That skinny little bastard's no more than twenty years."

"Your humanity's admirable," Howe said. "I share your compassion, Sir Henry, but a ship's a ship. Discipline's discipline. You don't want to double that bet?" he asked Burgoyne.

"You're on."

The drums rolled, and the first lash fell, curling around Merton's back and leaving a red welt on the white flesh.

"Creative little bugger," said Burgoyne. "Imagine—a rat in the officers' soup."

The second lash, and then the third and the fourth and the fifth. A pattern of red lines appeared on the bony little back. At the tenth lash, Merton began to scream. At twenty-two lashes, he stopped screaming. At thirty lashes, the pattern of red lines disappeared from his back; it was a red, bubbling froth of meat, and he had lost consciousness. At forty-two lashes, the second officer signaled for the flogging to stop. He went over to Merton, lifted the seaman's head and then an eyelid.

"Cut him down. He's dead," the second officer said.

"Heart gave out," Howe said, accepting defeat. "Never know about a man's heart."

"Could we go now, gentlemen?" Clinton asked, an edge of anger and disgust in his voice.

When they were in the ship's boat and being rowed to shore, Gage pointed out that it was precisely such an incident as they had just witnessed that produced rage and resentment in the taverns and meeting places of Boston.

Burgoyne disagreed. "They are a stinking, narrow lot," he said. "In this time of enlightenment and understanding, they burn witches."

"Enlightenment and understanding," Clinton reflected.

"They have stopped burning witches," Howe said.

"Recently."

"I don't think they give two damns about a seaman's punishment," Howe continued. "Use it for agitation—no doubt. I wouldn't put it beyond Sam Adams and his crowd. But as far as compassion is concerned—*pah!*"

"We have compassion," said Sir Henry Clinton.

"The trouble with you, Clinton, is that you're a bloody Continental yourself. Too much time in America."

Clinton shook his head and remained silent. He had closed his eyes and given over his body to the sway of the boat. He felt sick and empty and dirty, and he tried to comfort himself by pretending that the salt spray in his face was an anointment of some sort, some holy liquid whose secret God shared with Britain, as in the past he had shared it with other nations that made the sea their wall and salvation. Merton was a single skinny little cockney whose life or death made no difference whatsoever, and this was not the first time, not even the fiftieth time, Clinton had seen a man flogged and often enough flogged to death.

Gage, on the other hand, was more deeply troubled. He had lived twenty years in America, married to the daughter of a wealthy Jersey landowner, and he had come to think of himself, at least in part, as a colonial. Here was his home, and here he had a wide circle of friends, Tories most of them, but enough of the Puritan bent to have adopted some of their egalitarian notions. He had fought alongside the Americans during Braddock's campaign, and he had more respect for their fighting ability than either Howe or Burgoyne. He knew that the story of the whipping of Seaman Merton would soon be all over Boston, and he could picture Presbyterian and Congregational clerics busily scribbling sermons on the subject of British brutality and disregard for human life, while Sam Adams applied himself to the publication of another fiery pamphlet.

Like Clinton, he would have preferred that the punishment had been less severe—at least while the fleet was in the port of Boston.

The boat touched the dock, and Sir William Howe exploded, "Goddamn it to hell, I had the company of a lady today, and I clean forgot it!"

"Do you ever think of anything else?" Burgoyne asked.

"Not when I am off duty, laddy. I'll see you gentlemen." Then he hurried down the street, half-running.

"Amazing man," said Burgoyne. "Utterly preoccupied with fucking. He literally exists for it. Here in Boston just a fortnight or so and he knows every lady available."

"It's not the screwing," Clinton said. "He wants to be loved, Johnny. We all do."

"Turned Christian?" Burgoyne grinned, and Gage said, why don't they amble along to his place and have some tea and some sensible talk about what was to be done?

"I'll have something stronger than tea," said Clinton.

They walked on, a squad of Gage's troops marching six on either side, accompanying them through the almost deserted city of Boston. Clinton wondered how many had gone and how many were left. He saw only two civilians, and they were hurriedly on their way.

"One in three, perhaps," said Gage. "The others have taken off. They have relatives everywhere. They're a close-knit lot."

"And what's left are loyal?"

"You tell me."

"They bolt their doors and stay inside," Burgoyne said. "I'd root them out, and damned if I wouldn't make them declare themselves!"

"To what end?" Gage asked tiredly. "It's not a war and it's not a peace, and I can't say that I know what it is."

"If we're going to talk seriously," Clinton said, "and it's high time that we did, we'll want our happy lad Howe with us, won't we? Why the devil can't he do his fornicating at night."

"Because he's screwing a lady called Amanda Blaketon whose husband spends his days plotting with the rebels and his nights at home."

"Why not arrest him and make it easy for Sir William?"

"For what? For being her husband?" Clinton asked.

"Plotting with the rebels," Burgoyne suggested.

"Good heavens, Johnny, where do I start, and where do I finish? You really have no idea. It's not a simple question of loyalty or disloyalty. They regard themselves as proper Englishmen."

"Proper Englishmen?" Gage wondered aloud.

"The column into Concord botched it. I know that."

"They shot the very hell out of us. Proper Englishmen be damned!" Gage said.

"Then you tell me, dear fellow. Do we start a war?"

"It is a war," Burgoyne snapped.

"It's not a war," Clinton said sourly.

"My business is war. That's why I was sent here," said Burgoyne. "You deal with a war by ending it. I would have put every one of the bastards into irons."

"How many? A thousand? Five thousand? Ten thousand?" Gage said.

"That wretched seaman Merton spelled it out."

"I don't follow you."

"He died."

"I haven't heard two sensible words about this whole mess since I have been here," Clinton said. "Suppose we drop it now and have a spot of tea and put our heads together sanely. It's quite ridiculous, you know. The best army in the world backed by the best navy in the world bottled up here in this wretched Continental village by a lot of hotheaded, disorganized farmers. We are supposed to be hardheaded, intelligent military men. Or are we?"

Then they were at Province House, Gage's home and executive mansion, where Mrs. Gage greeted them almost somberly. It gave Clinton the thought that already she knew about the disgusting mess of the flogging, but then he realized that that was impossible. They had come straight from the ship. As they entered the house, Howe joined them, mumbling something about thinking better of the whole thing and that they ought to get down to business, after all. His big, shambling form took on the stance of a penitent little boy, and looking at his swarthy face, Clinton realized that he was blushing.

"I don't believe it," Burgoyne said. Howe told him to shut his bloody mouth and then apologized profusely to Mrs. Gage.

Clinton, watching Mrs. Gage, realized that she had apparently heard neither Howe's oath nor his apology. Margaret Gage was a lovely, intelligent woman, and Clinton had fallen into the habit of flirting with her, not crudely or even noticeably but with the smallest and gentlest of gestures and courtesies. Gage himself never noticed, or if he did, shrugged it off as a matter of no importance. The truth of it was that he was so utterly entrapped and frustrated by his situation that he might hardly have noticed had Clinton and his wife embraced in front of him.

"Is there trouble, Margaret?" Clinton asked her. He had fallen into calling her by her first name the first day they met, cozened it out of her with his easy manner, and with that her permission to use it. Sir William noticed. He envied both Clinton and Burgoyne for their easy manner with women. Arriving with them in America a few days ago, he as a Whig, had expected that his reputation as a great friend of the colonies would have preceded him, and since he lived with a dream of politics as seduction, he was almost always disappointed.

In reply to Clinton's question, Margaret Gage told her husband that Dr. Benjamin Church had been there.

"We'll have tea, my dear, if it's no trouble. With a bottle of sherry or Madeira. I think the Madeira would be better."

"I don't want him in my house again!" Mrs. Gage said.

"Really, my dear."

"Please understand me, Thomas. He is a disgusting man, and he disgusts me."

"But why suddenly? You know how useful he is to me."

"You want to know why? In front of these gentlemen?"

"I have no secrets from them."

"Very well. He made advances."

"Dr. Church?" Gage exclaimed in amazement. "That fat, foolish little man! Oh, no, my dear. You must be mistaken. What advances?"

"He fondled my tits, if you must, sir!" she cried out in rage then turned on her heel and left the room.

Burgoyne stifled his grin, and they all looked at Gage, who whispered, "Well, I'll be damned!"

"None of our business," Clinton said.

"Talk for yourself, son," said Howe. "I'm dying of curiosity, and devil take the niceties! Who is this bastard? The man wants a whipping."

"Dr. Benjamin Church." Gage sighed. "Oh, no. No indeed. You don't want to whip him, Sir William. He's a fat little man, half your size, and he's a sort of nasty treasure to me. I always think of him as a toad. You see, he's a very important muckamuck among the rebels. Great patriot. Member of the Committee of Safety. Sits in on all their important meetings. Absolutely invaluable. And I bought him. Offer and purchase—fifty pounds for the dirty little swine. But I can't treat him like a gentleman. He's much too important to me. You can see what a wretched mess this whole thing is." And with that, he followed his wife out of the room.

"I'll be damned!" said Howe.

Burgoyne wandered around the room, studying the hand-blocked wallpaper, the paintings, the beautifully wrought Queen Anne side chairs. Good taste. It astonished him how well they managed to live here at the edge of the wilderness. Clinton watched him. Burgoyne was a playwright, a rotten one, as Clinton appraised him, but still a playwright. If I ever write anything, it'll be better than his, Clinton thought. Books. We're here to destroy, not to write books. Still, he gets his silly plays produced.

Howe was muttering, "Fondled her tits, did he."

"Henry," Burgoyne said to Clinton, "this is a damn strange place, this America of yours. How do you feel about it? I mean, how do you see yourself? One of them or one of us?"

"That's an odd question."

"You grew up in the colonies. Where? In New York?"

The servants were setting up the tea, and Howe poured the Madeira. Gage rejoined them.

"Terribly sorry," Burgoyne said to him.

"She's in a pet. I don't blame her," Gage said. "She loves this place, you know. And she blames us. We're going to make a war and destroy it."

"Not necessarily," Howe said.

The servants put the chairs to the table, and Gage motioned for them to sit down.

"Not necessarily," Howe said again.

Sir William Howe had a reputation to uphold. All the Howes were friends of America, a great, powerful family, a general, an admiral, a foot in the court. They sat down with the king and talked to him face-to-face.

We can deal with our enemies, Clinton thought. God save us from our friends. Us, he repeated to himself. Who is *us* and who the devil am I? He had grown up here in this place, ten years of his youth in New York City, where his father was governor. The whole thing made no damn sense whatsoever—a British army pinned down in the little town of Boston by fifteen thousand boys and grown men and old men who were filled with a senseless rage generated by a senseless act. The act was Thomas Gage's fault and Gage's stupidity. Gage had sent the army into their land, to the village of Concord, to take away from them the gunpowder and the shot they had so carefully stored. They were playing a game, a game filled with words of freedom and independence and the right to do as they damn pleased, and then Gage joined their game, and the world went mad. You don't send generals to do a man's job; you send the generals to kill.

"Let's have a toast." John Burgoyne lifted his glass. "His Majesty, gentlemen." He was grinning.

The bastard was thinking of Margaret Gage's tits. This afternoon, perhaps, they would decide the fate of the world, and Burgoyne was sitting there trying to decide whether it was worth his while to seduce Margaret Gage. Well, how far was that from his own thoughts? Howe wondered.

The servants brought cake and hard-boiled eggs and bread and sliced ham. Gage and Howe ate hungrily. They had finished lunch an hour ago, and here they were stuffing themselves again. Burgoyne sat with his smile and his thoughts. Clinton poured himself more wine.

"What do you mean, not necessarily?" Clinton asked Howe.

"Do nothing. They'll cool off and go home. They're not soldiers. No one is paying them or feeding them. They'll be bloody well disenchanted in a week or two, if they're not already. Ask Thomas here," Howe said, nodding at Gage.

"I am offended," said Burgoyne.

"He's right, you know," Gage said. "They're breaking up already. They're in a much more impossible situation than we are."

"I said I was offended," Burgoyne repeated.

"Oh, Christ, Johnny," Clinton said, "what in hell are you offended about? Why don't you take your bleeding honor and shove it up your ass."

"How dare you!" Burgoyne exploded.

"Come on, chaps," Howe said. "We're a lot of paunchy middle-aged men, not children. You've been bitching all day, Henry."

"I'm sorry."

"The hell you are!" Burgoyne snapped. "Talk to me like that again, Clinton, and so help me God I'll put you on a field of honor. So help me, I will!"

"Oh, yes, yes, indeed," Howe said, and Clinton reflected that he was nowhere such a fool as he appeared. "They send the three best iron-assed generals they have over here, and Henry Clinton and John Burgoyne work out the problem on a field of honor. Score one for lunacy. Eat something, Henry. I can't tolerate a man who sneers at food."

"Johnny, please end this right here," Gage said worriedly.

Burgoyne shrugged. "Ended."

"I'm sorry," said Clinton with cold formality. "That is an apology."

"Now about the Yankees," Howe continued. "Tell us, Thomas. What does it add up to? Have they been going home? You have people like this wretched Dr. Church. What do they say?"

"It's a matter of hay—feed for their stock."

"You mean for their horses here?"

"No, no—you know, most of them are farmers, what we call yeomen farmers back at home, but they have land. Good God, that's the crux of this place, all the land in the world and no end to it as you move west. Well, they put pastures of it to grass, and the grass is ready for the cutting between the middle of May and the middle of June. That's how they raise their stock—so much grass to feed so many animals. They cut the grass now, and they cut it again in six or seven weeks. It's not fine grain, but it serves for feed. Well, today is the twelfth of June, and it's on to the end of the time for them. If they don't cut the grass, they will have to kill the animals."

"Then they'll go home?" Clinton asked with sudden interest.

"Come on, come on, you don't win wars that way," Burgoyne said.

"Not proper wars, but damn it all, this is no proper war, Johnny. They have no army, no uniforms, no tactics. Heavens, they don't even have a table of organization, and the men from—well, say Connecticut—they won't even tolerate officers. They're damn sodden with the leveler business, and when they don't like an officer, they hold a meeting and vote him out."

"No!"

"God's truth. Now, according to Church, on the ninth, about two hundred walked out, two hundred and fifty or so on the tenth, and yesterday almost three hundred. They just pick up and off they go, and the food is so tight that no one complains. After all, it's a bit of a bore—no drill, no discipline, just sitting out there and chewing their nails."

Clinton was aware of Burgoyne's anger before the others sensed it. "A maggot's eating the man," he said to himself. "He's full of maggots." The others didn't know him. He was Gentleman Johnny, who would rather write plays and screw the prima donnas than be out in the field. But that was a total lie and a pose, and it was blood the man wanted. Not like the other three. Howe had a taste for success and a soft spine, and Gage had a taste for comfort. That was the worst disease for a military man, to prefer comfort.

At this moment Clinton's whole being ached to be away from the three of them and naked in bed with a woman, but comfort wasn't entirely what he wanted. Then what was? Did he have a taste for glory? Or did he have a taste for nothing at all, which would be the final jest.

Burgoyne was on his feet, pacing across the room. Suddenly he turned and thrust a finger at the three men and half-shouted, his voice high-pitched, "To let those lousy peasants walk away from here and eat shit. No, gentlemen! Give me a thousand grenadiers and this wretched rebellion will be a memory!"

The three generals sat in silence. Howe continued to eat, his black eyes fixed on Burgoyne.

"You let them go home, Thomas. Go ahead. You command!" he shouted at Gage. "I am an Englishman. I represent the majesty of the most splendid empire this world has known."

"I don't believe it," Clinton told himself. "I truly don't believe it. The horse's ass is writing himself into his own play."

"Ah, now, Johnny, calm down," Howe said. "We haven't a thought among the lot of us. Thomas spelled out some facts, and likely enough we'll see the farmers in hell, but we'll deal with fewer of them. Tell you what my notion is." He turned to Gage. "Put a map on the table, Thomas, and we'll see where we are and what's to do.

"After all," he said to Burgoyne, "we're a trio of tyros. Nice phrase that, don't you think, Johnny? We're the new elegance from the homeland, and poor Thomas has been sitting on this powder keg for months. I am not one to suggest a war, not with Englishmen, don't you know—and they are Englishmen—but a battle's another thing. A purgative effect. They caught us by our cocks at Lexington and Concord, and it's time we did a bit of gelding."

"I'll get the map," Gage replied gloomily, and left the table and went into the next room. Howe poured a glass of wine and offered it to Burgoyne. "Come drink with us, Johnny." Burgoyne stood his distance. "Ah, Johnny, Johnny, you have a quick temper." Gage came back into the room with a servant, who cleared the table, and then Gage spread out the map. Burgoyne, mollified, joined them.

"This is Clifton Trowman's work," Gage explained, "and he's a damn good cartographer. I'm sure you know the lay of the land, gentlemen, so I will simply orient you. Here's the neck of Boston, here the Charles River, here the Mystic River. These are Dorchester Heights, and this is the village of Charlestown. The broken line traces the Yankee position."

They studied the map for a little while, and then Clinton wondered how many men they actually had out there.

"Ten, twelve, fifteen thousand—I don't think they really know themselves," Gage said. "They come and they go."

"Who's in command, and what's the beggar like?" Burgoyne asked.

"That's hard to say," Gage admitted. "and it's questionable whether anyone is truly in command. There's this old gentleman from Worcester, Artemus Ward's his name. Pleasant enough chap—bit fanatical, but that's the Puritan in him. He's in command of the Massachusetts men, if you call it command. He has a bellyful of trouble."

"What kind of trouble?" Howe demanded.

"He pisses in agony. Stones in the bladder or something of the sort. Drives him crazy with pain, so mostly it's John Thomas who does his work. They both style themselves generals. Thomas has something less than half the Massachusetts men here"—Gage traced it on the map—"between Dorchester and Roxbury, covering the Boston neck. The rest of the Massachusetts contingent is over here at Cambridge, spread out. With them, perhaps two, three, four, thousand from Connecticut and Rhode Island. I get different figures every day. And some of the same lot are over at Roxbury. A good bit of shifting from day to day. And here, right at the water edge, about a thousand more from Connecticut. They're a bad lot."

"Why?" Clinton wanted to know.

"Two reasons," Gage said. "First of all, they're led by a cold-blooded and nasty son of a bitch named Israel Putnam. We trained the old bastard ourselves, back in the French wars, and now he's giving it back to us. He's hard and heartless, and I offered to make him a rich man if he'd come over to us. Second reason—do any of you know what the levelers are?"

"Half a notion," said Howe. "Back in Cromwell's time, wasn't it? A daft set of loonies, if I remember right."

"Well, it's a current disease in Connecticut. Pure and simple hatred of anyone who has more than two shillings. No proper New Englander, mind you. A Boston man will sell his mother, if you can only make the price right, and there's nobody worships money and rank like these Yankees, with all their talk of equality. But these levelers are something else indeed. They have a thing about equality. No rich, no poor. Or put it all poor. Every man on the same level. Every piece of property the same. It's a madness with them."

"And when you face muskets in the hands of those," said Clinton, "it will be no ruffle of drums to send them running. You mark my words."

"Who else is there?" Burgoyne asked.

"Over here," Gage said. "Stark and six or seven hundred men out of New Hampshire Grants. They put them back a few miles because maybe old Artemas Ward don't know what to do with them. They are a most peculiar lot, you know, some of them just riffraff, but most of them a crazy Presbyterian lot, and they don't rightly hold their land with any clear title. That, by the way, is the crux of it with half the men out there—a deadly fear of losing their land with the shaky title they have, and so help me God, if we could guarantee title to all their holdings you could go home and drink your port in peace. But these men from the Grants with Stark are riflemen and bloody good marksmen, and I have seen them pop the head off a turkey at a hundred paces. They are an ignorant, bigoted lot out of the woods, buckskin men who live half like animals, but if they were on that road back from Concord, not one of my men would have returned from Boston."

"I am not bugged by riflemen," Howe said. "They have to reload, and that's the business of ramming down the lead. Give them a touch of cold steel and they'll run like bloody rabbits."

"Well, let me tell you this," Clinton interjected. "I have seen them at it. They'll make a line of the hundred best marksmen, and the rest will simply load. That means they will fire every ten seconds, and there is nothing like it."

"I have seen that," Gage agreed, "but they will not stand in an open field. You know, that's the maxim of that old bastard Putnam, that the Yankee, having an empty head, don't give two damns for it, so if you put him behind a stone wall or a log of wood he's brave as a lion. But his legs and belly are another matter, and he will not have them shot at. They were lined up across the field at Lexington, and at the first shots they ran like rabbits, but coming back, they were behind the walls, and that was a horse of another color."

"Did you try to buy John Stark?" Howe wondered. "He's a good man, you know."

"I sent him a letter," Thomas Gage said, "offering him a hundred golden guineas and his own ranger commission. I told him that if he raised a company of five hundred men, I would uniform them and pay them. He replied in two words."

Burgoyne raised a brow. "Two words?"

"Fuck you. It's standard King's English with them, and they suffer a paucity of vocabulary. Do you know old Putnam's order to his men? It has become a sort of slogan with them. Let me quote him: 'If one of you fuckin' shitheads shows his ass to the enemy, I will slice his balls off personally.' And they love it. The old man has the reputation of the foulest mouth in the colonies."

"I wouldn't call it paucity of vocabulary," Burgoyne said.

"Perhaps not," Gage continued. "Still, it always strikes me as an odd concomitant of their Puritanism. They say Boston has the highest percentage of whores of any city in the empire, and while that may be an exaggeration, it is a most peculiar element of their holiness. That about does it," he said, pointing to the map. "Over here, to the north of Willis Creek, there's a chap called Reed, with another band of New Hampshire men, facing this little neck of land to Charlestown."

"What's in Charlestown, Thomas?" Clinton asked.

"It's a deserted village. It was a rebel stronghold, and they all cleared out of it. I suppose the houses are empty now. They were last week when I sent a company through it."

"Why didn't you occupy it?" Howe asked.

"Because I don't want to loot it." Gage explained. "You can't put soldiers into an empty town and expect them not to loot it. Hell, you couldn't put saints into an empty town and ask them to keep hands off, and these people are insane on the subject of looting. With all their fine talk of liberty, it's property they worship. Take a piece of silver or china and they go mad."

"Why don't they occupy it?"

"It's all wood, shingle and siding. One broadside of hot shot and it goes up in flames. So we leave it alone."

They stared at the map in silence for a while, and then Clinton pointed to the delicate topographical swirls beyond the village of Charlestown. "This hill?"

"Breed's Hill. And just beyond it, Bunker Hill."

"What's there?"

"Nothing."

"Why don't we occupy it?"

"Never occurred to me," Gage admitted. "I mean, what for?"

"Then the whole harbor is ours."

"Interesting," Howe said.

"It's a question of what we intend to do here and how long we stay here," Gage said, "and I'm damned if I know the answer to either question. We have three thousand men. They have fifteen thousand. If we split up and go into the Charlestown neck, we're no better off and a lot thinner."

"With the marines we muster better than three thousand," Howe said. "Suppose they occupy Bunker Hill and Breed's Hill. That would be sticky, wouldn't it?"

Staring at the map, Clinton said, "That would be the answer to our prayers, Sir William. We would cut them off and let them starve, and your whole bloody rebellion would collapse like a bag of wind."

"What makes you think they would sit there and starve?" Howe asked.

"What else could they do? We put our ordnance here on Copp's Hill, bring up ships and barges, cut them off by water, and turn that little bridge of land into pure hellfire." He glanced at Burgoyne. "Not to your taste, is it, Johnny?"

"You don't win wars that way."

"You win a war any bloody way you can."

"I'm afraid I agree with Johnny," Howe said. "They have a vision, which I suppose we gave them." He turned to Gage. "I don't speak in criticism. Heaven knows, you could not have anticipated what happened at Concord, but the plain fact of the matter is that they ran our asses off. We have the best damn army in the world, and that is not boasting or vainglory. It's a matter of plain fact, which the world knows, and as far as I am concerned, the world must continue to know. I never wanted this rotten mess. My sentiments are with the colonies, and I have never made a secret of that, gentlemen. But the fact remains that they have a vision of a British army running like a pack of beaten dogs, and all Europe knows and all Europe is farting with delight. What if we starve a few thousand of them into surrender? What will it change? No, sir! We must see these bleeding bastards face-to-face."

"Hear! Hear!" cried Burgoyne.

"Does that finish it, or does that start it?" Clinton wondered.

"Devil only knows," Gage said hopelessly. "It's inconceivable that they want to make a war with us. There's no reason for war. Their complaints are petty, and we've given into one demand after another. Except land," he added hopelessly. "God knows, there's enough land out there for everyone. Most of it never touched or explored. They want it, and the Crown wants it. They are a stiff-necked, ignorant, and vulgar people—and righteous. They are the most righteous folk on the face of this earth. I know, gentlemen." He sighed. "I married one of them. I'm sure you know that my wife is a Kemble, out of New Jersey, and while they are not this devilish Puritan strain down there, they share the arrogance."

Margaret Gage came into the room in time to hear the last of this conversation. Clinton saw her enter and noticed how her face tightened and her body stiffened.

"General Gage," she said very formally to her husband.

He reddened and rose with the others to face her.

"I have no desire to interrupt important councils, and I know your distinguished companions speak of nothing but matters of the greatest import, still, we are all of us to be at dinner with Reverend Hallsbury at eight o'clock. There is only time to change."

"Of course, my dear. I had forgotten."

She turned and left the room. Howe wanted to know who Reverend Hallsbury was.

"Very important High Church. He's the grandson of Lord Hallsbury, the old man in Suffolk who died a few years ago. He's it with the handful who are totally loyal."

"Also," Burgoyne added, "a young wife whose fire he stokes poorly. By God, she's a beauty—gifted as the fairies are, and with a magnificent pair of tits."

Clinton noticed how uncomfortable Gage had become. Too long among the Presbyterians and too long away from London. The disgraceful, running reteat from Concord only two months ago, a British army chivied and torn to shreds by a pack of loutish farmers, had broken his ego. The empire's response to his disgrace was to send to his aid the three brightest lights in the British military, all of them men who had fought in America during the French and Indian Wars. Gage would not cross Burgoyne, or any of them, and this was a pity, Clinton thought, since he was the only one among them who had any real knowledge of the situation.

Gage saw them to the door. Howe had a house of his own, as befitting his ranking position; Clinton and Burgoyne were quartered together in a fine brick house that had belonged to a cousin of James Otis's and which he had vacated some weeks before. They walked there together, followed by four grenadiers—a fact that irked Burgoyne.

"It's a pain in the ass, Sir Henry," Burgoyne remarked. "I'll talk to Gage about it. He's an old woman. It's utterly ridiculous, walking around this city and trailing a military guard."

Clinton agreed with him. "Of course you could simply take off, the way Sir William does."

"We're none of us Sir William, are we?" Burgoyne smiled. "I was a bit of an ass before, wasn't I?"

"I've forgotten the whole matter," Clinton replied.

"That's jolly good of you."

"I think we're a bit tight underneath, aren't we? It's the strangest damn place. I grew up in the colonies, but that gave me no intimacy. I was the governor's son, and that set me apart."

"It's the emptiness of the place that does it," Burgoyne commented. "Ever been in a half-empty town before?"

"In Germany," Clinton remembered. "Bizarre."

"Notice the damn bloody dogs. Always slinking around."

They were at their quarters now, and each went to his rooms. Clinton's quarters, on the second floor of the house, were hot and air-less. He began to sweat the moment he entered his sitting room. Where the devil was O'Brian? Why hadn't he aired the place? Why weren't his clothes laid out? He was irritable, tired, and then it occurred to him that he experienced this state of mind whenever there was a portend of dis-aster. But what conceivable disaster? Out in the harbor lay a mighty British fleet. The three generals had brought with them from England fifteen hundred of the best troops in the world. Add that to the fifteen hundred troops already at Gage's disposal and there were better than three thousand.

He tore himself out of his reverie and shouted for O'Brian, and when there was no response, he stormed out of the room and down the stairs two at a time. He felt some relief in the use of his body and his muscles. He was forty-five years old and going to fat, but a look in his mirror pleased him, with its reflection of blond hair and a boyish face. Outside the scullery, he heard the shrill voice of O'Brian's wife:

"Devil take you, me boyo! You sit on your bloody ass, and here I am with five shirts and twelve singlets and all the stinking lace that adorns the high and the mighty and you tell me I am a slut not to have it fin-ished. Call me a slut once more and as sure as Mary is the mother of God, I'll cut your bleeding heart out."

"It was a loose word came from me lips."

"Loose words and loose britches. Ah, ye make me sick."

"And what are you, me lass? Some shining inspiration?"

"O'Brian!" Clinton shouted, and then entered the room, reflecting on the curious madness of the British military that allowed wives to accompany their husbands overseas. Mary O'Brian sputtered her apologies. She was a large, stout woman, quite comely but with most of her teeth missing. Her husband was lean, fox-faced, and given to stealing anything he could. Yet he was a good servant and a good soldier, with a sergeant's rank and twenty years of military experience behind him.

"Sure, and what the devil was I thinking?" O'Brian said. "It's the time that does me an injustice, and me thinking it's no more than noon and at least two hours before Your Excellency would be coming."

"It is six o'clock in the afternoon," said Clinton. "I want hot water and my dress uniform and clean linen, and so help me, I will break you if it is not ready and waiting in half an hour."

He turned on his heel and mounted the stairs again. In his bedroom, he stripped off his sweat-soaked clothes and looked at himself in the mirror. The roll of fat around his belly was fast becoming a paunch. He kneaded the belly fat with his hands and regarded himself with disgust and despair.

O'Brian entered with a tub of hot water and began to rub down Clinton's back and buttocks with a hot towel. Suddenly, Clinton found himself staring at the rug and at the spreading pool of dampness. It was a Chinese rug, a pale blue background decorated with intertwining dragons, a thousand pounds in the best London carpet shop and probably brought from China by one of those incredible Yankee square riggers that roamed the whole world as if it were theirs without doubt or question; and suddenly he was aware of the seat of his disquiet and misgiving—the arrogance of these people, not guts or gallantry but simply an astonishing and righteous arrogance that he alone among the four generals appeared to sense and respond to.

"Goddamn you," he exploded at O'Brian, "we are not in a stable, you stupid Irish sot! See what you are doing to the rug—if you know what a rug is! Get me a towel to put under my feet and stop slopping the bloody water."

"Yes, sir, Your Excellency. Goddamn me for a pig, and not knowing even the smell of the finer things," he said, leaping into the next room and returning with a thick towel for Clinton to stand on. "There ye are, me lord. Sure as there is a God in heaven, ye'll be giving me thirty lashes for the stupidity of me behavior."

"Oh, shut up," Clinton said.

"Yes, sir."

He washed Clinton expertly. Lost in his own thoughts, Clinton stood there while O'Brian parted his buttocks, lifted the testicles and penis, washing and currying him as a mother washes a child. His wife came into the room, carrying the freshly ironed linen, paying no more attention to the naked general than she might have given a piece of furniture. But suddenly Clinton was aroused, not only conscious of her but hot with desire.

"Get me my robe!" he snapped at O'Brian.

As if O'Brian had a map of every nerve in his body: He grinned as he handed the robe to Clinton, and Mary O'Brian, laying out the linen, watched the general covertly as he covered himself. O'Brian went after her as she left the room, and at the door out of the sitting room, he whispered to her, "Now there's a bit of humping would make me a master sergeant before ye could say Paddy's pig, and it ain't no small thing, me love, to have a bastard out of the nobility."

"Ye're a dirty louse, O'Brian." She swept off, grinning out of her toothless mouth.

As for Clinton, he had been dead for weeks, and now he was wonderfully alive, his blood coursing through his veins, his sex throbbing, his mind filled with pictures of taking the great, fat Irish woman to bed. Watching him, O'Brian read his thoughts and made his own plans. Clinton did not dwell upon what had happened to him. He simply allowed himself to fall into the fact that it had happened, and reserving Mary O'Brian and thoughts of her for the future, he began to dwell on Reverend Hallsbury's wife. His pique faded. It would be an exciting evening. By and large, he had found no pleasure in Boston women. They were dull, narrow, obsessed with their own tiny class structure.

He was almost dressed, O'Brian hovering over him, when Lieutenant Parker, Burgoyne's aide, entered and told him that the general was waiting. Parker was a pink-cheeked, handsome, ebullient lad of twenty. He took the occasion to observe to Clinton how positively splendid he looked, as indeed he did in his scarlet coat, his white linen and lace, powdered wig, white silk trousers, and fine boots.

"Well, Parker, an old man does his best, doesn't he?"

"My good fortune to look like you someday, sir."

"Well said." Clinton smiled. "You'll do, Parker."

Clinton and Burgoyne were the last of the guests to arrive, and even as the servant ushered them into Reverend Hallsbury's rather splendid sitting room, Clinton noticed Howe deep in conversation with one of the most beautiful women he had ever seen, a tall, slender, but full-breasted blonde with bright blue eyes and exquisite features. Unquestionably, Clinton decided, she was the reverend's wife. Nor was he at all disturbed by Howe's initial place on the starting line. He had no small opinion of himself in that direction when it came to William Howe, or to Johnny Burgoyne, for that matter. The reverend himself was a gray-haired, turning-white gentleman in his middle sixties. He had his own money from his family, and it was reflected in the imported furniture, the rugs, the silver, the great chandelier, which held at least a hundred candles, the diamond set in the cross that hung on a gold chain from his neck, and the simple string of priceless pearls his wife wore.

Gage and his wife, Margaret, were already there, as was Howe, along with a tea merchant, John Stibble by name, late forties, and a dark, handsome woman who was his wife. There was a widowed Mrs. Plunkett—her husband had been an officer in the marines—and two toothy young ladies in their twenties to complete a genteel pairing with the British generals.

Madeira and sherry were being served by a man in livery. Clinton relfected upon the fact that in this half-abandoned town, where a population was being slowly starved by twelve thousand rebels who encircled the place, there was nevertheless no shortage of anything the rich required. He and Burgoyne were moved around and introduced, Mrs. Plunkett clapping onto Burgoyne, to whom she insisted upon being distantly related. When Hallsbury brought Clinton to his wife, the people in the room marked the contrast, Howe, so large and dark and slow of movement and speech, and Clinton and the woman, both of them pale and fair, their blue eyes grasping at and holding each other. Against them, Howe was Calaban, a clumsy, shuffling beast who was suddenly speechless as Clinton and Mrs. Hallsbury recognized each other's need. She gave Clinton her hand, smiled her most dazzling smile, and murmured how delighted she was finally to meet Sir Henry Clinton, of whom she had heard so much.

"Well, he's yours for the evening, my dear," her husband said, the haughty, aristocratic churchman suddenly humble and beseeching.

It was a very quick and subtle byplay, yet Clinton marked it as he said the required thing. "Much that is bad, Mrs. Hallsbury, but certainly very little that is good. I am charmed."

"Ah, no, no, indeed, Sir Henry. Much that is good."

"Which proves that no one speaks the plain truth about anything," Howe put in. "You interrupt a first-rate lecture upon strategy, Henry."

"I fear for you, Sir William," Clinton said lightly. "To lecture the loveliest woman in the colonies on anything is all too close to the original sin."

"Dear gentlemen, I will have no talk of sin tonight. My husband is well versed on the subject, and I am his apt pupil." She threw her smile from one to another. "You cannot imagine how delighted we all of us are to have Britain's proudest generals not simply in Boston but here in our house tonight. Oh, I know that wisdom and courage are so matter-of-fact to you. But think of a poor woman living day to day in a jungle. And good Sir William here was only reassuring me that we have nothing to fear. So you must not scold him, Sir Henry."

Clinton felt magnanimous. "But no one scolds Sir William," he hastened to explain. "Not even the king. And Sir William is my commander, you know."

"Bosh," said Howe.

"I will have no favorites. I have seated myself between you."

At the table, Clinton waited for the pressure of her knee. The game had begun earlier. Mrs. Hallsbury was a user, a manipulator. She used Howe because to an observer it was plain that a woman flirting with two men was less serious than a woman flirting with one. She used her aging husband with something less than contempt. And she was using Clinton to assuage an aching loneliness and desire so desperate it came to Clinton like a silent scream. Yet she played the game step by step. When she took his hand, there was a slight extra pressure, and coming into dinner, she mentioned in a whisper only for him that some of the red Indians in her land were loath to reveal their true names for fear it gave one power over them. "My name is Prudence," she said. "Does that give you power over me?"

"I would not want such power," he answered gallantly. "Still, it is unquestionably one of those damned Puritan names."

"I am married to a High Church priest, sir. And do you always swear in front of women, or is that the current fashion in London?"

"Forgive me the swearing. I will forgive you the marriage."

"You are too bold, sir, and rather nasty." And with that, she turned her conversation to Howe, who sat at her right.

Mr. Stibble was regaling the table with a monologue on the British Empire and the tea trade. Burgoyne was finding Mrs. Plunkett interesting. And Sir William Howe was listening to Mrs. Hallsbury when Clinton felt the first pressure of her knee. Then her leg caressed his, and he dropped his right hand beneath his napkin to rest on her thigh. She turned from Howe to Clinton, and their eyes met.

"I think," Clinton whispered, barely moving his lips, conscious that her husband was watching them, "that I want you more than anything on earth."

"More than a great victory, Sir Henry?" She smiled. "And in a battle, do you move so directly and quickly?"

"I do."

Her light, high-pitched voice cut across the tea merchant's peroration like a knife. She demanded, "Then how would you see us out of our predicament, Sir Henry?"

The tea merchant halted in mid-sentence, and the table listened. "I would take two thousand men," said Clinton, "and I would deal with them as I would with a snake."

"And how does one deal with a snake, Sir Henry?" Gage asked.

Aware that he was speaking only for her, boasting the way a small boy does, yet becoming increasingly enamoured of his words as he spoke them, Clinton said, "I would slice through the belly first, and then I would cut off the head, and then I would cut off the tail."

"But my dear Sir Henry," Burgoyne drawled, "a snake dies slowly. What if the head and the tail decided to come in here to Boston while you were dealing with the belly? That might be a bad show for our good friends here."

"Devil take all generals," Howe said. "Here I sit with as fine a roast as I ever tasted in England, lovely ladies, and good company. I will not have this talk of war. To our host, gentlemen!" He raised his glass. "And to his lovely companion. I am a poor churchgoer, sir, but I pledge you my presence at your next service."

"Which may be a while off," the Reverend Hallsbury replied sourly, "since my church is behind their lines—if indeed they have not burned it to the ground."

Gage drank the toast and reassured Hallsbury. "My intelligence is dependable, sir. As of tonight, your church still stands. They have some nasty ways, but they don't burn churches."

Softly, Mrs. Hallsbury asked Clinton, "Were you just talking? Or would you do as you said you would?"

"That I want you more than anything on earth?" he whispered.

"Your two thousand soldiers, sir."

"I think I would," he said slowly.

"Will they listen to you?"

"No."

"Why not?"

"I have never fought in America. Only in Europe. They have."

"Why aren't you the commander?"

"Dear lady, the questions you ask."

"It would be better, Sir Henry, if you took your hand from my thigh. You are so hot with passion, sir, that I can smell it. If you continue to look at me that way, not only my husband but everyone at the table will know."

"I don't give a damn for your husband."

"But I must give a damn for him, sir."

"As you might for your father or your grandfather."

"Your hand, Sir Henry." He placed his hand upon the table, in conspicuous view. "You see, Sir Henry," she went on, "we all fight our battles as best we may, and we are all in some sort of servitude. Isn't that what your military discipline teaches you?"

"Don't make a fool of me."

"When you are so willing to make a fool of me?"

"He's old enough to be your grandfather."

"I think we have whispered enough. A few minutes are permissible. More than that invites scandal." She raised her voice to catch her husband's attention. "Sir Henry has been amusing me with his experiences in Europe. What a sight it must be to see two great armies in all their splendid ranks and uniforms meet in battle! I should think that no sight in all the world can equal it."

"I would think, my dear," her husband replied, "that there is more agony than joy in a battle. Wouldn't you say so, Sir William?"

"Depends on who wins and who losses."

"As God wills it. God has blessed England."

"Not this past April," Gage said.

"That," said Burgoyne, "was not a battle, if you will forgive me, Sir Thomas. They set on us like a pack of dogs, yet you brought our troops out of their country. The battle still awaits us."

"I sincerely hope not," said Margaret Gage.

"Then are we to live forever in this beleaguered city?" the reverend asked.

Clinton took the opportunity to whisper to Mrs. Hallsbury, "I must see you."

"Perhaps. If our fates will it."

"To hell with our fates. Tonight."

"You know that is impossible."

"Nothing is impossible."

"I am not a British general, Sir Henry. I am a woman, and to a woman most things are impossible."

"Forgive me."

"There is nothing to forgive. I would like very much to see you alone, but tonight is impossible."

"For five minutes?"

"What will five minutes achieve?"

"Just to stand face-to-face with you, alone."

Mr. Stibble was talking about furniture. He had ordered a breakfront and ten chairs from the workshop of Mr. Thomas Chippendale. He wanted Burgoyne's opinion of Mr. Chippendale's work. Not that he would ever receive the shipment, the way things were today, but only to know what he would miss.

Burgoyne was bored with Mr. Stibble. To sit at dinner with a man of great wealth in London, who might back a new play, was one thing; to do the same with a Continental ass was an imposition. Before he had an opportunity to reply with a sufficiently clever insult, Margaret Gage explained that the very chairs they were sitting on were out of Mr. Chippendale's workshop.

"Wait an hour after you leave," Mrs. Hallsbury whispered. "There is an arbor behind the house."

After they had made their farewells, they went out to where Gage's carriage was waiting. Clinton said that he thought he would walk and clear his head. "I would not advise it, Henry. The city isn't safe at night."

"Safe enough."

"You're not armed."

"He's armed with his dreams," Burgoyne said. "The lucky devil had all good things to himself. Do you want company, Henry?"

"I'd as soon be alone," Clinton replied. "Thank you."

As the carriage drove off, Burgoyne said, "He's a surly devil, isn't he?"

"Ah, well, that's understandable. The place is new to him. We've all fought here in the French wars."

"He grew up here, didn't he?"

"But not as a soldier. He feels isolated. He can't understand why we don't take two thousand regulars and march from one end of the continent to the other."

"I think you do him an injustice," Margaret Gage said unexpectedly. "Perhaps he can't understand why there should be a war at all."

Yet war was as far from Clinton's thoughts as China as he walked slowly through the empty streets. It was almost midnight now, and the city was as dead and silent as some ancient, abandoned ruin. Not a sound, not a voice, not a light in any window. A pack of dogs came racing around a corner and swirled around Clinton, who ignored them. He suffered from many difficulties, but physical fear was not one of them. He found himself on King Street, and he walked slowly out onto the Long Wharf. There were soldiers on guard there, and they saluted him, but if they wondered what a general in full-dress regalia was doing wandering around Boston at this time of the night, they kept their silence and asked no questions. He walked to the end of the wharf. The moon was in the sky now, and the June night was warm and pleasant.

Clinton stood at the end of the wharf, staring at the dark hulks of the British warships in the harbor. His ardor had cooled sufficiently for him to contemplate himself, a process that never brought him great satisfaction. In affairs of the heart or the groin, he always in time reduced his image to that of a small boy, with a small boy's voyeuristic dreams, and now the spectacle of his headlong assault upon Mrs. Hallsbury made him feel both the fool and the lout. Nevertheless, he had the appointment, and peering at his watch in the pale moonlight, he realized that he had only enough time to return to the assignation.

As he walked back through the deserted streets, his process of self-examination dwindled, and now he thought only of the fact that he had assaulted what was certainly one of the most beautiful women in the colonies and won at least her acquiescence, and all of it in whispers at a dinner table where her husband was present. With the name of Prudence she was either a Puritan or a Presbyterian, which only meant that the fires had never really been stoked. What had motivated her to marry the elderly High Church priest, he could not imagine, except that Hallsbury was very rich and that a few years she would endure as a wife might give her many years as a free and wealthy widow. All of which meant that she was manipulative and calculating, and the thought occurred to him that she had seduced him rather than the reverse. Well, be that as it may, she was beautiful and clever, and more than that he asked of no woman.

His first reaction when he reached the house and moved stealthily through the garden to the back door was one of wretched disappointment. She was not there, and he had been made an utter fool. He stood in the moonlight, looking at the brick walks that edged the herb and rose gardens, deflated and humiliated, and then he heard her whisper, "Sir Henry?"

He turned, and she was standing by the door. She came to him, took his arm, and silently led him to a grape arbor at the back of the garden. Still, he had spoken no word, and in the darkness of the arbor, he suddenly embraced her, found her mouth and then her tongue darting between his lips like the quick thrusts of a small snake. Then she drew away from him, breathing heavily.

In the bits of moonlight that crept through the leaves, he saw her as a dappled, shadowy figure in a long silken night robe. He reached out, then parted the robe and fondled her breasts. She did not resist or indeed make any response, and then he slipped the robe off her shoulders, and she stood naked in front of him. He clutched her in his arms, kissing her face, her neck, and her shoulders. She trembled and sighed and then pleaded with him, "Not here. Please, not here,"

"I must have you."

"I know. I know. But not here, not tonight."

"I must!"

"Tomorrow. Please," her voice quite terror-stricken.

He let go of her and stepped back, and she stood there naked, with her arms crossed over her breasts. Then he picked up her robe and placed it over her shoulders, feeling suddenly empty and deflated.

"Oh, God, I'm so sorry," she whimpered. "But he's awake. Don't you understand? He's still awake."

"Will he look for you?"

"I don't know. Call for me tomorrow. To look at one of the warships. He won't mind that."

"What time?"

"When you please. I'll wait. I must go. Give me a few minutes." And with that, she fled from the arbor.

There was a bench in the arbor, and Clinton sat there for perhaps ten minutes. Then, as he slipped away through the garden, a dog began to bark, and he found himself half-running. He rounded a corner and, panting, slowed to a walk. The dog came after him, a large brown mongrel beast, snapping at his heels. Clinton ignored the animal, and presently the dog gave up the game and turned away. Clinton walked on, trying to compose the events of the following day in his mind, recalling that Howe had ordered a review of the grenadiers for the fourteenth of June, trying to remember what time the event was scheduled so that he could think of some excuse that would allow him to be elsewhere.

On the other hand, why not invite her to the review—unless that would bring her husband along with her. The old man was quite a fire-eater. As this and that plan went through his mind, he found himself losing interest. It had been a full day; he would think about it tomorrow. He recalled the feel of her naked body, her lips, her breasts, and slowly a feeling of satisfaction replaced his sense of loutishness and loss.

The two guards at the door of the house where he was quartered regarded him without curiosity. They were well trained. Had he come in with Mrs. Hallsbury upon his arm, they would have been equally graven and silent.

Slowly, he climbed the stairs to his rooms. It had been a long day, and he was, after all, forty-five years old. His sitting room was empty. O'Brian should have been waiting there with warm water and freshly done nightclothes, and his first impulse was to fling open the door and roar out the bastard's name. Then he realized that the house was asleep. Burgoyne and their aides would not bless him for awakening them at this hour, unless, of course, they were still away, bedded down in the arms of less fettered Boston ladies.

His eyes drifted around the room. The candles had been lit no more than an hour before, so O'Brian must have been there and then given up like the lazy bastard he was. He wondered whether Mrs. Hallsbury's sitting room had this same restrained elegance that one found among the upper classes in the colonies: the hand-blocked wallpaper, the simple yet lovely wing chairs that flanked the fireplace, the oriental rugs, the plain yet beautiful silver that they wrought so well in America—all of it carefully protected by Sir William's mania against looting. At least that—and beyond her sitting room, what? Would she be in bed with the old man now, warming his cold, ecclesiastical bones?

He sighed and went into his bedroom, pulled off his boots, and began to strip himself of his uniform. He was naked except for his singlet when he heard the door to his sitting room open and then a light knock on his bedroom door.

"Come in, you wretch," he said, thinking that it was O'Brian.

It was Mary O'Brian who opened the door and entered, a pitcher of warm water in one hand and his freshly laundered nightdress over her arm. She had washed her hair and set it up high on her head, and she was clad in a long linen robe that fell to her ankles yet revealed the curves of her full, womanly figure. There was just the slightest smile upon her lips, and as earlier in the day, she accepted his nakedness matter-of-factly. She laid the nightdress upon the bed, poured water into the hand basin, and then dipped a towel into the water and squeezed it out.

"Where's O'Brian?" Clinton asked her.

"Sleeping, the lazy pig. Take off the shirt, General, and I'll be refreshing you."

He stared at her for a long moment, pulled his singlet off over he head, and then stood by the bedside while she sponged his body with the towel. Then she took a fresh towel and dried his body, her fingers gently massaging his flesh throught the cloth. He had no thoughts in his mind, indeed no mind at all, only a luxurious sense of the passion rising inside of him. She finished drying him, then turned down the covers of his bed.

"Will ye be wanting a nightdress, me lord?" she asked, a note of archness creeping into her voice.

He shook his head.

"Then will ye have the left or the right side of the bed, me lord."

"I am no lord, as you damn well know."

"In my eyes, me lord."

He grinned at her, and she grinned back.

"Is O'Brian really asleep?"

"Who the hell cares!"

She unbelted her robe and slipped it off, a great mountain of a woman, as tall as Clinton, yet not fat, as he had thought, her breasts high and enormous, her hips wide and womanly, and quite beautiful, with her dead white skin and her mountain of red hair.

Clinton crawled into the bed. She stood at the foot of the bed, naked, until he growled, "What in the devil's name are you waiting for?"

"For your sweet summons, me lord."

Then she snuffed the candles, and a moment later he felt her warm body next to him.

June 14

*F*eversham did not like Dr. Church, and as always when he disliked a person, he found himself bending backward to disguise his distaste and replying to the obvious with inanities. The small, fat man played the roll of patriot and fire-eater—a condition which Feversham despised—and at the same time he toadied to Feversham's English accent and English manner. He had assumed Feversham like a garment; Feversham was his.

"Did I not tell you, sir," said Dr. Benjamin Church. "that Joe Warren is my friend. Friend and student. I said to him, I am bringing around a Dr. Evan Feversham. Connecticut man, but born and trained in the old country. You will want to meet him, I said to Warren. Just those words. You will profit from meeting him. Are you a married man, Doctor?"

Feversham nodded. They were walking their horses through Cambridge in the early afternoon of a lovely June day. On both sides of the road, shoulder to shoulder, it would seem, in two unbroken lines, stood the endless tents, shelters, lean-tos, and brush huts of the volunteers who had flocked in from all over Massachusetts, Connecticut, and Rhode Island, and even from Vermont and New Hampshire and Maine, with their muskets and bullet pouches and not much else. Now they lay around, sunning themselves, picking lice from their clothes, shaving, cooking, urinating, playing games of lacrosse and Johnny-jump-the-pony and tag or flirting with the girls and women, who were almost as numerous as the men.

"Good heavens," Feversham said, "how many of them are there?"

Dr. Church shrugged. "Who knows! We try to make a count, and one day it comes out fifteen thousand and the next day perhaps ten thousand, and then maybe twelve thousand. They drift in, and then they go home, and then sometimes they come back again. Or a captain will come in with a band of a hundred or so, and he'll make his camp in one place, and then, by golly, off he goes to another place, or maybe he marches them through the back country to scrounge for food. Now if you were not a married man, you could get yourself as fine a little filly as you'd want to look at for a shilling for a night."

"Where do the women come from?" Feversham asked.

"Everywhere, Doctor. It's in the nature of women."

"Is no one trying to make something out of it? They're wallowing in their own filth. If someone doesn't take it in hand, the British won't have to move out of Boston. Disease will do the job for them."

Church smiled smugly and nodded. "So you're one of them."

"What the devil does that mean?"

"Oh, yes, Dr. Feversham, I know the story, dirt breeds disease. It's one of Warren's small pets."

"And you don't think dirt breeds disease, Doctor?"

"Rank superstition. The evil humor comes from within, not from without."

"Does it? Then how do you account for plagues?"

"Not from filth but from man to man, sir. It awakens the evil humor within."

Feversham stared at him in amazement. There was no retort to such an argument, nor did he see any profit in persuading Dr. Church to accept his views.

"How much farther is it?" Feversham asked.

"Watertown. Just a few miles. He's staying with the Hunts, you know." Church was a name user and a name dropper. "We're all doubling up, since we've been kicked out of Boston. Joe and Betsy Palmer are there—she's Hunt's daughter—and Joe Warren's children. Well, these are sacrifices a patriot makes. Hunt is a patriot."

He broke off as a cluster of men in front of one of the shacks moved out into the road. One of them pointed to Church.

"That's him!" another shouted. "That's the bastard!"

"Hey, Doctor. Hold on!"

They were a wretched-looking lot to Feversham's eyes, four of them, unshaven, barefoot, their shirts stained and dirty. When Church would have ridden by, one man grabbed his bridle while another caught him by the arm and tumbled him into the dust. For all of Feversham's dislike, he felt pity for the fat little man lying facedown in the road. Other men and women came running to see what the excitement was all about, and by the time Feversham had reached Church and helped him to his feet, there was quite a crowd around them. The man who had tumbled Church off his horse grabbed him by the lapels of his jacket and began to shake him violently.

"Let go of him!" Feversham snapped.

"He put death's touch on my brother."

Church tried to speak, but he had lost his breath, and he could not get a word out. "The devil you say!" cried Feversham. "No one puts death's touch on anyone. Suppose you talk sense."

"Who are you?"

"He's a limey, that's who he is," said the man who was still hanging on to the bridle of Church's horse.

"I'm Dr. Feversham. Now what's all this about your brother?"

Church found his voice and remembered. He had been called there the day before and had given the boy medicine. He had a bit of fever and vomiting.

"What kind of medicine?" Feversham demanded.

"Salts."

"No one dies of salts."

"Are you a real doctor?" the man asked him. Feversham simply stared at him. At the coldness of his look, the crowd quieted.

"Is your brother dead or alive?"

"Alive."

"Where is he?"

The man pointed to the shack. Feversham started for the hut, and the four men stood still, watching him silently. Then, when Feversham reached the door, the man with the brother ran after him, grasped his arm, and whispered into his ear, "Smallpox."

Feversham took a deep breath. "How do you know?"

"I seen it plenty. Don't go in. Make that little bastard go in. He give it to him."

"Don't be an ass," Feversham muttered, and went on into the shack. It was hot, dark, and airless inside. A boy of fourteen or fifteen lay on a blanket, and as Feversham bent over him, he began to whimper.

"I got the pox, mister. Don't you come near me."

"Sit up," Feversham told him brusquely.

"I be sick nigh to death."

"Sit up!"

He sat up, and Feversham peered at his face. From outside, Church whispered hoarsely, "Get out of there, Feversham. It's the pox."

"Look, son," Feversham said gently, "I want you to get up and come out into the light."

"I can't. I'm dying."

"You're not dying. Now do as I say!"

The boy groaned, climbed to his feet, and then followed Feversham out of the shack. By now almost a hundred men and women had gathered around from the sprawl of tents and lean-tos. Feversham looked at the boy's face and touched one of the sores with his finger.

"Church!"

The doctor hung back, just in front of the crowd that was carefully keeping its distance. Now a tall, lean man, who had an old sword slung over his shoulder, pushed through the crowd and made his way over to Feversham.

"I'm Captain Hawkins," he declared. "What's all this? Has the lad the smallpox? If he has, it's sure enough hell in store for us."

"Goddamn you, Church," Feversham said. "Will you come over here and look at this boy, or must I drag you over?"

Church came with slow steps, stared, and then smiled.

"Chicken pox?" asked Feversham.

"Chicken pox," Church agreed. "Plain as the nose on his face."

"Chicken pox!" Hawkins yelled to the crowd. "Chicken pox!"

"Ignorant louts," said Church as they mounted their horses. Feversham made no comment. "Connecticut," Church went on. He was thick-skinned. His feelings were not to be hurt, or else they had been hurt so often that it no longer mattered. "There's the most benighted place on earth, and what a pretty rabble they sent us here!"

"I'm from Connecticut," Feversham said.

"Well, no. Only in a manner of speaking."

Feversham could endure it no longer. "Dr. Church, I asked you to bring me to Dr. Warren, and now I am bloody damn sorry that I ever did. Ride with me if you wish, but keep your mouth shut. I cannot tolerate your conversation."

"Well, now—" He rode on a few paces more, took a deep breath, and exploded, "You are an arrogant son of a bitch. Just who in hell do you think you are? How dare you speak to me like that. I am Dr. Benjamin Church, member of the Committee of Safety. Do you know what that means? How the devil would you know? You, a damned Englishman. Or a spy. Would you be a spy, sir? I find you intolerable, sir. To hell with you and be damned."

He reined his horse aside, and Feversham rode on, regretting his own outburst. The little man had done nothing so terrible. It was his own malaise operating here, his doubts and loneliness, his sense of disorder and chaos, riding for hours through the disorganized rabble that called itself an army, and then turning it against the wretched little man. It was arrogant of him, and he felt sick at the thing that was eating his craw and tying him up in knots. Well, it was done, and if he wanted to see Warren, he would have to do so on his own. Certainly he would have no trouble finding his way to Watertown, since the little village was now the functioning capital of Massachusetts, and for all of his guilt, it was a relief to be traveling alone.

Asking the way, he was told to follow the path along the river and that it would bring him to Watertown in no more than and hour. In any case, he could hardly desire a lovelier day to be traveling. The river path was shaded by great elms, maples, and oaks, and the countryside was as pretty as anything he had ever seen. As he made his journey away from Boston, he left the tents and shacks of the militiamen behind him—and this with a sense of relief. It was beyond his comprehension that an army of several thousand British regulars should consider themselves besieged in Boston. Why didn't they simply cut their way through, or was the memory of how they were decimated on their march back from Concord too much for them? Or were they simply unwilling to make war?

He found the latter thought comforting, at least to some degree. He had insisted to his wife that there would be no war, and then her question was inevitable: "Then why must you go there?" His action was not connected with anything he could put to words.

Yet now, as he pondered it, he realized that he had fled her and the responsibilities that went with her, and his home and his practice, for war was the ultimate male liberation, especially the war that was no war but only an eloquent excuse for the children to escape from the school room. Men were a race of children, he thought, more sadly than bitterly, and war was a child's game until death and horror brought maturity. And then the young were old, and there was no interval to mark the passage of time.

So it had been with him. He once had a childhood, but no youth, and now, past forty, he comforted himself with the thought that he was a healer, not a destroyer. But even such small comfort was fraught with deceit, for he had shed all responsibility except the bundle of surgical instruments in his saddlebags. Even the label of patriot was no rationale, for the sense of himself as a Roman Catholic in this rocky bed of Protestantism never left him, nor did he truly know whether his taste for New England was so much deeper than his distaste for old England, whether he was a man of principle or a turncoat. As always, such musings always led Feversham to accept the fact that he knew himself very little.

His period of introspection had carried him some miles on his way, and now, ahead of him, he saw a cluster of buildings that might well be Watertown. And coming toward him, a group of twelve mounted men in striking, if outlandish, uniforms of yellow and green and pink. He hailed them to ask directions. The leader of the group was a bright-faced young man of nineteen or so who hastened to inform Feversham that they were the Independent and Loyal Third Company of Mounted Artillery out of New Haven, Connecticut, that they had been assigned to duty in Dorchester, whence they were bound—and while they did not have any cannon at the moment, they had been promised two of the guns that were captured at Fort Ticonderoga—and that he himself was Capt. Emil Williams. Through it all he grinned with pride, for what could be more fun than riding through the countryside on a delightful June day in their wonderful uniforms?

Feversham informed him that he himself was from Ridgefield, in Connecticut.

"By golly, isn't that a fine thing," Captain Williams said.

Feversham said that he was looking for Dr. Warren, who was staying at the Hunt house in Watertown.

"That's Watertown," the boy said, pointing, "and the Hunt place is the big house on your right as you ride in."

With that, he saluted and trotted away, his grinning fellow artillery-men trotting after him, and such was their pride and pleasure in what they were and how they looked that Feversham found himself smiling in response. Certainly they were the envy of the army, twelve uniforms in twelve thousand.

He rode on into Watertown, and there was a crowd of more than a hundred men, women, and children milling in front of the big house on the right, waving their hats and cheering. Obviously, he decided, the Hunt house, and obviously an occasion of importance. He dismounted and led his horse to the edge of the crowd.

They were applauding a man who stood at the front door of the house, looking hesitant and uncomfortable as he shook hands with one person after another. He was a man in his mid-thirties, tall, well built, with bright blue eyes and a great head of sand-colored hair—a very handsome man whose uneasy and embarrassed smile was most win-ning. He wore a loose white comfort shirt, black trousers, and white stockings. Feversham suspected that this was Joseph Warren. After watching him for a minute or two, he decided that he liked him—and felt that most people did. There was something totally outgoing and ingenuous about the man. Feversham had no notion as to why they were congratulating him, but he appeared to accept their praise with such boyish gratitude that his manner was most winning.

Bit by bit, the crowd drifted away. Feversham remained, his arm through the reins of his horse. Still engaged with two men at the front of the house, the tall blond man noticed Feversham and nodded at him. A few words more, and then he walked over to Feversham and looked at him inquiringly. "I'm Dr. Warren," he said. "And you, sir?"

"Dr. Feversham. Evan Feversham."

"Oh, of course, of course. I knew you would be coming by. General Putnam told me. What a pleasure. Indeed, what a pleasure."

He shook hands with Feversham, and now the two men who had been speaking with Warren joined them. "You must forgive all this fuss and bother," Warren went on. "You see, they've just made me a major general, that is, the Congress did, and the news is just arrived. Incredible, isn't it? A bit ridiculous, too. It boggles my mind, and you must forgive me if I make no sense whatsoever. I simply say it in the way of explanation."

"Not ridiculous at all," said a short, stocky, middle-aged man, bespectacled, his shirt and hands ink stained.

"This is Benjamin Edes, who prints the *Boston Gazette*. He's in exile here, like the rest of us, chased out of Boston and making the lives of the poor folk in Watertown utterly wretched, and this"—indicating the second man, stocky, wide-faced—"is Paul Revere, who's printing money for us, although heaven knows what we can buy for it." And to them: "And this is Dr. Feversham, who worked and studied with Dr. Suffolk in London when he did away with the hot-oil nonsense and developed his method of tying off the vessels. That makes no sense to you two, does it? It does to me. But come inside. You must be dog weary."

He called a stable boy, who took Feversham's horse, and the Edes and Revere left, and Feversham followed Warren into the house. It was a large house, but all too small for the population it contained, and Feversham's first impression was of unlimited confusion. At two sawbuck tables in the sitting room, half a dozen men were at work scribbling in record books and on sheets of foolscap paper. Journals, rolls of paper, and stacks of newspapers were piled everywhere. At least a dozen shouting children of every age were darting in and out of the room, chased by women, dodging, playing their own games.

At one side of the sitting room, half a dozen men were in a heated discussion, voice raised over voice in anger, despair, disgust, and frustration.

"No, sir! No, sir! I will not have you treat me as a fool!"

"When you are a fool."

"And you, sir, are a goddamn horse's ass."

"Why? Because I counsel common sense?"

"What in hell's name has common sense to do with it? Do you think these men will lay around forever? No, sir. They are going home."

"A fortnight."

"He's right. A fortnight."

"No army. Goddamn you, there will be no army."

"There is no army."

"I piss on that."

"You piss where you please, old man."

"Shit in your blood. Not you, Prescott. The others."

"By God, even for New England, that's the foulest mouth I every heard," Feversham said to Warren. "Who is it?"

"Israel Putnam," he answered, smiling. "He speaks well of you."

"What a turn of phrase!"

"He's contained here. There's women and children about."

"I'd sooner put a hoe up a pig's ass!" Putnam shouted.

"What is he?" asked Feversham.

Warren smiled. "He's hard to like. You have to know him. He's one hell of a soldier, the only one of us who is born to it, made for it. No fear of man or God or the devil, no reluctance to kill. It's a quality I do not comprehend, but God Almighty, we do need it. What a stupid, bloody business war is, Feversham!"

"How old is he?" Feversham wondered.

"Fifty-five. But he's vigorous. The tall man next to him is William Prescott. The British wanted to buy him out, but he stayed with us. Good man. That's Gridley next to him. The only engineer we have that's worth a fig, and the small chap next to him is Artemus Ward. He's the commander of the Massachusetts army. That's Farraday, the fat one. He's from Rhode Island, and he'll be back there soon, he's that nervous. And the other is Stompton, a shipmaster."

Feversham regarded the group with interest and curiosity. In this incredible situation that had pitted some thousands of New England farmers against the power of the mightiest empire on earth, these were the men who commanded the rebels: Putnam, short, stocky, filled with hostility and anger; Prescott, a head taller, handsome, his eyes almost hypnotically blue—forty-two or forty-three, Feversham would guess; Gridley muscular, compact, confident; Ward, aging, tired, his face creased with pain. And there was Warren beside him, who had just been made a major general by a Congress miles away and totally unaware of the chaos here at hand.

"Stompton," said Warren. "I mean, one wonders, do we need a navy. So one calls a committee meeting. Subject, navy. Of course, we don't know exactly what we are, an army, a rebellion, a state, or what. I'm a physician, so they make me a major general. Of course. Perfectly natural. Stompton is a shipmaster. Should we make him an admiral?"

One of the men at a table called to Warren to know whether he desired to check the food figures. Of course, it was only the roughest estimate. The violent argument had washed out now. Warren said he would get to the figures later, and he introduced Feversham to Putnam and Prescott and the others. "I heard about you," Putnam said. "You saw action in Spain and Germany, if I am not mistaken." His words were a challenge, but apparently there was no other level upon which he could conduct a conversation.

A little girl of three or four years clung to Feversham's leg, and by now three more men had entered the room and were engaged in arguments with the tabulators at the tables. His fingers in the child's silky hair, Feversham smiled and wondered how Putnam knew.

"Damn little in Connecticut that I don't know about. You're from Ridgefield, aren't you? Married one of the locals?"

"I have a practice there," Feversham said. "But action is too strong a word. I'm a surgeon."

"And one of the very best there is," Warren added. "What was all the heat about? The hill again."

"The hill again," said Gridley.

"How much have you seen of real war, Doctor?" Prescott asked Feversham. "I don't mean what we have here, skirmish and woods fighting—God knows, we all saw enough of that in the war with the French. I mean the real thing—forts and redoubts and great armies moved across a field of battle?"

"I've seen it," Feversham said.

"From the inside?"

"At times, yes."

Feversham realized that there were no real distinctions of rank here, no levels that made a thing private to one and public to another. The men at the tables left off or finished what they were doing to crowd around and listen, and other men entered and joined the crowd that already packed the sitting room. Women pushed through, some of them searching out children, grabbing them by the ears and dragging them away squalling, while two giggling teenage girls pressed through the crowd of men to place fresh candles. While it was still light outside, the room was darkened by the crowd of people. The candles would be there when needed, and Feversham decided that somewhere there were people who lived in the house which had become a public place.

"Never been to Boston before?" Putnam demanded.

"No, sir."

"Then how the hell would he know?" Putnam said.

"No one asked him anything," Warren said.

"You know damn well Gridley's going to drag him into it."

"Good heavens, the man's just here," Warren said. "He could be starving, and I haven't offered him a crust of bread. You've been at this all day, with that cursed hill of yours. Leave off."

"Who's in command now?" Gridley, the engineer, demanded of Warren. "You, sir, are now a major general."

"Enough of that," Warren pleaded.

"Goddamn it, Doctor, look a fact in the face. We're already so ass-wise confused we don't know which side is up. Ward here commands the Massachusetts men—"

"Which means three-quarters of all the men out there!" someone shouted.

"Goddamn it, no," Putnam growled. "By no means three-quarters. Say half."

"Not now," Warren begged them.

"Then when?" Gridley insisted. "You're major general by an act of Congress—"

"Which means not one damn thing in Massachusetts," said Prescott.

"General Ward is in command," Warren said firmly. "That's the way it is, and that's the way it remains. Now, suppose we go to our respective places, gentlemen, and give their home back to the Hunts. It's been a long day."

Artemus Ward, commander of the Massachusetts troops, lingered as the room cleared out. Ward was pale, dark rings under his eyes, tired and sick. Feversham decided that he would leave and find some place to stay the night, but Warren clung to him, and Feversham recognized in Warren some aching need but argued that he could not stay there. "They tell me there are twenty people here in Hunt's house."

Hunt, a stout, gray-haired man with a bewildered smile, came into the room and heard that. He was introduced to Feversham and hastened to add his invitation to Warren's.

"But there's no house in Watertown in better case," he assured Feversham. "Where will you stay, Doctor? The Otises have twenty-two heads under their roof, the Blakes have almost forty. I'm not offering you a bed. No one offers beds in Watertown these days. But there'll be half a dozen men stretched out here on the rug tonight, and one more makes no difference. And better the rug than the grass outside, wouldn't you say? We'll have food in the kitchen. We make no attempt to set a table these days—you can understand why—but we have meat and cheese and pudding, and no one starves. So stay with us, and for heaven's sake, if you are as good a doctor as Joseph here says you are, then look at him and find what ails him. For as God is my witness, if something happens to him, I don't know what we should do."

"I'm sorry, are you ill?" Feversham asked Warren.

"He makes too much of a case of it," Warren said impatiently. "Of course you will stay here. Hunt, give us just a few minutes with General Ward."

"Shall I go?" asked Feversham.

"No, no," Artemus Ward put in. "I want your advice. Warren says you know more about things military than any of us, and unlike him, I want not only for my health but for my brains as well." He grimaced with pain. "Stones. I stand in agony, sit in agony and piss in agony. War is for younger men, believe me."

Hunt left the room, and Ward went over to the trestle tables and picked up one of the ledgers. "This is where we are. Bookkeepers. We are trying to make rosters—men, guns, gunpowder, food—but it's a charade. The plain fact is that we don't actually have an army but just a mess of men strung out around Boston and waiting for the British to do whatever they are going to do, except for Putnam and Prescott and Gridley, and they know what they want to do, but so help me God, I don't."

"What do they want to do?" Feversham asked.

"Warren, get the map."

Warren left the room and returned a moment later and unrolled a large map of Boston and its environs. The three men huddled over it.

"You've been to Boston before? Or is this your first visit, Feversham?"

"My first time, I'm afraid."

"Then you'll follow me. Here are two islands in the harbor, Boston and Charlestown. Properly speaking, neither is an island, because each of them has a neck of land connecting with the main. Then again, both are islands, because in each case the neck is narrow and of no consequence. Now here is the spread of our men—" His finger moved north in a circle. "From Roxbury here up the bank of the Charles River, where we have built some defenses around the Great Bridge across the Charles. Then our lines go past Harvard College, through Cambridge to the Charlestown neck. We are on both sides of the Mystic River, here and here, and we have men in Chelsea and men in Malden."

"How many men all told?" Feversham asked.

"Thirteen thousand, we think."

"It's always in flux," Warren explained. "You must understand, Feversham, they are all volunteers, just ordinary men and boys. No one is paid. There are no enlistment papers, no controls."

"You mean there are no regular troops anywhere?"

"Good heavens, man, from where? These are New Englanders. We have no army. Oh, yes, you'll find a company in uniform here and there, local militia, made uniforms, marched a little. But it was a game, like a turkey shoot or a clambake. No, we haven't any soldiers as such."

"Do the British know all this?"

"We must presume that they know as much about us as we know about them."

"And what do the British have in Boston?"

"Well over three thousand men if you include the marines. The Fifth and Fifty-second of light infantry, the Forty-third and Thirty-eighth, and the grenadiers. They have a fleet of warships in the harbor, and I suppose they could arm and put ashore a thousand sailors if they wanted to." Warren looked up at Feversham and said, "I know what you're thinking."

"They're as good as any troops in the world."

"They don't have to be that good," Ward said.

"If they have the warships," Feversham said, "they can come ashore anywhere. How can you stop them?"

"We can't."

"Not the way you're spread out. I rode through Cambridge. I saw the encampment."

"What are we to do?" Ward asked plaintively. "Suppose we fortify one spot. All they have to do is to land in another place and walk around us. Then it would be panic. It's one thing to be a soldier. It's another thing to be a seventeen-year-old kid with a fowling piece and off you go to fight the British because everyone else is doing so. We don't even have a command they'll listen to. I'm in command of the Massachusetts men, when they listen. And if they say, Shut your yap, old man, and I'll do it may own way, there's nothing I can do but let them. Putnam's in command of the Connecticut men, except when they tell him he's not, and today, Warren here is put in command of everyone by the Congress, who are in Philadelphia and don't have a notion of things. But he doesn't want any command and—forgive me, Joseph—damned if he knows one blessed thing about war."

"It's as senseless as everything else," Warren admitted. "Why me? I'm a physician, not a soldier." He turned to Ward and demanded querulously, "Feversham would have made more damn sense. He's been on half a dozen battlefields in Europe. Even Putnam says he knows the lousy game better than any of us."

"I'm British," Feversham said, "and I'm a physician, and I am no commander."

"Lee is British, and so is Gates, and no one holds that against them."

"What is—well, it is," Feversham said. "The point at hand is this: What will happen when the British attack?"

"If they attack," Ward said.

"They must attack. Otherwise, they'll starve, and Boston will starve."

"It's not quite that simple," said Warren. "The question is whether we are at war or who is at war. Massachusetts against the empire? Does that make sense, Feversham?

"And the Connecticut men and the others?"

"It's a matter of emotion. We don't truly know whether any of the colonies will support us. They don't know, either, but if they attack, well, it's a war then, isn't it? That's how the whole question of the hill comes into it, the question of Charlestown."

He pointed to the map. "As I said before, there are two islands. They have causeways to the main, but to all effects they are islands. The British hold Boston. We have a perimeter around them, and it's not worth two damns. But no one holds this island, Charlestown and Breed's Hill and Bunker Hill. That's the argument now, Feversham. Putnam and Prescott and Gridley—yes, and Ward, too—they say, occupy Bunker Hill and hold the Charlestown island and we force the British hand."

"How do you force the British hand?" Feversham asked.

"We mount cannon there. Then we can blow them out of the city and their stinking ships out of the bay."

"I saw no cannon," Feversham said.

For the first time, Ward smiled. "We got the cannon, Doctor. Just a matter of getting them here. We took them at Ticonderoga, seventy-eight cannon, every kind you can think of—howitzers, mortars. By God, we even got twenty-four-pounders that can throw a ball for a mile—more balls and gunpowder than you can shake a stick at."

"Still, that's at Ticonderoga, and how far away? A hundred miles, two hundred miles? How do you bring them here? If I remember, there's not even a road."

"We sent Harry Knox up there," Warren said. "He's a very solid young fellow, a bookseller, but then he's read every book on artillery that's been published. It's just our good luck that it's been a hobby of his."

Feversham could hardly believe his ears. "How old is this Harry Knox?"

"How old is Harry, Artemus?"

"Twenty-two?"

"No, he must be older than that. Twenty-three at least."

"Then he never fought with guns."

"Now look here, Feversham," Warren said a bit testily. "We are not an army. Good heavens, we have to make out, don't we? Well, we do what we can. We do have two cannon, small ones, and Harry Knox has been drilling with those guns for two months now. He's a hardheaded young man with guts, and if he says he'll bring those guns here, by God he will."

"When?"

"In two weeks, three weeks at the most."

Feversham said, "Then how in hell's name can you hold that Charlestown island for two or three weeks without guns? And when he brings the guns, how are you going to get them there. There's only the narrow neck of land connecting it, and the British would be a pack of bloody fools if they didn't bring their ships in and cover the causeway."

"The water's too shallow for their big ships," Warren protested

"Then they'll use gun floats and flatboats. I have seen that operation. They can put a twenty-four-pound cannon where there's a foot of water, and they can blow that causeway to pieces. If you try to hold Bunker Hill or Breed's Hill, they'll bring up their guns and blow you off without ever coming into musket range."

"Gridley says he can build a redoubt," Warren explained.

"In full sight of the British?"

"In one night, he says."

"Gridley is a good engineer," Warren said. "Try to see our position, Feversham. You're from the outside, and we appreciate that. You can be objective. But we have to do something."

"Why?"

Both men stared at Feversham in silence for a while before answering, and then Warren shook his head and said that it would wash out.

"Just wash out, Feversham. We can't hold fifteen thousand men around Boston here. We can't pay them, and we can't feed them, and now it's time for the first cutting of the meadow grass, and then it's the first crops, and meanwhile, the wives are bitching like mad. I suppose you could ask why not let it wash out, but we're committed, and the people down in Philadelphia know that we're committed, and if it ends here, it does so down the line. We have our dead, and we had our bloodletting. At Lexington, they shot us down like dogs, and then we fought them, and there's more dead to pay for that. We're a close-knit lot, and it's a cousin here and a nephew there and a son and a husband. So we don't just let it wash out. There's no way we could do that."

"If this were a meeting of the Committee of Safety," Ward said almost sadly, "you'd hear us rave and rant. We make great orations to each other, and I suppose we do it to keep up our nerve. But I am a sick and tired old man, Feversham, and tonight I feel it in every bone. The God's truth is that it makes me want to say, Give up and go home. But we can't. We have been here for a hundred and fifty years, and this is our place. They must go home, and here we must sit until they do."

"What about the other colonies—New York, New Jersey, Pennsylvania, the South?" Feversham asked. "Will they send men to help?"

"God knows."

"And if they do, it will be next month or next year," Warren said.

"Then you have to make a move," Feversham agreed. "But why Charlestown?"

"What else?"

"Boston. Seize the causeway at night. You have fifteen thousand men. The British have less then four thousand. Pour into the city and take it back."

Ward shook his head. "We have farm boys. They have soldiers."

"We can't attack, " Warren said hopelessly. "We don't know how. It's as simple as that. Our men won't go up against the regulars. They won't go up against bayonets."

Staring at the map, Feversham said, "The hill is a death trap. Surely you can see that. If you held Boston, it would be different. But if you go into Charlestown, they will cut the causeway, and you'll never get out."

"We have bled it enough," Warren said. "We'll have some food, and we'll talk to the women and pretend for a little while that things are as they should be." He rose and took Feversham by the arm. "Come! Be a good colleague and a physician now. We'll have a medical talk, which is the best talk of all." He turned to Ward. "Eat with us, Artemus. We are all good Englishmen, and God wounds us for hating our mother. Have you ever felt that way, Feversham?"

"At times, yes."

That night, five men slept on the rug in the Hunts' living room, Putnam and Prescott among them. Feversham shared the rug for a while, but what with the wheezing and grunting and snoring and his own thoughts, sleep evaded him, and finally he gave up the attempt and went into the kitchen. A four-inch-thick night candle burned there, and Feversham took foolscap and pen and ink from the trestle table and then sat down in the kitchen to write a letter to his wife.

My dear Alice, I am here safely at Watertown in Massachusetts, where I have been welcomed at the house of Mr. Hunt, even though the house is so crowded already that men sleep on the floor in every room. I myself have been quartered in the sitting room, where, on a very splendid Chinese rug, I share very distinguished company. Perhaps you remember an Israel Putnam, who says that he remembers you and that he dined at your father's house on two occasions. He has been made a general in this strange army that is besieging Boston and the British army there. He is one of the rug sleepers, and I must say that when awake he has by far the foulest mouth in New England— and asleep, a snore like a bugle. I decided that rather than lie in the sitting room awake with my own thoughts, I would share them with you, and since the kitchen is the only room in the house without sleeping guests, here I am.

I must explain that this condition of the little village of Watertown is due to the fact that half the population of Boston has fled to the suburbs and that right now Watertown is in the way of being the nerve center of this strange war. And a very strange war it is—if indeed we are at war—with this tiny colony of Puritan and Presbyterian farmers facing the might of the British Empire.

Strangely, I find them a more worldly and understanding lot than your Connecticut countrymen, for they are not shocked by the fact that I am Catholic, and they regard my being English and trained in the English army almost with worship. They are desperately looking for English officers to help them out of the almost indescribable confusion of affairs that exists here, and they constantly express the hope that if the colonies to the south decide to send men to reinforce them, such troops will be put under the command of either Charles Lee or Horatio Gates, both of them Englishmen, as I am given to understand.

As to who is actually in command of the fourteen or fifteen thousand men who have gathered around Boston, it is almost impossible to say. Nominally, the command would be in the hands of an elderly gentleman named Artemus War, but he is quite ill and suffering from stones. A certain Dr. Church, whom I have met and find most distastful, bled him for the stones, which I think only worsens the pain, and Dr. Warren here agrees with me. Both Dr. Warren and I concur in grave doubts about the whole process of bleeding for cure, but I am afraid that our voices will little prevail on the subject.

This Dr. Warren, whose full name is Joseph Warren, is quite a remarkable man—one of those men whose plain manner of greeting and response is so gentle and, if I may use the expression, so noble, that he is virtually adored by everyone around him. He is a tall, handsome man, with wide shoulders and a shock of yellow hair, and simply by virtue of personal integrity has become the most valued and admired of the whole Boston crowd, many of whom I would not give twopence for. His reputation has become known in Philadelphia, and this incredible Continental Congress of yours—or should I say of mine as well—has responded by making him a major general and thereby adding to the current confusion. For not only is Joseph Warren the last person on earth to command an army, but he is ill with what I suspect to be milk fever, and since he asked me to examine him, I prescribed a week in bed with emetic salts—but with no hope that he will follow my advice.

Thus, we have two men in command of the same army, which is no army at all, but only a mob of men and boys gathered around

Boston, without uniforms or more than a few rounds of ammunition or a few days' supply of food, and neither men have even the vaguest notion of what to do or when to do it. If anyone is in command of this motley lot, it is Israel Putnam, a wild old man whose contempt for the British will surely lead us into some kind of disaster. He and an engineer named Gridley have some idea of fortifying a hill outside of Charlestown and thereby gaining the upper hand over the British. They talk of doing this tomorrow night or the night after, but perhaps they will think better of it, since Charlestown, as you may remember, is almost an island and to fortify it in face of the British fleet is to be cut off and destroyed.

As to what the British may be thinking or doing in the face of all this, I cannot image. We hear that they have almost four thousand men, among them some of the best regiments in the army, and it would appear to me that they have only to march onto the mainland and there would be nothing to oppose them. I think they hesitate to make a war. It is not yet a war, and perhaps if things go well, there will be no war, and please believe that I hope for this as much as you do. How many times have you heard me say that of all the obsessions of mankind, war is the most stupid and the most beastly. To think that intelligent men can find no other way of settling disputes is to lose heart and hope in man.

It is well past midnight now, and I have written much of the conditions here and the men I have met but little of myself. Why is it so easy to communicate when we are far apart—and so hard to find proper words to speak to each other when we are together? Of course you were right in charging me that I was not what you like to think of as a patriot and that it was no great surge of emotional indignation that took me away from you and brought me here. I think that as a physician I know better than most how complex people are and how difficult it is for them to know why they do what they do, much less to explain coherently to others.

I wonder how many of the thousands of men around Boston could explain the truth of what brought them here. I know that I cannot. But you were wrong, my dear, to say that I fled from you. Better have it that I fled from myself and, like all men who engage in doing so, found that the flight was quite futile.

What will be of my coming here and what will ensue over the next few days, I cannot imagine. But let me say that I am filled with unease, for there is something morose and heartbreaking in the making here. I would not say this and leave you in uncertainty if I intended to send this letter off now. But rather than do that, I shall hold it for a few days so that perhaps I may have a more cheerful postscript—or indeed find that there is no immediate need for me here and that I can make my way back to Connecticut. . . ."

Then Feversham sat pen in hand for a while, brooding over what he had written. His eyes were heavy, and he put the pen into the ink bottle, pushed it away, and thought that he would rest his head on his arms for just a moment and doze. When he opened his eyes, dawn was creeping through the many-paned windows. He spread his cramped arms and yawned, and a voice said, "I bid you good morning, Dr. Feversham."

He turned to see a lovely young woman kneeling by the great hearth and gently breathing an ember to life. It caught, and as she fed wood shavings to it, she explained that her name was Betsy Palmer and that she was Mr. Hunt's married daughter and that they had met the evening before.

"And I deplore the awakening, sir. Forgive me."

"Let me help you with the fire," Feversham hastened to say.

"No, no. It's not fitting. And see, it's already alight, and there's wood in plenty. Just rest you, Doctor, and I will have coffee for you. The coffee is dreadful, but we have heavy cream and sweet honey, so you will not drink it with too much distaste. Let me pamper you, for my heart is gladdened by your presence."

Smiling, amused by her prim speech, Feversham asked, "But why, my dear?"

"Because you are a physician," she replied simply. "I am gifted with sight, and I can hear them crying as they die."

June 15

Maj. Gen. Sir William Howe, a tall, dark, heavy-set man of forty-six years, had two passions in life, whist and women. And since he was a military man, he often observed that war without both would be intolerable. Thus, his first inquiry upon his arrival in Boston was whether there was a club? He was informed that indeed there was, the Anacreon, and there, on any given night, two or three games of whist would be in progress. He was escorted there the night after the dinner party at the home of Reverend Hallsbury by his-junior, Henry Clinton, where he was introduced to his partner for the game, a tall, good-looking, richly endowed woman by the name of Elizabeth Loring.

"I will be of service to you," Sir Henry had said to his commander in chief upon Sir William's arrival in Boston.

"I expect no less."

"There is a lady, name of Elizabeth Loring."

"Oh?"

"She is a prime beauty," Sir Henry said.

"I trust your judgment. On the other hand, if you are throwing me a bone you picked dry—"

"Sir William, believe me, I am otherwise involved."

"She's a colonial?"

"Loyal to the Crown."

"I see." The general stared at Sir Henry Clinton thoughtfully.

"This business that these wretched peasants have thrust upon us is no small game. It could go on for weeks or months."

"So it could. Or we could finish it tomorrow," Howe said.

"Hardly likely," Clinton replied.

"This Elizabeth Loring, is she married?"

"Oh, yes, to a Mr. Joshua Loring."

"Also loyal to the Crown?"

"Oh, yes," Sir Henry Clinton said.

"And what is he like, this Joshua Loring?"

"Loathsome. A wretched, dirty little man. He wants to be of service. I let him know that there might be something for him. He's useful, and he's so full of hate for the rebels that it's like a sickness with him."

"It doesn't speak for the lady's good taste," Sir William Howe said. "Why the marriage?"

"He had money. She had none. I speak of the past. He was a shipowner with a warehouse. They burned him out. I would guess that if the price is right, he would sell his mother."

"And this lady, this Elizabeth Loring, does she play whist?"

"With a passion."

"I would not like to think, sir," the general said, "that you are offering Johnny Burgoyne's leavings?"

"Rest assured, like myself, he is otherwise occupied."

"He, too? War is a heavy duty for both of you."

"Boredom is a heavy duty," Clinton said.

"And you wish to lessen mine. I would enjoy a game of whist tonight."

Boredom, General Howe decided, might easily be overcome and perhaps laid aside for the duration of this campaign. He faced a woman whose beauty was on the edge of being wanton, whose full figure was on the edge of being fat, at least five feet ten inches tall, her breasts overflowing her bodice, her dark eyes bold and direct. For all of her physical form, there was nothing soft or easily pliable. He felt immediately that this was a woman no one owned or dominated.

The large, generous gaming room of the Anacreon, with a beamed ceiling, green wainscotting and lovely hand-blocked wallpaper, boasted a hearth that could take a five-foot-long log. But the night being warm, no fire burned, only half a hundred candles in three chandeliers. And in their unsteady light, Mrs. Loring was almost unreal. Her eyes welcomed General Howe, and her slight smile convinced him that Sir Henry Clinton had prepared the ground well. She held out her hand, and when Sir William took it, the pressure was firm.

"General Sir William Howe," Clinton said, "and this, sir, is Mistress Elizabeth Loring."

Sir William bowed and lifted her hand to his lips. All eyes in the room observed them, the big man in his glittering red-and-gold coat, his gold-embroidered waistcoat, his white trousers and silk stockings, and facing him, this extraordinary woman, her black hair piled on top of her head, her handsome face framed in tight curls.

"I am delighted, madam" Howe said.

"And I am honored. I have heard a great deal about you, Sir William."

"Things to the good, I hope."

She bowed her head.

"I am told you favor the game of whist."

"Times I have played a hand. Yes, indeed, sir."

"Then shall we be partners this evening?"

"I would like nothing better, sir."

They joined Clinton at a table where a pretty woman sat, her head bent demurely. She smiled at Sir William. "Mistress Prudence Hallsbury," Clinton said.

"We met at General Gage's home, Sir William."

Earlier, Clinton had whispered to Howe a few words of explanation. "Temper your language if you would, sir. Not that her heart's cold. There's fire there, believe me, but she's the wife of a priest."

"No! You don't mean—"

"Just as sure as hell. The same Prudence Hallsbury, and she's the wife of the Very Reverend Hallsbury, who is High Church and most loyal."

"Then what in hell is she doing in a gambling club?" Howe demanded. "Of course, I remember. She hides her face."

"I put her down last night. She is a darling thing."

"Does her husband know?"

Clinton shrugged. "I really don't give a damn."

"Is that wise?" Sir William wondered.

"You mean we might disturb his loyalty? But where would he go with his stinking loyalty? He's very rich, more sterling on his dinner than you'll find in Westminister. The rebels would tear him to pieces."

"Still and all—"

"Oh, believe me, Sir William," Clinton assured him, "if he had serviced her properly, he might have cause to howl."

"And you tell me she plays whist?"

"So she says. After all, the reverend's not a Presbyterian. He plays himself."

When the four of them were seated at the table, Howe partner to Elizabeth Loring and Clinton partner to Prudence Hallsbury, each with a glass of bright red wine, Sir Henry offered a toast:

"To you, Sir William, my commander in chief, and to these lovely and gracious ladies, and to the fortunes of war, may they be neither brief nor demanding!"

Mrs. Loring shuffled the pack and dealt the cards. General Howe was impressed by her dexterity, her long, strong fingers sending the cards to each of the four players with never a moment of hesitation, until finally she dealt the last card faceup, the king of hearts.

"How so!" Clinton snorted. "I don't believe it."

"For you, sir," Mrs. Loring said to her partner. "Hearts are trump."

"As always," Howe replied gallently.

She smiled at him, and her smile defined the relationship. Howe arranged his cards. He had seven hearts—ace, jack, nine, eight, six, five, and two. Mrs. Loring folded the king and played hearts to Prudence Hallsbury; a bold move to force the trump and challenge the enemy. Howe recognized it and nodded slightly. Prudence played the queen, a forced or a stupid move. Since she had not hesitated when she cast the card, Howe decided that she had only a single trump, and he covered her queen with his ace. They finished the game with twelve tricks, and Howe raised his glass to salute his partner.

"You play well, my dear Betsy," he said.

"Too bloody damn well," Clinton observed.

"Ah, now," Mrs. Hallsbury said soothingly, "the evening has only begun, Sir Henry. Shall we double the stakes?"

"Is your hand that deep in your husband's purse?"

"For shame?" Howe snorted.

"For shame, indeed," Prudence said. "The purse is mine, Sir Henry."

"Touché!" Mrs. Loring cried. "Pru's father owns half the shipping that sails out of Boston Harbor."

"Or did before this stupid war started," Prudence added. "You haven't answered me, Sir Henry. Shall we double the stakes, or does Sir William shy away from a rich game?"

Mrs. Loring answered to that. "I think," she said, "that in games or love or war, Sir William has yet to meet a situation that frightens him."

When the rubbers were over, almost at midnight, General Howe had won sixty guineas for himself and sixty more for his partner. Sir Henry Clinton and Mrs. Hallsbury stepped into a carriage that was waiting, offering a ride to the other couple.

"Would you go with them?" Howe asked Mrs. Loring, and dropping his voice, "They can take you home. On the other hand, my quarters are only a short walk from here."

"I should love to see your quarters, as you call it."

The carriage drove off, and Elizabeth Loring took Sir William's arm with firm, possessive pressure. It was a cool, moon-washed evening, the wind from the bay fresh and salty, the docks deserted of any presence except for the grenadiers standing guard. More than half of the houses were empty, their owners having taken refuge behind the Continental lines. Sir William and Mrs. Loring walked slowly, comfortable with each other. There was no need to speak now. The night of whist had bonded them, And as for who she was and what she was and where her husband was, all that would come later, after the fire that burned in both of them had been quenched. Their only conversation now was a question from Elizabeth Loring:

"Do you believe in fate, Sir William?"

"I am a Christian gentleman, my dear."

"It is no accident that brought us together."

No, indeed, he thought, but Sir Henry, who, with another station in life, would be a remarkable pimp.

Aloud, he said, "Accident or not, you are the most desirable thing I have encountered in these cursed colonies."

Howe had taken over one of the best houses in the town, a fine structure, well furnished and with Chinese rugs that would have brought a fortune in London. His orderly had waited up for him, Sergeant Hawkins by name, well trained, with neither a smile nor a look of surprise at the presence of Mrs. Loring or the lateness of the hour. He spoke of hot rum toddy or tea or wine, to which General Howe replied curtly, "Go to bed, Hawkins."

"The candles are lit in the bedroom," Hawkins noted, and with that he disappeared. In the bedroom, the general and Mrs. Loring stood facing each other, Sir William thinking that here, in this candlelight, she was both more and less than real.

"Will you want privacy, Betsy? To undress?"

"Betsy? Will that be your name for me?"

"What do you fancy? Elizabeth?"

She smiled, unloosed her dress and let it fall, and then her petticoats. "Unhook me, sir," she said, "and call me what you will." She bent to peel down her stockings while he unhooked and unlaced her corset. Her tall, full body was on the edge of being fat, her breasts still high and firm. Sir William had never felt this way before, half crazy with desire as he tore off his uniform. "Gently, gently, sir," she cried, laughing. "Such feathers are too fine to spoil."

She sprawled on the bed, and still in his silk stockings, he fairly leaped upon her. "You will rape me, sir," she whispered.

And he replied, "That and more," and then, pressing his lips to her open mouth, drove into her.

When they had finished, both of them perspiring and exhausted, lying naked side by side, after a space of spent silence, she said to him, "Well, sir, how do you find me?"

"I am no callow youth, my dear Betsy. I am almost forty-seven years old, but as God is my witness, I have never come this way before. You are mine. Do you understand me?"

"Only too well, my lord."

"What about your husband?" he asked bluntly. "I have not spoken about him before, this Joshua Loring. Shall I have to challenge him and kill the bastard?"

"Why should you?"

"Does he know where you are?"

"My dear, dear Sir William, my husband does not know, nor does he care, and if he dared to object, I would break his wretched neck. I do not fuck my husband. I have never fucked him. He fucks whores, and he is quite happy with them."

"What are you telling me.?"

"The truth, sir."

"My God, woman, how did that happen? You could have had any man in Boston——"

"As a husband, sir?" She burst out laughing. "Do you really want me, Sir William? Oh, I don't mean to ease that raging cock of yours, but as a woman, to be with you, to stay with you, to go back to London with you, to be your lady?"

Now there was a long silence before he answered, and then he spoke slowly, "Yes. As I said before, as God is my witness. I have played an evening of whist with you, and I have fucked you, and I know you, and I will kill Mr. Loring as cheerfully as I would tread on a cockroach."

"Now listen to me, William Howe," she said, "before you dig a hole too deep to crawl out of. You say I could have had any man in Boston, which only goes to show how little you know these blue-nosed Presbyterians. I was nothing, my father a drunken fisherman, my mother a nameless slattern. I didn't want any man in Boston. I wanted a man with enough wealth and position to take me out of the slough of filth and poverty that I was born into. God gave me wits and beauty, and I would be a lady. Do you understand! A lady. I married Joshua Loring for his money, most of which has been washed away in this stupid rebellion. If you want me, you don't have to kill him. He had a fine house in Roxbury, but the rebels have taken it, and now we have rooms at the inn."

"What kind of a man is he?"

"He's a wretched dog. Throw him a bone."

"What kind of a bone?"

"He would sell his little soul to be an officer in your army. He will do whatever you wish him to do. Yes, he'll empty the chamber pots if you make him Captain Loring. But after tonight, I will not go back to him. If you want me—"

"I want you."

"Then make love to me again. I'm tired of talking."

Evan Feversham was a bit in awe of Dr. Joseph Warren. His own medical education, in the Old Hospital in London, had been highly unorthodox. He had worked under Sir Evelyn Dundeen, a man both honored and mocked for his insistence that wounds festered not because of evil humors or the night air—a belief widely held then and for years to come—but because of filth and creatures too small to be seen. Sir Evelyn's success won over Feversham and became the basis of his own practice of medicine. Dr. Joseph Warren, the head of the Continental Committee of Safety and, under Artemus Ward, the head of the American army, agreed with him. Now, on this morning of June 15, Evan Feversham awakened to see Warren standing over him. It seemed to Feversham that he had barely closed his eyes.

"Forgive me, Dr. Feversham," Warren said. "I know how precious sleep is to a man who must sleep on a wooden floor, but I need your cooperation, and the day is only too short."

"No apology, please, " Feversham said. "I had my few hours. Give me leave to piss and wet my eyes."

"There is hot coffee, and a chamber pot in the closet there." He spoke in a whisper, the room filled with men who still slept. Feversham did his toilet and then took a cup of hot coffee from a pot in the hearth and joined Warren outside. Fourteen men were gathered around Warren, all of them in knee-length leather or linen aprons. The sun was just rising.

"Here is our medical brigade," Warren explained, speaking softly and unhappily. "Only six are surgeons, euphemistically. The others are barbers and leeches."

"And that's all of them?"

"All we have available." He walked Feversham a few paces away from the group and, still speaking very softly, added, "It's been decided,

Feversham. We're going to defend the Charlestown peninsula, and that will mean a nasty battle. Once we're there, the British must drive us off or quit Boston. They have no other choice."

"What about the cannon?"

"Not yet, but Ward and Putnam insist that we can't wait. Perhaps they're right, perhaps not. We're going to fortify the heights, Bunker Hill and Breed's Hill. The British can put three thousand men into the attack, and to level the field, we must double that. And the neck of land that connects the peninsula to the mainland is only a hundred paces across. Still, it's our only hope to drive them out of Boston, and it will mean a battle. There's no way the British can endure us on those hills."

"Why didn't they take the hills before this?"

"There's the question. They had the hills, and then they left them. Good God, I don't know. Perhaps they're as stupid as we are. But I do know one thing. Over there are our surgeons, and they're all we have, and I want you to talk to them. They'll listen to you. You're from the old country, and they respect that."

"All right, I'll talk to them," Feversham agreed. "But what about litters and litter bearers and bandages and catgut?"

"The women are taking care of that. Joe Palmer and his wife are organizing it at their house."

"How much time have we?"

"We're fortifying the hills today. I don't know when the British will decide to attack. Today. Tomorrow. The next day. God only knows. Feversham, we had a sort of battle a few weeks past, when we drove them back from Concord, but we never faced them. We were behind the stone walls and the trees, and we were strung out over miles of countryside, and every man was fighting his own war and could run away when the mood took him. We never tried to stop their retreat. We never stood up to them."

"Even at Concord?"

"We surprised them there," Warren said. "We had the river and the bridge, and we took them by surprise." Warren was a tall man, his face red and flushed. He took a deep, painful breath.

"You're not well," Feversham said, and reached out to touch Warren's brow. "You have a fever, sir. You should be in bed."

"Damn it," Warren exclaimed, "I can't afford illness! Not now. A rasping throat. It will pass."

Feversham nodded, aware that you did not argue with a man like Warren. "At least drink lots of water. It's a beastly hot day."

Warren led him back to the waiting cluster of doctors, barbers, and leeches, announcing, "Here is Dr. Feversham. He was trained and schooled in London, and he's seen three campaigns on the Continent, and he comes with the blessing of General Putnam. He's a Connecticut man, with his home in Ridgefield." Warren ticked off their names: "Haddam, Carter, Bones, Woodly, Preston." He paused, his finger directed at a tall, thin, dark-eyed, dark-haired man whose leather apron had a wide pocket filled with a surgeon's tools. "Dr. Gonzales—he's out of Providence with the Rhode Island Brigade. He thinks as we do, Feversham, regarding infection."

Feversham said, "Dr. Benjamin Rush spoke highly of you. I met him in Philadelphia last year. Are you Spanish, Doctor?"

"Jewish," Gonzales said with a thin smile.

"Well, now, you are the first of the tribe I ever met. Myself, I am Catholic, but unhappily a fallen one."

"Then you must come to Providence, Feversham, where you'll find a round number of Catholics as well as Jews."

"Someday, certainly."

Warren went on with the introductions, the attention of the other men fixed on these two rather astonishing outsiders in a world of Protestants.

"Make yourselves comfortable," Feversham said. "I'll try not to bore you." There were two benches in front of the Palmer house. Some of the men sat on the benches. The others squatted. Warren sprawled wearily on the ground. "Who of you were with the wounded after Concord?" Three of them raised their hands, two barbers and a young man, who apologized that he was merely a leech, only a few months into learning his trade. Bones, a Welshman, explained that he had been with the British army years before.

"Then you know what a musket ball will do," Feversham continued. "The habit is to probe for the bullet, and I've seen men bleed away their lives while a surgeon probed and cut away. There are simply not enough of us to take the time to probe in a wound. The thing is to close the wound and put the man in a litter. Stop the bleeding and get him to the hospital—"

"We have no hospitals," someone interrupted.

"There'll be at least three houses for that," Warren said. "We have two in Cambridge and another in Roxbury. We'll portion them out. There'll be men and women there to help."

"Do we try to amputate where the battle is?" Gonzales asked.

"I would say no. And unless the tibia or the femur is smashed by the ball, we don't rush to amputate."

"And the humerus and the radius and the ulnar?"

"No, not on the battlefield. If the arm or leg must come off, the poor devil has some small chance in the hospital, where the light is good and the surgeon can work slowly and carefully. The odds are all against the man who is hit, but if you try to cut away with bullets flying around you, he has no chance at all. Use a tourniquet, stop the bleeding, and pack the wound. But above all, wherever the wound is, we must try to keep it clean."

"What difference does it make?" someone asked.

"The difference between life and death," Gonzales put in.

"Now let me tell you this," Feversham said. "If we had a fortnight, we could argue this matter. We don't. Dr. Warren tells me that we are already fortifying the peninsula, both hills beyond Charlestown. So you hear me well. A wound festers because the living filth spreads through the body and poisons it. It is not evil humors; it is not even the bullet. It is filth. You must carry water to wash the wound, and you must have a flask of rum, and when the wound is washed, pour a measure of rum into it—"

"What!" "Be damned!" "Are you mad, sir?" The outcries exploded all around Feversham.

Bones, white-haired and gaunt, cried out, "Be damned, Doctor, sir, here's a man in screaming pain and you want to pour a liquor in the wound? I'm no tyro, sir. The very pain will kill."

"The pain won't kill, and better the pain than the fester. You were a surgeon in the French war. How many men have you seen to survive an amputation or a belly wound?"

"Some do. I never served one who did."

"Have you used the liquor, Feversham?" Gonzales asked.

"I have."

"And did it do a miracle?"

"There are no miracles. But I've seen a man here and there who survived when the odds told me he was dead."

"Will you provide the rum, Dr. Warren?" a leech asked him.

"You come to Hunt's place. I'll have the rum there. You all come by Hunt's this afternoon and bring your tools and probes and saws and forceps and knives. Ay, bring a couple of buckets. We'll have some kind of plan and give your orders."

Finally, they drifted away. Feversham asked Gonzales to stay. Warren remained sprawled out on the grass, telling Feversham, "I want desperately to sleep, and I don't sleep. They'll be after me—God's curse. The stupidity of making me the commander. I'm a doctor, not a military man."

"Let me look at your throat," Gonzales said. Warren climbed to his feet. "My throat's sore, yes." Gonzales took a small stick and depressed Warren's tongue. "It's a springtime humor, flushed." He fingered the glands in Warren's neck. "Coddle it with hot flip and rest."

Warren laughed. "Rest, you say."

"Where did you learn, Dr. Gonzales?" Feversham asked him.

"In Rhode Island. We have a hospital in Providence."

"Have you seen any war?"

"No, but I've had cuts and hunting wounds, and I've done amputations. I had good mentors. The ships come in, you know, and the seamen are knocked about. I'm fifty-two years, so I have a lifetime behind me."

"Warren," Feversham said, "we'll not make it with a handful of barbers and leeches. "It's going to be a bloody, dreadful mess. If you could find a dozen men to help Gonzales here and myself, it might make a difference. And where is this Dr. Church?"

"God knows! Come inside and we'll talk to Hunt about the men you want. As for Dr. Church, Feversham, he's too damned elusive for my taste. He's supposed to be a member of our Committee of Safety, and I wish to God he weren't. The man raises too many doubts in me."

June 16

*I*n a royal rage, Sir William Howe, Fifth Viscount Howe, pillar of the British armed forces in America, commander in chief of the Royal Expeditionary Forces in the colonies, strode back and forth across the tastefully furnished living room of the Boston mansion appropriated for his use. Then he halted, his huge six-foot, one-inch bulk towering over Henry Clinton. He drove an accusing hand at him and shouted, "You dare, sir! And with what conscience, sir? You will preach me morality! You have taken the wife of a priest of the Church of England and are fucking her like a damned stallion with all the world to see and you dare to teach me propriety!"

"I beg you to be calm, sir," Clinton said softly. "I apologize for my forthrightness. For God's sake, let's speak like gentlemen. We are comrades in arms. I honor you. I beg you, sir."

Rage was never a lasting mood with William Howe. The anger passed, and for a long moment he stood silent, staring at Henry Clinton. Then he said quietly, "You don't understand."

"Perhaps not," Clinton admitted.

"You know me very little, sir. You take great liberties."

"My duty speaks, Sir William. In all of England there is no more honored family than yours. Your brother, the Earl Richard, more than any other man, is an emblem for the Crown. For seven years, he commanded the fleet that was England's wall against the French. You are a peer of the realm, with a wife and family in England."

"I'll thank you not to read me my honors," Howe said sourly. He fell into a spacious armchair. "I am no schoolboy," he said. "I am no callow, horny subaltern looking for ass. Something happened to me that never happened before in all my life. I am in love, sir. I have encountered something I never believed existed. This is my woman, now and forever."

Sir Henry groped for words. Later, describing the scene to Burgoyne, he would say, "I was bloody speechless. Here's this huge, overaged, overweight top dog—mind you, top dog at home as well as here—talking like a lovesick schoolboy. And over what? Over a low-born hussy, a whore, if you will, because she has been fucked over and diddled by anyone willing to pay the price. Oh, she plays a magnificent hand of whist, and she has tits that would make a vicar's tongue hang out, and I'll give you her looks, but the woman's a slut, and she married a gelding for his money—and Sir William is most certainly Sir William." But at this moment, staring at General Howe in speechless disbelief, Henry Clinton could only say, "I don't understand, Sir William—now and forever?"

"Now and forever. That's plain, straightforward king's English. What do you fail to understand?"

"Forgive me, do you intend to marry her?"

"That's a stupid question to a married man."

"Yes," Clinton admitted.

"She is to be my mistress, do you understand? Mrs. Loring will be with me through this campaign. She will share my quarters. She is to be treated and addressed as in every way a lady of quality. Any insult offered her—and hear this clearly—will call for a response on a field of honor. She will be the hostess wherever and whenever I propose a social occasion. I want this to be known around."

Clinton nodded.

"I would like an audible reply!" Howe snapped.

"Yes, Sir William. I understand."

"Good."

Very tentatively, Clinton responded, "May I simply say, that as you propose this, it cannot be sub rosa."

"I don't give a bloody fuck," Howe said flatly. "And damn it to hell, will you sit down and stop standing there like some bleeding school-master."

Sir Henry seated himself. "It will be an incredible scandal."

"I suppose it will."

"Not only here but in England and in Europe."

"Yes, but I don't choose to discuss that, Sir Henry. I wish to discuss the lady's husband, Mr. Joshua Loring. Have you met him?"

"Oh yes, He's been ass licking around for a commission."

"I gather he's queer."

"He makes no secret of it," Clinton said. "He married her to give himself some probity in the Tory crowd."

"What is he like?"

"Despicable."

"I want you to talk to him. Be open. Tell him exactly what I have told you. His wife will live with me. He is not to open his mouth concerning that, and if I hear a tittle of gossip or complaint, I will cut his balls off, that is, considering he has any."

"What do we give him?" Clinton wondered.

"He wants to be a captain in the grenadiers."

"Oh, does he? And how long would the officers in the grenadiers put up with him?"

"Not very long, sir." Howe began to chuckle, and Clinton waited patiently to share his humor.

"How many rebel prisoners do we have, Sir Henry?"

"I don't have an exact count. Not many."

"And what do we do with them?" Howe asked.

"Do with them? Well, damned if I know what to do with them!"

"Where are they?"

"We put them in Boston jail. Where else?"

"Who's in charge?"

"No one, Just a few guards."

"Well, by God, we'll soon have many more. Give our friend, Mr. Joshua Loring, the commission he wants so badly. Make him Captain

Joshua Loring and give him a command over the rebel prisoners. Find a dozen louts that you want to rid of and make them his brigade."

Clinton hesitated before replying, and then he shook his head uneasily. "These are prisoners of war, Sir William. They should be in the charge of a gentleman."

"These are stinking rebels, and they are no more prisoners of war than any footpad or highwayman at home. Captain Joshua Loring, in charge of His Majesty's prisoners. Does he hate the rebels?"

"Oh, that he does, and with a vengeance. They stripped him clean."

"Good," General Howe said. "I know his kind. Give him a little power over another and he'll be a happy man."

Evan Feversham was troubled that Dr. Benjamin Church had absented himself from the gathering of doctors and leeches. When he raised the matter with Dr. Warren, Warren was disposed to shake it off. "He's an odd lot, Dr. Benjamin Church," he said, not willing to go into details and explain to Feversham that when he, Warren, had raised the matter of the impending battle with Church, the little man had fumed with anger and denounced Feversham as a damned papist and Englishman, with whom he desired no further intercourse. Warren had heard the tale of the misdiagnosed smallpox incident and of Feversham's rescue of Church from the angry crowd, and he thought it best to let the business rest.

"Still and all," Feversham argued, "he's a member of the Committee of Safety. He's an established physician, and we are in desperate need. If he nurses a grudge against me, I'll try to talk him out of it."

"And if you do," Warren said without enthusiasm, "you'll never get him up there on the hills."

"Where can I find him?"

"He's with the Middlesex men, over by Willis Creek. He has a tent there, and he dispenses."

"Really? What does he dispense?"

"Poultices. He has a leech who bleeds for a shilling. It's not a business I care for."

"Those fourteen men," Feversham said, shaking his head. "Surely we could find a dozen more. Good heavens, there must have been a dozen doctors in Boston town alone.'

"And they're still there," Warren agreed. "Tending the British, who pay in real coin."

It was about two miles to where the Massachusetts farmers had encamped at Willis Creek. Feversham walked his horse through as noisy and disorganized a crowd of men as he had ever seen. Officers, many of them self-appointed, shouted orders, trying to form their men in ranks. Still other units were on the move, more or less orderly, marching three abreast. There were town militias from as far away as Pennsylvania, units that numbered anywhere from a dozen to a hundred men, a variety of uniforms as colorful as they were improbable, small brigades, large brigades, either carrying banners or calling out their origin—Albany, Stamford, Marblehead, Basking Ridge, Bridgeport, Providence, Fall River, Cape Cod, New London, Philadelphia, Baltimore, Norfolk, Newport, New Haven, Milford, Springfield. There was even a company of two hundred riflemen from Virginia, smart and romantic with their six-foot-long rifles, their doeskin leggings, and their fringed smocks. The uniforms were as colorful and different as the sewing circles in a hundred different villages could devise—red coats with white facings, blue coats with red facings, green coats, yellow coats, brown coats, pink coats, and shirts and vests and sashes in all the colors of the rainbow.

On the day before, the great army of thirteen or fourteen or fifteen thousand men had been sprawled all over the circumference of Boston. No count was valid, and no one actually knew how many they were, and it seemed incredible to Feversham that now they were at least somewhat organized and on the march to a great battle. Here and there were mounted units of twelve or twenty or thirty men, never many more than that, but in wonderful fettle, one unit with metal cuirasses and lances and feathered helms, making their horses prance and rear to the hoots and jibes of the men on foot. And in and among them, women and children, the children strutting with sticks of wood, and in front of every house along the way, the women and children of the house whistling and cheering.

Feversham had tended the wounded in three battles on the Continent, European wars, where the men stood against each other in solid ranks, and he had watched men die like pigs in a slaughterhouse. These men were ebullient. They knew of war only what they had seen or heard of the long, stretched-out battle of Concord, where each man was an army unto himself, where he could pot away at the retreating British soldiers from behind a stone wall or from the shelter of a tree or a barn or a house. War was like a turkey shoot, and as long as one kept his head down, he could come to no harm. And here he was with six-teen doctors, including himself and Joseph Warren, who was walking his horse to participate in eternity. He was too old for this. He was too far from home, and these men were as strange to him as men on the moon, if indeed there were men on the moon. He was a Catholic and fallen beyond redemption. He had married a lovely woman in Ridgefield in Connecticut, and he had left her to be a part of this mad-ness for reasons beyond his understanding. He was not good at under-standing himself.

It was a hot June day. Feversham saw a girl standing in the doorway. She had a pitcher in one hand, a mug in the other, and poured water into the mug for a thirsty young fellow to drink. She had hair as yellow as corn silk, and her firm breasts were bursting from her bodice. Her blue eyes fixed on him, and he pulled up his horse, his body seized sud-denly with desire so strong it weakened him.

She took the mug back, poured water, and cried out to him, "Here, Captain, wet your throat."

He had no sense of himself as a good-looking man, his long, dark face bringing him no comfort when he regarded it in a mirror. He had his Welsh mother's brown eyes, her black hair, now streaked through with gray. But he cut a fine figure on his horse, with his black boots and doeskin breeches and loose white shirt. The girl handed him the mug, watching him with pleasure as he drank.

"More, Captain?"

"Oh, no. Thank you." He found himself smiling at her. What a blessing to find something to smile at. He leaned down to hand back the mug, asking her, "Why do you call me captain, lass?"

"The officers ride, sir. The common men walk."

"I'm a common man, but I am a doctor, which earns me a horse."

"And what a strange way of speech you have, Captain!"

"I'm English."

"Ah, so you are. And why are you not over there with the lobsters?"

"I would find no such beauty as you over there with the lobsters."

"Come inside out of the heat, " she said. "The war will wait."

He was almost sick with desire. Cursing himself, he rode on without looking back, the foot soldiers passing by, grinning and hooting and offering themselves as substitutes. As so often, he wondered what strange forces drove him that he should be here of his own will, among these alien bumpkins who lived cheek by jowl with their angry Protestant God and were making this bloody war out of slights that English commoners had endured for centuries without protest.

A cluster of tents caught his eye, and he turned his horse toward them, enduring the curses and shouts of a column of marching men that had to give way for him. In front of one oversized brown tent, a man on a horse was shouting a stream of profanities at a small, fat man, whom Feversham recognized as Dr. Church. The man on the horse he knew slightly, Israel Putnam by name, whom he had met and spoken with two days ago. Putnam was an older man, almost sixty, a farmer from Pomfret in Connecticut and given to fits of anger. A handful of men stood around, listening to the exchange between Church and Putnam, and as Feversham came on the scene, Putnam was shouting, "I do not give a tinker's fart for your damned headaches, Dr. Church. This whole lousy day is a headache. Joe Warren tells me he called for all doctors to be assigned, and you refused."

"I am unwell," Church protested. "I have the runs. I am here at my tent, and I will do my duty here. I will not be spoken to like some common lout. I am a member of the Committee of Safety."

"You could be a member of the angel's chorus, for all that I give a damn. Your place is up on the hills, and you will set up a surgery there or I'll burn this fuckin' tent down on your head!" He paused for breath and saw Feversham. "On the same mission, Dr. Feversham?"

Feversham nodded.

"He'll be there," Putnam said, spurring his horse away and waving an arm for Feversham to follow him. Feversham was intrigued by the short, stocky, grizzled man, half bald with what remained of his hair flowing down in long white locks over his shoulders. In spite of the heat, he wore heavy leather trousers, knit stockings, and old shoes. He carried two horse pistols and over the pommel, hanging from a chain loop, an enormous cutlass. Though his shirt was drenched with perspiration, he wore a leather waistcoat and, on his head, a broad-brimmed farmer's hat.

"Come up alongside of me," he shouted to Feversham, and when they were side by side, he said to the English doctor, "I'm for the hills. Will you ride with me?"

Feversham pulled up alongside of Putnam, who said, "That man is no damn good. It was in my mind to tie a rope around his neck and drag him over to the peninsula. As much as anyone, I'm in command of this army, and I had to come here myself to talk to that little bastard. He's a big muckamuck on the damned Committee of Safety, and no one will touch him. The committee holds a meeting, and two hours later, the British know every word spoken. As sure as there's a God in heaven, it comes from Church. What kind of spell he has over them, I don't known."

"Do you have any evidence?" Feversham wondered.

Putnam shrugged and shook his head. "Devil take him! We have other fish to fry. Warren tells me you fought in Europe? Why are you with us?"

"I'm Catholic. They took all that our family had, all that my grandfather had. But that's a small thing. I had a bellyful of them and a land where a poor bastard is hanged by the neck for stealing a loaf of bread. The crux of it came when I served the wounds of a French soldier. They cashiered me. I came to America."

"We're going to defend both hills, Breed's Hill and Bunker Hill. Gridley insists that the whole defense hangs on a redoubt. I don't agree with him, but I'm going along. Have you ever seen a proper redoubt?"

"I'm a surgeon, not a soldier or an engineer."

"Warren says you have brains and eyes in your head."

They were now at the Charlestown neck, the sliver of land that connected Charlestown peninsula with the mainland, the road crowded with Continental troops marching across the neck toward the two high points that dominated the peninsula. Putnam waved at two men who sat their horses alongside the road. Feversham recognized Dr. Warren and Artemus Ward, and remembering the order of battle he had seen in Europe, the marvelously disciplined French and Prussian and British troops, the lines of attack and defense, of movement and countermovement, the rush of musket fire like eruptions from the mouth of hell, he couldn't help thinking that this was a tragicomic opera, a disaster on its way to happen, the half-disciplined files of farmers and clerks and hunters and woodcutters, the confusion, the babble of voices. Next to him rode the tactical commander of the whole movement, who had taken time to seek out a fat little doctor, suspected of being the enemy's master spy, and over on the other side of the causeway there was an elderly man ridden with the pain of kidney stones and a gentle doctor who was running a fever and ought to be in bed.

They pushed through to join Warren and Ward, Putnam explaining that he had run into Feversham and had brought him along. Putnam asked about the redoubt.

"The redoubt? I'm not sure that we ought to build a redoubt," Ward said. "Suppose they attack immediately?"

"My men are on Bunker Hill," Putnam said. "Prescott is there with his men. I'm going to move Nutting's brigade through Charlestown to the shoreline." He pointed to the ridge that connected the two hills, Breed's Hill and Bunker Hill, the slope to the ridge spotted with men climbing to take their position across the ridge toward Breed's Hill. "They're Prescott's men," he said.

"Where's Prescott?" Ward demanded. "I don't see him."

To Feversham, they looked like an aimless mob, without direction or leadership. Why the British did not attack immediately was beyond his understanding. There were no more than a few hundred men in Nutting's brigade. "How many? With Nutting?" he asked Putnam.

"Two hundred." The houses of Charlestown obscured the view.

"There's at least a mile of shoreline," Feversham said, and then bit his lips. It was actually none of his damn business even to question them.

"We'll reinforce them," Putnam said shortly.

"Feversham," Warren said, "would you go up there to the top of the hill. I told Gridley that you have seen redoubts in action."

"I'm not equipped to interfere," Feversham said.

"Goddamn it, sir!" Putnam snarled. "Do what you're ordered to do!"

His abrupt change of mood startled Feversham. Without another word, Putnam spurred his horse down the road toward Bunker Hill.

Artemus Ward shook his head anxiously. "That's the way he is," Warren said. "At least he has the make of a commander. Even if he doesn't know what to do, he does it."

Feversham nodded, shook his reins, and rode off on a path across a meadow toward Breed's Hill. He dismounted to lead his horse up the slope, passing by a division of about sixty men, stripped to the waist, dragging four pieces of artillery up the hill. They had three horses to help with the struggle, and when they saw Feversham, they began to shout, "Lend us your horse, Captain!" Evidently, captain was the proper address for anyone astride a horse.

Feversham grinned and passed them by, thinking that if they were British, no questions would be asked; the horse would simply have been appropriated. As the slope lessened, he mounted again and rode to where men were digging earnestly, looking around until he located Gridley, who was squatting over a large sheet of paper that rested on a flat stone.

From their position, Feversham had a view of the whole harbor, with Charlestown just below at the base of the peninsula and Boston town across the peninsula, and in the Charles River and off Hudson's Point, five British warships. The sight made his heart sink as he measured the chaos he had just passed through against the mighty force of the British fleet.

He dismounted, and Gridley glanced up to greet him. Col. Richard Gridley was a big man, wide and strong and well over six feet in height, with reddish hair, a two-day growth of blond beard, and tired, bloodshot blue eyes. He squinted at Feversham for a moment then nodded. "Feversham. Right?"

Feversham nodded.

"Warren said you'd be coming by." He called to one of the diggers, "Lenny, get over here and take the doctor's horse."

Feversham gave up the reins and bent over the sheet of paper on the stone. Gridley had sketched out the shape of a redoubt in charcoal. "Look at this, Doctor. I swear I don't know what the devil I'm doing. I saw redoubts when we took Quebec during the French war, but they were built of stone and concrete. We have fieldstone and common soil, but how on God's earth I can build a proper fortification out of that, I don't know. If we pile up earth walls, the British cannon will blow it to pieces. We could dig trenches, I suppose, but Warren insists on a redoubt. How do they do it in the old country? Warren says you've seen European battlefields."

"Some, yes."

"And redoubts?"

"I've been trying to remember."

"The thing is, what holds the walls together."

"Yes. I remember that well enough. They take young trees—saplings, we call them in Connecticut—and branches the thickness of my thumb, and they weave them the way you weave a basket, and then they wrap the basket weave around the bastions and face the wall with the same woven stuff."

"Of course! I've seen pictures of that, and if we had a fortnight or a week or even two days—but we don't." He stood up and pointed to the British warships. "We have the rest of today and tonight. Feversham, why don't they attack? We're spread out all over these hills. They could land their troops and cut through us like a scythe cuts wheat? Why don't they?"

Feversham thought about it.

"You're one of them. You know them. Tell me why."

"I don't know them that well," Feversham said. "They know what we're doing. But they're so damned arrogant and bloody well sure of themselves. To my way of thinking, they're simply taking their time. They can't see what's on the other side. There's the possibility that they want all of us up here, and then they cut the causeway and here we are. Or maybe not. Who knows how they think and what they think. They had the hills. They were up here, weren't they?"

"They surely were."

"And then they pulled out. Stupidity?"

"They must have had a reason," Gridley said.

"I suppose." Feversham pointed to the rooftops of Charlestown. "When they do attack, Colonel, they'll fire those houses."

"Why?"

"Because it's easy and because you might have riflemen in the houses. All they have to do is drop hot shot and those wooden houses will burn like torches. I hope to God you have gotten the householders out."

"The houses are empty," Gridley said. "There's no one left in Charlestown."

"You're sure?"

"Of course I'm sure."

"Where are they?"

"Roxbury, Cambridge, Dorchester," Gridley said. "They saw the handwriting on the wall, and they fled—modest folk, no Tories there, and they're no different than anyone else. We all think about a rope around the neck."

"The houses are empty?"

"I told you they were."

"Now listen," Feversham said. "Here's a way to build the redoubt. Think about a bed, any bed. You have a wooden frame with leather strips woven through it, crisscross. Do you follow?"

"Go on," Gridley said.

"Theres our basket weave. Face both aides of the wall. They've likely taken the pallets with them, but they'd leave the beds. Send a party down there and take every bed in the place."

"My God, Feversham, that's looting. We're not barbarians. Those beds belong to our own people."

"I tell you, they will burn Charlestown. Can't you believe me? There is no way in the world that place can survive."

Gridley was silent, staring at the rooftops of the little village at the edge of the peninsula. Three of his aides had gathered to listen.

"How would we keep them in place?" Gridley finally asked.

"On the outside face and the inside face. Rope them together as you build it."

"And to keep the earth in?"

"Jackets, shirts, coats, boards. Use everything you can find."

Gridley turned to one of his men. "What do you think?"

"It might work."

Gridley sighed and nodded. "All right. We'll try it."

At eleven o'clock, on the night of the sixteenth of June, in the year 1775, Sir William Howe and his partner, Mrs. Joshua Loring, finished their seventh rubber of whist, taking twelve or thirteen tricks and causing

Henry Clinton to exclaim, "The woman's a witch. A hundred years ago they would have burned her at the stake, and I would be one hundred and twelve guineas richer."

"Oh, for shame," Mrs. Loring cried, laughing. "Would you burn me at the stake, Sir Henry? And then what would poor Sir William do for a partner at cards?"

"Surely he was jesting," Prudence Hallsbury said. "And you are not to take my losses as your own, Sir Henry. If I had played well, they would be far less."

"Nonsense!" Clinton said gallantly.

"Nevertheless," Sir William said, "I shall, if you wish, my darling Betsy, take this poltroon to a field of honor. Witch indeed."

"Absolutely not! What should we do for a hand at whist? Or two hands, for that matter, since I am certain that both you excellent gentlemen are splendid marksmen and would end up shooting each other."

"Hear! Hear!" Clinton exclaimed.

"Of course," Mrs. Hallsbury said, "there is always that very handsome General Burgoyne."

"My dear Prudence," Clinton said, "how can you." And turning to Mrs. Loring, "I apologize most humbly."

"Sir William, shall I accept his apology?"

"I think so, my dear. We have a limited number of talented officers, and I am too old for fields of honor."

"Never too old!" She rose, went around the table, and bent to kiss Sir William demurely on his cheek. "Now, excuse me for my toilet. Will you accompany me, Prudence?"

Prudence rose, dropped a curtsy, and then, along with Mrs. Loring, went off to the closet the club kept for ladies. Sir William leaned back in his chair, rubbed his hands together, and said to Clinton, "Would you regard this rebellion as misfortune or as good fortune, Sir Henry?"

Clinton took snuff before answering, shook out his lace cuffs, and replied to the effect that no military man should regard war as misfortune. "Any more than a musician might regard music as a misfortune."

"The best of situations."

"Sir?"

"My wife is three thousand miles away."

"And when this is over, sir?" Clinton wondered.

"That is a problem I shall face when the moment comes. Meanwhile, I am a happy man. That is, insomuch as any man can call himself happy in this vale of tears. I have had many women, Sir Henry, but in all my life—which has not been without adventure—I have never met a woman like Mistress Elizabeth Loring. Have you spoken to her husband?"

"As you requested, Sir William."

"And pray, what was his response?"

"I think I can say that he, too, is a happy man. All he could talk about was how he knew a tailor in Boston who was the best uniform maker in the colonies. He wanted the grenadiers because he fancies the headgear and the sword, but he's a little man, and he would be laughable in the grenadiers. I think he's in love with the motto—"

"*Nec Aspera Terrent*," Howe murmured.

"Do not fear the use of brutality."

"Very fitting," Howe said. "Evidently, we've found us a proper jailer. No unhappiness about Mrs. Loring?"

"The man's as happy as a pig in an outhouse."

"And did you find him a berth?"

"With the Fifth Irish," Clinton said, smiling "Entirely proper, since the Irish know pigs. As the number of prisoners grows, we'll have to find more commodious quarters than Boston jail. Perhaps the hold of one of the larger merchant ships. That would keep him out of our hair."

"Indeed." Sir William poured wine and raised his glass. "To Captain Joshua Loring of His Majesty's Service."

The ladies returned now, and Mrs. Loring asked what was the occasion of the toast.

"To the peaceful and adoring cohabitation of the sexes," Sir Henry answered.

"Then I think that we should drink to that," Prudence declared.

"I think we should drink to America," Sir William said.

June 17

*F*eversham slept uneasily on the floor of the holding room in the Palmers' house, that is, when he slept at all; bits and pieces of half slumber, awakened each time by his dreams. They were not pleasant dreams. He had been a surgeon in three great battles, and he hated war with all his heart, and for the first time in years he longed for a priest to hear his confession. But there were no priests in the army, and here he was awaiting a battle that could be as bloody and awful as anything he had ever seen. These were strange people, these Americans, with their endless talk and bluster about equality and freedom. But they were an antidote to all that his life had been, and they were the only hope he had found in his tortured existence. They possessed a kind of innocence he had never encountered anywhere else.

In eight hours of backbreaking work, first under the burning sun and then in the darkness, they had built the redoubt on Breed's Hill. No orders were flung at them. Gridley knew each of them by name, and his instructions were gentle and easy. They were unhappy in taking the beds out of the abandoned homes. The soldiers were poor people, and to take what belonged to other poor people sat badly with them. They used their own clothing to back up the webbing and hold the earth in place. Feversham had lived long enough in the tiny Connecticut village of Ridgefield to know the work that went into these homespun garments and how precious and irreplaceable they were.

They were highly conscious of his status among them, an Englishman who had come over to their side, a gentleman and a doctor. Their attitude toward him as a doctor was a sort of veneration. A pickax, swung by a weary man, cut into the leg of another. They watched Feversham clean and sew and bind the wound. He overheard them talk about the incident. "You'll stay with us tomorrow?" a boy of no more than sixteen years asked him. It was up to Gridley. Quietly, Gridley told him, "Warren is going to command here. The men have a feeling for you, but we can't have two doctors in one place. You said there were only fourteen beside you and Warren?"

"Only fourteen."

As the redoubt was raised, the problem of placing the cannon faced them, the main difficulty being in depressing the angle so that the shot might sweep men advancing up the hill. Feversham's respect for Gridley grew. One of the men, and older man, had been with Gridley on the Plains of Abraham in the French war. There would have been no victory for the British then had not Gridley managed to raise the cannon up to the heights.

As Feversham lay on the floor at the Palmers' house, he lived over the struggle to build the redoubt. He had left before the work was finished, summoned by Warren to meet with the doctors once more and to oversee the division of bandages and catgut and surgical tools. It was past midnight when he finally reached the holding room, pulled off his boots, ate a few mouthfuls of bread and cheese, washed down by hot coffee as thin as tea, and settled himself to sleep and dream. He had meant to write another letter to his wife, but sheer weariness and the impossibility of lighting a candle in a room where at least six other men were sprawled on the floor asleep made writing impossible. "Perhaps tomorrow," he told himself, if there was to be a tomorrow.

He tried to dream of his wife, but he had never been able to control a dream or direct one to his desire. He was awakened from a dream of a battlefield covered with dead soldiers, and he walked among them, searching for one he could minister to. There were none. He had seen men with a slight bullet wound in the flesh of one arm bind it up, ignore it, and go on fighting, and the wound would fester, and the men would sicken and die. The whole world was wedded to the notion that arguments could only be settled by death, and here was a British army that had come three thousand miles to spread death among the farmers who had toiled all their lives to scratch a living out of the soil of this hard New England land.

Sheer weariness allowed Feversham to sleep, but it seemed to him that he had hardly closed his eyes when someone shook him gently. He rolled over to see Betsy Palmer holding a candlestick. "Forgive me, Dr. Feversham, but the officers are to have a meeting here in the holding room, and I must make it clear for them."

"What time is it?" he asked thickly.

"Two o'clock in the morning."

He sat up and sighed. "All right. It's warm, isn't it?"

"Quite warm."

"I'll find a place in the courtyard."

"No, no. I wish you could sleep. I don't know how any of you can stand it. But General Putnam wants you here. There's water at the pump outside, and I'll have hot coffee."

Feversham rose and looked around him. A woman was lighting candles on the kitchen table. The other men who had used the holding room as a place to sleep were picking themselves up and wearily shuffling through the doorway. Feversham followed them. Some of the men who had slept on the floor went off to a clump of bushes to urinate. Others were at the pump. Feversham noticed Joseph Palmer, who was lighting a post torch. The officers were arriving, tying their horses at the hitching rail.

As Feversham waited his turn at the pump, he observed Putnam and Gridley going into the house. He splashed cold water on his face, rinsed his mouth, and felt better, almost awake, almost alert. As he turned away from the pump, he heard his name called, and he peered through the torchlight to see Warren dismounting. Warren joined him and shook his hand warmly.

"How do you feel?" Feversham asked.

"I think there's medicine in excitement, don't you?"

Feversham touched his head. "You're feverish. No, I won't instruct you."

"I want to thank you for what you did at the redoubt. This is our place and home and life, but when a stranger like yourself comes to us, I feel God smiles at us a little. Forgive me for being sentimental. It's the fever, I'm sure."

Embarrassed, Feversham only nodded.

"You'll come inside?" Warren asked.

"I need the bushes over yonder. I'll be inside." Feversham went to the thicket to urinate, thinking how easily manner and custom collapsed at a time like this. "Naked we come and naked we go," he said to himself. "It strips away so easily. What poor creatures we are, with our pretense at civilization."

When he entered the holding room, it was already crowded with the officers: Israel Putnam, Artemus Ward, William Prescott, John Stark, Tom Knowlton, Richard Gridley, Dr. Joseph Warren, and half a dozen others who were unfamiliar to Feversham. They crowded around the table, some on benches, others standing.

Feversham tried to remember rank. Warren, Ward, and Putnam were all generals, but as to the others, who were colonels and who were captains he could not say. Since only a handful were not in civilian clothes but in uniforms of one militia company or another, there was no way for him to know until an officer was addressed. For all of that, Feversham was sensitive enough to feel the drama of the moment, the earnest, tired faces of the officers in the flickering candlelight, the silence of fatigue that substituted for the chatter that such a meeting in daylight would have occasioned, the strong smell of sweat, the dirt on their shirts, and the curious setting in the holding room, with the hams and sausages and cheeses hanging from the beams above them, the kitchen of a serious and hardworking householder.

Mrs. Palmer and her husband were handing out wooden or clay mugs, whatever they could find to drink from, and pouring coffee for the officers. Only now, in the relatively greater light of the holding room, with a dozen candles on the table, did Feversham become aware of how Joseph Warren was dressed—trousers of white satin, a gold-embroidered waistcoat over a silk shirt, a jabot of lace, and a coat of beautifully embroidered silk.

He stood up at the end of the long board table and tapped with his ring to gain their attention and end the whispering. Again, Fevesham remarked to himself what an interesting man this was, so tall and slender, with the long, sensitive face of a poet.

"Let me being," Joseph Warren said, "by apologizing for my festive garb. Those two wise men, Colonel Gridley and Dr. Feversham, worked out a unique manner of building a redoubt. But having only sand and stones to back up the webbing that holds the walls in place, they called for pieces of cloth to reinforce the sand and keep it in place. I decided to give them my entire wardrobe, and my good wife would not do less. So I stand before you in the only clothes that remain to me, and I am sure that before this day is over, they will be less ornate. With that said, may I offer my heartfelt praise for what you and our loyal comrades have accomplished these past fifteen hours. Where there was confusion, there is now order, thanks to your tireless efforts. And where we were a crowd, we are now an army, in position to fight. I now give the floor to General Israel Putnam, our most beloved brother from Connecticut. He will deliver the order of the day."

Putnam rose, his gnarled hands clasped in front of his chin, stood for a long moment, glancing from face to face, and then said bluntly, "Here is how we stand on the Charlestown peninsula. Colonel William Prescott, as you know, is in command of the general defense of Breed's Hill and Bunker Hill. He has established our position. The order of the day is that we will fight to the death so long as our ammunition holds. If we must retreat, we retreat in good order, facing the enemy."

He sat back, and Prescott stood up, leaning over the table. "We are in a good position from Bunker Hill and across the ridge to Breed's Hill. The men stationed there have the protection of stone walls. They have been working to connect the separate pasture walls. General Putnam and his Connecticut men have taken up a position on Bunker Hill. To protect their flank, Colonel Stark has taken a stand with his riflemen, from the slope to the Mystic river. Colonel Stark," he said, nodding at a rangy, sunburned man who sat next to Gridley.

"We have a fence of sorts where we are," Stark said. "I wish we had a wall of stone, but there's no time for that. The hay in the pastures at our position is baled, and God forgive me for taking the crop of honest farmers—we're all of us Hampshire farmers—but it's our lives. We made a wall of the baled hay against the wood fence. It won't stop a bullet, but it will cover us. These are good Hampshire riflemen, and I swear we'll hold our side."

"The redoubt?" someone asked.

"Not completely finished," Gridley said, "but it's in place. If you want the whole picture, it's four-square, forty paces to a side. The main attack side is reinforced with woven leather and cloth. The rest is dirt and rocks. There are slits and firing steps. Tomorrow, if there's time before they attack, we'll dig a trench all along the one side where they can attack directly. There's an old clay pit there and good shelter, and that anchors Colonel Knowlton's division. He has a proper stone-wall barricade, maybe two hundred paces to connect with Johnny Stark's New Hampshire men. Am I right, Tom?"

Feversham saw the man called Knowlton smile grimly, a hard-faced man in his forties with a pair of tired blue eyes. "Yes, Richie, you paint a fine picture, and we've been breaking our asses to make something of that two hundred paces, but every time I turned around, half my men were gone for the building of your damned redoubt. They're so tired they can't stand. I told them to sleep. There are stones enough for Breed's Hill. We never needed that damned redoubt. You have a hundred men on the redoubt. What in hell are we building the bloody fortress for! It's indefensible!"

"We had the argument yesterday and the day before," Putnam snarled. "Let it go, Tom!"

"He's right!" someone cried. "It's a death trap."

"Ah, please, please," Warren begged them, rising and spreading his arms. "What matters most is for us to be together."

They had enormous respect for him, and the hubbub of voices died down. Feversham realized that this slender, aristocratic physician occupied a unique place among these men. Feversham was new to the group, and he wondered what circumstances led to their choice of Warren, a man with limited military knowledge, as their leader. He had heard that

Warren defied the British openly in a manner that only Samuel Adams dared to match. Now the man was seriously ill, if Feversham was any judge of sickness. Yet some fire within him rejected sickness, as if spirit alone could make him whole.

"You gave me the command of our forces," Warren said gently. "Half of you fought in the French war, and I bow to you. But if I must command, then I must. It was my decision to build the redoubt. Now it is built. There are more important matters to discuss."

"You are damn right!" Putnam boomed. "I didn't want the redoubt, but it's built. You can't saw sawdust. But it's true that we wasted ourselves. Ward tells us that they'll attack tomorrow—"

"Today is tomorrow," someone interrupted.

"I don't mean that. Today is the seventeenth. Ward said on the eighteenth. I know today is tomorrow. It's three o'clock in the morning. Suppose they attack today. Suppose they attack at dawn, two hours from now."

"God help us."

Artemus Ward rose. "We only know what we know," he said, his face tight with pain. "We have one man with the British, but the Almighty Jehovah has given us his voice and his truth."

"If you believe him."

"He risked his life to come to us," Ward said. "You must trust me. I have spoken with him, and I believe him."

"Why can't we know his name?" Knowlton demanded.

"Because I gave him my sacred trust that no one but myself would know his name. He is an officer in the king's army, and he came to me because he believes in our cause. He says that they will attack on the eighteenth of June. Gage wants to hold off, but Clinton and Burgoyne have convinced Howe that an attack will succeed. Mostly, it's Burgoyne. To Burgoyne, we are a joke, a witless crowd of peasants. They have only three thousand men, but Burgoyne said they will sweep us away like so much dirt. At the first sight of their bayonets, we will break and run."

"I heard Gage wanted out of the whole thing," Prescott said.

"Our friend says that Gage is more or less in disgrace. It's Burgoyne and Clinton, and both of them in a rage to destroy us, and they use Sir William Howe as they will."

"General Ward," Putnam said stiffly, "I put my trust in no man who serves the king. When the sun rises today—today, mind you—they will see that damned redoubt. It stands up on Breed's Hill like some stinking castle. They will see men digging, and unless they are brainless, they will attack."

"General Putnam," Warren said, "if they attack today, we will fight them today. If they attack tomorrow, we will fight them tomorrow. And now there is still work to be done, and we have argued enough. We will have a prayer, and then we will go to our commands." He put his hands together and bent his head. "Great Lord of Hosts, we place our lives and our cause in thy trust. Grant us to be of stout heart and good will."

Yet they talked on and argued and argued, and while they talked, the first light of dawn touched Breed's Hill. His Majesty's warship *Lively*, a brig of twenty guns, rested at anchor in Boston Harbor off the meadowland that sloped up to Breed's Hill. On board the bell sounded the third watch. Midshipman Earnest Copeley crawled out of his hammock and, rubbing the sleep out of his eyes, climbed up to the main deck and urinated into Boston Harbor. It had been beastly hot below, and it was none too cool on deck. Knowing that he would be officer of the deck until the next watch, Copeley took the liberty of appearing in shirt and trousers, barefoot. Midshipman Copeley was fourteen years old, and this was his first assignment aboard ship. He was totally intrigued with Boston and the rebellion and with the posibility that he might witness a great battle. Until now, his life in Boston Harbor had been dull indeed, with only two short shore leaves and both of them under the supervision of Lieutenant Kent. Now, as he came on deck, he was called over by Henderson, the midshipman he was to relieve.

"Barefoot again," Henderson said, being two years Copeley's senior and entitled to rebuke.

"Too bloody hot for shoes."

"Tell that to Lieutenant Kent. All right, have a look up there on the hill," he said, pointing to the top of Breed's Hill.

"Oh?" Midshipman Copeley stared and squinted. "It's a damned fortress."

"Precisely. And was it there yesterday?"

"No, it was not."

"Exactly. Now get below and put your bloody shoes on and wake the Lieutenant Kent."

Midshipman Copeley scampered below and a few minutes later appeared again, followed by Lieutenant Kent and Captain Dexter, the latter with a spyglass, which he trained on Breed's Hill. "Well, I will be everlastingly damned, it's a bloody redoubt! Here, have a look," he said, handing the spyglass to Lieutenant Kent.

"So it is," Kent agreed, "and rebels all over the place, digging away like maggots in an offal pit."

"What will you do, sir?" Copeley asked, fairly hopping with excitement.

"We'll soon put and end to that," Dexter decided. "Rouse the drummer and beat to quarters, Copeley. Clear for action, Mr. Kent, and you, Henderson, get up topside and report."

Copeley dashed off, fairly tumbling down below, while Henderson scrambled up the rigging to the lookout station. Minutes later, the drummer's beat to quarters sounded across the bay, while Lieutenant Kent supervised the launching of the ship's longboat so that the *Lively* could be swung around so that its guns might bear on Breed's Hill. Captain Dexter and his chief of gunnery checked the elevation of the guns, and within fifteen minutes of Midshipman Copeley's arrival on deck, the ship was swinging into proper target position. Just before 5:00 A.M, on the morning of the seventeenth of June, *Lively* launched its first broadside at the redoubt of Breed's Hill.

Sir William Howe slept in his singlet but without covers, for his room was hot. Next to him, Mrs. Loring lay naked, in defiance of the attitude that attributed the custom to whores. As she had explained to Sir William, since all the ladies, both here and in London, would call her a whore, she might just as well sleep in comfort. Her forthrightness endeared her to Sir William, and when he was awakened on the morning of the seventeenth, thinking that he had dreamed of gunfire, he looked with warm pleasure at the sight of Elizabeth Loring's abundant pink buttocks. For a bit less than a minute, he allowed this pleasant contemplation to continue, feeling his own groin come alive, and then a second salvo of guns made him realize that this was no dream. He tumbled out of bed, threw open the door of his bedroom, and roared, "Hasgood! Hasgood, get the hell up here!"

Awake, her knees drawn up, her arms across her breasts, Mrs. Loring cried out in alarm. "What is it, sir? What is happening?"

"Cover yourself," he said as his orderly, Hasgood, knocked at the door. She drew the sheet over herself, and Howe threw open the door for Hasgood.

"What the devil is that, Hasgood?"

"Cannon fire, Sir William."

"I know that, you idiot! What cannon?"

"If I may open the shutters, sir?"

"Open them."

Sir William followed Hasgood to the window that looked out over the bay.

"The *Lively*, sir," Hasgood said. "I believe she's firing broadsides."

"At what? Move aside."

"At Breed's Hill, sir, as near as I can make out."

"Yes—yes—there it goes again," he said as a third broadside thundered out. "What's that up on the hill?"

"Some sort of fortress, sir, as near as I can make it."

"It wasn't there yesterday."

"No, your lordship. No, it was not, as nearly as I can remember."

"Well, it's there now. Where's my glass?" He turned to Mrs. Loring. "Betsy, where did I put my glass?"

The night before, he had been showing her the wonders of the moon through his spyglass. "There on the chest. What is happening, Sir William?"

He took the spyglass and strode to the window. "Be damned," he exclaimed. "They're as thick as fleas up there on the hill. Bad aim, bad aim. Who commands *Lively*, Hasgood?"

"Captain Dexter, sir."

"Yes, of course. Dark chap with a stupid look. The idiot quoted Dryden to me. I can't tolerate people who quote poetry. Can you, my dear?" turning to Mrs. Loring.

"Of course not. Bores, Sir William. Bores."

"Hasgood, turn out Lieutenant Jefferies and tell him I want him to round up Clinton, Burgoyne, and Gage. I want them all here not later than"—he paused to look at a tall cabinet clock in one corner of the bedroom—"no later than six o'clock. And Admiral Graves. He's aboard ship, so tell Jefferies to send a lolly boat for him. And then you get back here. They'll want breakfast, tea and sausage and hot bread—"

"Oh, leave the breakfast to me, sir," Mrs. Loring put in. "I'll wake the kitchen and take care of it."

Another volley of gunfire thundered out across the bay.

"Get to it, Hasgood," Sir William said. Hasgood left the room, and Howe peered through his spyglass. "He'll piss off all his gunpowder for nothing."

"What a gift for words, dear sir. Piss off his gunpowder."

He turned to face her. She had cast off the sheet. "What does it mean? All this shooting?"

"They're becoming insufferable. We have to dress."

"Now? This moment? You wake me at this ungodly hour and tell me to dress?"

"There's work afoot, my dear one."

"And a little play," she said, smiling. "What do they say—all work and no play makes Jack a dull clod. Come kiss me."

He threw up his hands in dispair and fell into the bed.

Betsy Palmer stopped Feversham as the officers were leaving. "About Dr. Warren, he's not well, is he?"

"I'm afraid not."

"I have a room upstairs where he could rest."

"I don't think he means to rest," Feversham said.

"Would you talk to him, please? As a favor to me?"

Warren was in the dooryard, speaking to Colonel Prescott. Without meaning to eavesdrop, Feversham realized that they were talking about the redoubt. In the pale light of dawn, there was not even a touch of breeze to disturb the early heat, and Warren mopped his face constantly. "It was my own notion from the beginning, and God help me if I have forced a death trap upon us."

The other officers were untying their horses at the hitching rail. A few had mounted and were riding off. Others were clustered in the road, still talking.

"Who's to say it's a death trap?" Prescott shook his head in annoyance. "Knowlton? Does he have a crystal ball? Stop whipping yourself, Doctor. It may turn out that the redoubt is our salvation."

I won't urge him to bed, Feversham thought, convinced that Warren would die before he took to his bed. He saw Artemus Ward approaching and moved to step away.

"No, stay here, Feversham. You're a doctor, and that may give you the best chance of surviving what's coming. I've been thinking about our informnant. If I should be killed, someone must know his name."

"Feversham's British," Prescott said shortly.

"Colonel, he's my friend and colleague. If we lose on the hills, he'll hang as high as any of us."

"I'll leave you," Feversham said.

"No!"

"I'm sorry," Prescott muttered. "We're all too tense and tired. He nodded at Artemus Ward. "Go ahead, General."

"Johnny Lovell," Ward said.

"No!" Warren exclaimed. "Lovell's son?"

"His father's the worst swine in the whole lousy Tory crew," Prescott exclaimed. "Lovell's son! Well, I'll be damned!"

"He's given me every move, every step, they planned. It comes from his father, who's trying to organize a Tory brigade. He put his life in my hands, and now I put it in yours. I have business now, gentlemen. God willing, I'll see you later." With that, he turned and shambled away to where his horse was tethered.

"Johnny Lovell," Warren murmured. "I tried to speak to his father once. I tried reason, but the man is filled with bile."

"I would guess," Feversham said slowly, "that there are more men in London who pray for our cause than over there in Boston, where they lick the ass of the redcoats and open their homes to them and wait to see us all hanged."

The three men mounted their horses. The other officers had left. They rode slowly toward the causeway that led to the Charlestown peninsula. In the east, the sky turned from gray to pearl, and as they rode toward Charlestown, they heard the first salvo of guns from the warship *Lively*.

"A proper breakfast," Sir William Howe said, "after a proper roll in the hay, equips a man for whatever the day might bring." He moved along the sideboard, heaping his plate with eggs, sausage, ham, turnips, and parsnip. "You have a talent for the best things in life, my dear," he said to Mrs. Loring, who was pouring tea. "I prefer my eggs boiled hard rather than coddled, but these look delicious."

It was half-past seven in the morning, and the thunder of guns from the ships in the bay shook the house. They were all gathered in the dining room of Howe's house—that is, the house which he had appropriated for himself, the largest and best rebel house that Boston boasted—Sir Henry Clinton, Maj. Gen. John Burgoyne, Gen. Thomas Gage, and Adm. Thomas Graves.

"All ships firing, " Admiral Graves said. He was a large man with a protruding stomach and bright pink cheeks, hunched over a plate piled to abundance. "The sweet rolls are delicious. My compliments to the cook, Mrs. Loring."

"The rolls are my doing. I thank you, Admiral."

Burgoyne, helping himself at the sideboard, opined that it was all noise and bluster.

"I beg to differ," the admiral said.

"Admiral," said Burgoyne, seating himself at the table, "if you had a mind to wager, I'd say that all that storm and sound outside won't kill half a dozen rebels. Meanwhile, you're shooting away your cannonballs as if they grew on trees."

"I resent that, sir."

"My word," Clinton said, "you worry about cannonballs as if they came out of your pay, Johnny. On the other hand, they built that damn redoubt up on the hill. That's an insolent piece of business. Do you think you can knock it down, Admiral?"

They turned to Graves, who shrugged and shook his head. "It's a piece of work. No. We're not having any real effect on the redoubt. I ordered Dexter on *Lively* to halt his fire. You know, he opened up on his own. Then Gage here countermanded me. He ordered a bombardment of Breed's Hill by all ships. Goddamn it, gentleman, who is in command here?"

"I am in command," Sir William said flatly.

"Do you want the bombardment stopped?" Graves demanded.

"No."

"Sir William," Clinton said, "we are to attack tomorrow. Do you intend to go on shooting for the next twenty-four hours?"

Sir William finished chewing and washed his food down with a swallow of tea before he replied. "No, Henry, we will attack today."

There was a long moment of silence, broken by Burgoyne, who clapped his hands with pleasure. "Absolutely. From all I can learn, there's total chaos up there on the hills. The damn rebels are milling around like cattle in a thunderstorm. We watch them crowding over the neck into Charlestown, some going on to the peninsula, others running out of it. Dr. Church says every militia commander has a different notion of what they should do, defend the peninsula or abandon it. There's a brigade from Jersey that simply picked up and marched off. Old Artemus Ward is in agony over his stones, and Church says his mind is addled. They're tearing at each other over the redoubt. Putnam and Prescott never wanted it, and Gridley and Warren, who were the instigators, as I am given to understand, have fallen out with the others. They go on arguing endlessly on how to defend the hills and Charlestown, and Church says they're all over the place in total confusion."

"You want some meat," Howe said to Gage. "There's no bloody life in eggs and sweet rolls. Try the ham, sir. Betsy," he called out to Mrs. Loring, who stood by the sideboard, "put a slice of ham on General Gage's plate."

It was a deliberate slight, as the others realized. Sir William had small liking for Gage. "Thank you," Gage said coldly. "I have had quite enough."

"What I don't understand," said Admiral Graves, "is why we don't simply cut off the Charlestown neck and let their damn rebellion die on the peninsula. They'd soon run out of food and water."

"Yes," Clinton said, "but in spite of Johnny's enthusiasm with Church's intelligence, his word is not gospel for me. Who has counted the number of farmers around Boston? Ten thousand? Fifteen thousand? If we muster the Forty-seventh Marine Brigade along with everything else we have, it adds up to three thousand and two hundred men. If we place ourselves on the Charlestown neck, we are between two armies, the men on the peninsula and the damn mob outside of Boston. It's a position no army should ever be in."

"Thirty-two hundred of the best troops in the world," Burgoyne said. "Church says there can't be much more than a thousand of them on Breed's Hill and Bunker Hill. I'll hold that neck with a corporal's guard."

"What nonsense!" Gage cried. "Sir Henry is absolutely right."

"Oh, I wish I possessed your military acumen," Burgoyne muttered.

"I will not continue to take your sneers and insults," Gage cried angrily.

"Enough." Sir William roared. "You will not fight across Mrs. Loring's breakfast table. We will do what honor and England demands of us."

"And what is that, sir?"

"We will attack and clear the peninsula and end this insufferable rebellion." And turning to Mrs. Loring: "Betsy, bring me my map case." While she went upstairs for the maps, Sir William ate with energy. Breakfast was his favorite meal, and he saw no reason to forgo it simply because a battle was in the offing. Clinton nibbled at his food and voiced his doubts.

He said, "If they should put the cannon they have, even two guns, along the shore, they could blow us to pieces before we set foot on land."

"But they are not defending the shoreline," Burgoyne argued. "There is not a man or a gun on the meadows. It's not their style. They won't face up to our infantry. I had my glass on the shoreline. It's empty. They're up on the hills. The beggars learned one thing, to pot us from behind their cursed stone walls. From what I could see, they're digging a trench from that redoubt all across the ridge. Face 'em with a line of grenadiers and they'll run like rabbits."

"Admiral Graves," Howe said, "how long will it take to put our entire force on the peninsula?"

"What part of the peninsula?"

Mrs. Loring appeared with the map case, and Howe pushed the dishes aside and unrolled one of the maps. "All of you, gentlemen, gather around. According to what Dr. Church tells us, the main force of the farmers will take a position at the redoubt and alongside it, stretching over to here, I suppose. Prescott commands them. You know Prescott, Sir Henry?"

"He's a brave man."

"Is he smart?"

Clinton shrugged. "He's determined."

Burgoyne traced a line on the map. "Church says that John Stark holds this position, down to the river. He's there with a few hundred rifles."

"Only a few hundred?"

"Church says there are about three hundred of them, riflemen out of New Hampshire. No order, no discipline. They have the range for the first volley. Twice the distance of a musket. But then they have to pound the charge into their guns."

"Admiral Graves, I asked you a question," Howe said impatiently.

"I have been thinking and calculating. It's no simple matter. You'll want guns to back them."

"Of course I want guns."

"Johnny," Clinton said to Burgoyne, "Church is a piece of shit, and you take his word as gospel. He told me there are five hundred of the New Hampshire men."

Gage shook his head unhappily. "I listen to you," he said, "and you talk of facing a mob. I have been here longer than any of you. They are no mob. They are hellishly dangerous."

"My dear General Gage," Howe said soothingly. "I respect the knowledge you have of these people. Any man with a gun is dangerous. I accept the fact that they outnumber us five to one, but not on the peninsula. They are spread out from Roxbury to Cambridge to Chelsea. They don't dare risk their whole army on the peninsula. Or even a substantial part of it. As much as I can make out, they have their best men there, Prescott and Stark and Putnam, but no more than a thousand troops. So in that sense, we outnumber them."

"Then why not take them from the rear?" Clinton demanded. "We can land a thousand men on the Charlestown neck, and then they're bottled up like rats in a trap."

"Because like rats in a trap, they'll run," Burgoyne declared. "The Charlestown neck is four or five hundred paces wide. They're not going to try to break out. We'll have to climb the hills. If they decide not to fight, they'll go into the river, into the town. Meanwhile, the main army attacks us from the mainland. No, sir," he exclaimed. "I am with Sir William. We attack."

"If we break through here," Sir William said, pointing to a spot between the redoubt and Bunker Hill, "and turn their flank here on the river side—then it's over!" He was decisive now, filled with the excitement of a mighty coup that would end the rebellion, performing for Mrs. Loring.

"Follow me now," he commanded them. "If Stark is here on the right, we go up against him with my grenadiers in the center. The light infantry takes the right flank. The Forty-third and the Fifty-second will cover my left. The marines will go up against the redoubt, and on their right flank, the guards and the Forty-seventh. The Thirty-eighth will assault the redoubt from the right—" He broke off and turned to Graves. "For God's sake, Admiral, give me a time!"

Breakfast or not, Admiral Graves was in full-dress uniform—gold epaulets, white wig, sword by his side. Being at the head of the table, he had managed to continue with his breakfast while he, as he put it, cogitated. He swallowed a mouthful of sausage and complimented Mrs. Loring. "One doesn't eat like this aboard ship, not even an admiral, Mrs. Loring.

Turning to Howe: "Well, Sir William, it's almost eight o'clock. I'll have the marines on shore to secure the landing by ten, and if you'll have your men ready within the hour, I'll put your army on the Charleston shore no later than an hour past noon. Meanwhile, having listened to your discussion, I might be well advised to open a bombardment on the troops the rebels have in Roxbury and Dorchester.

That should keep them busy and make them think twice about reinforcing the lot on the Charlestown hills. What do you say to that, sir?"

"Splendid, Admiral Graves!" Sir William said. "And now I think a toast is in order."

Anticipating his wish, Mrs. Loring had two bottles of wine ready for pouring. Sir William raised his massive bulk, offered his glass, and said, "To our victory!"

The generals and the admiral drank.

"To His Majesty, the king!" Admiral Graves said, not to be outdone.

"Hear! Hear!" Sir William cried.

In the year 1770, Capt. Evan Feversham was court-martialed for his behavior in a small skirmish on shore on the coast of Landes in France. It was a contest of no importance, with only a few hundred men involved. When he appeared before the officers of the court-martial, the charge was read as follows ". . . that he gave aid and comfort to the enemy, namely, going to the assistance of a French combatant, when the wounded of his own brigade lay within sight, sorely in need of his surgical ministering, and deliberately ignoring the command of his superior officer." The charge was read by Col. Stephan Woodbury of the Seventeenth Marine Brigade, who then asked Feversham how he pleaded.

The barrister assigned to his defense had advised him to plead not guilty and argue that in the heat of battle, his confusion was reasonable. Feversham rejected his advice and pleaded guilty.

"Are you aware of what your plea entails?" Colonel Woodbury asked him.

"I am, sir."

"You will not reconsider it?"

"No, sir, I will not."

"Do you have anything to offer in the way of mitigation?"

"Only that I considered that I was doing my duty in terms of my pledge and oath as a physician."

"Do you, sir, consider that pledge a higher duty than your duty as an officer in His Majesty's forces."

Feversham considered the question for a moment or two before replying. He was thirty-six years old at the time, and he had spent the last nine years in the British army. Even the mildest sentence by the court-martial would amount to a dishonorable discharge and possibly a prison term; in any case, a mark black enough to end his career as a doctor. At the other end of the stick, he could be sentenced to death by hanging or punishment by whipping, a conclusion so ignominious that for a gentlman of honor, death was preferable, although in his case, he had never thought of himself as a gentleman of honor, the very term offensive to him, considering the usual circumstances in which it was earned and prized.

"I am well aware of my duty as a officer of the Crown," he finally said, "so I cannot in all honesty weigh the one against the other. I have no desire to alter or contradict the charge that has been read against me. I admit that the details of the charge are accurate. I will only plead that in the heat of battle, a surgeon's decisions must be made quickly. I saw a Frenchman gushing blood from a severed artery. It is quite true that a British trooper lay nearby. Yes, close enough for me to see his wound, a ball in his thigh, at the juncture of the gluteus. He was not bleeding to speak of, which meant that no major artery had been severed. His condition was not worsened or endangered because I chose to put a tourniquet on the Frenchman's arm." Even as he spoke, Feversham was thinking with a part of his mind that the encounter could have and should have been avoided.

"You still have not answered my question," Colonel Woodbury said.

"Only as I can answer it."

He was found guilty of disobeying the order of a superior officer, but the charge of "giving aid and comfort to the enemy" was dismissed, the court holding that a tourniquet could not be defined in either a political or a military sense and could be held as a medical action, apart from the rules of war, thereby freeing Feversham from either death by hanging or years in prison. His commission was taken away; he was given a dishonorable discharge and was publicly cashiered. A few months later, he sailed for America and the port of Philadelphia. He was alone in the world, a widower whose wife and child had died in a botched childbirth while he was in France.

In the *Pennsylvania Gazette*, he read an advertisement asking for a doctor to settle himself in Ridgefield, Connecticut. The advertisement offered "twenty acres of land, suitable for small cultivation and sheep grazing, as a gift of the township, and all help in the raising of house and barn." After he bought a horse and saddle, Feversham had three hundred pounds remaining to him. Since there appeared to be sufficient doctors, surgeons, barbers, and leeches already practicing in Philadelphia, the advertisement for Ridgefield, he felt, was worth looking into, and the journey there would acquaint him with the nature of America. It was in Ridgefield that he met and married Alice Cunningham.

And now, five years later, sitting his horse on the road to Charlestown Neck, listening to the thunder of guns from the bay and the shouting and questions from people on the road to Charlestown, he tried at once to comprehend himself as being here and guess where this day would end and what the meaning of the cannon fire might be. Since Cobble Hill separated them from the sight of the bay, they could only guess. "I would say at least two ships," Prescott ventured.

An officer on horseback, sighting Prescott, called out, "Colonel, who's guns are they?"

The militiamen on the road pressed around to hear Prescott's answer, and Feversham leaned over to speak in his ear. "Five ships. They signal firing time, so that makes the roll continuous."

"Nothing to fear!" Prescott shouted. "Nothing to fear! Now clear the road, and if you're bound for Charlestown, get along."

The officer who had spoken before said to Prescott, "There's a young fellow over there," pointing to where a young man of about seventeen with blue eyes and flaxen hair sat on his horse, apparently undecided which way to turn. "He wants to find General Ward."

"That's Johnny Lovell," Warren said.

"Bring him here!" Prescott shouted, and when the boy made as to turn his horse away, Prescott spurred through the crowd and grabbed his reins. "Hold on, young man!"

The boy was frightened. Warren and Feversham pushed their horses through to where Prescott, Lovell, and the officer—he identified himself as Lieutenant Jones—were pressed together against the hedgerow that lined the road.

"Where are you for?" Prescott asked Jones.

"Bunker Hill. I'm with General Putnam, sir."

"Then get the devil up there."

"Yes, sir, Colonel Prescott."

"You're Prescott?" the boy asked as Jones rode off.

"Well?"

"I must find General Ward. It's very important. Please," he pleaded, almost shaking with excitement.

"Listen now," Warren said. "I'm Dr. Warren. This is Dr. Feversham, and this is Colonel Prescott. We don't know where General Ward is, but if what you have can't wait, tell us."

"I can't."

"Look here, Johnny," Dr. Warren said. "Ward—" He dropped his voice. "General Ward entrusted us with your secret. I know you, I know your father. I gave you a mustard poultice when you were a lad of six. You screamed like the very devil."

The boy's face broke into a smile. He wiped his brow on his sleeve and nodded. "Yes, sir, I remember."

"General Ward confided in us. You must confide in us."

"Yes, Doctor. They just made their decision."

"Who?"

"The British, General Howe. I had it from a girl who cleans in the house he took for himself. They're going to attack today."

"You're sure?" Prescott demanded.

"I think I'm sure. I was shot at twice. I rode four miles, sir. I rode as if the very devils of hell were after me."

"What time will they attack?"

"Two o'clock, three o'clock."

"Johnny," Warren asked him, "are you sure it's today, not tomorrow?"

"Today."

June 17, 9:00 A.M.

*I*t had been arranged for the motley group of doctors or surgeons or leeches to meet with Warren and Feversham at the redoubt, but by nine o'clock, only Bones and Gonzales were there. Bones was born of a poor Welsh peasant family that scratched a living out of a stony hillside, as Feversham learned. He had walked to London, working for food along the way, and had found a job as a cleaning man at the St. Swithen Alms House. He was self-educated, and since St. Swithen was a sort of hospital, he picked up the beginning of his training as an all-around helper. Then he was apprenticed to a surgeon and eventually spent six years at a hospital in Glasgow. Bones—his full name was Gwynn Lewis Bones—had served for two years on a British man-of-war, deserting, finally, in New York City and opting for a life in the colonies. He was a short, hard-muscled man in his forties.

Both Bones and Gonzales, the Jew from Rhode Island, were at the redoubt when Feversham and Warren got there, engaged in a heated argument on the subject of amputation. Bones's point of view was that amputation was painful and useless. "I have done at least three dozen amputations and witnessed as many more, and not one of them survived. Not one of them, mind you."

"But if the tibia is blown away, if the knee is gone, if the foot is gone, what is the alternative?"

"To bind it up and let the poor devil die. He will die, anyway."

"I have seen men with a leg gone," Gonzales argued.

"One in a thousand. Have you ever done one?"

"Three times, yes."

"And did they survive, Dr. Gonzales. Tell me that."

Gonzales shook his head. "No, but we have to learn."

Feversham listened in amazement. The thunder of the British naval guns was almost unbroken as broadside after broadside was launched at the redoubt and at the entrenchment that was being dug along the ridge. It astonished him that the two men could stand on the firing step, leaning against the wall of the redoubt, absorbed in their discussion.

"Damn it, get down from there!" Warren shouted.

Bones and Gonzales stepped down. "No danger, Doctor," Bones said. "They've been at it all morning. They shoot off their stupid cannon, they hit nothing. This is a fine piece of work, this redoubt."

There were at least forty men packed into the redoubt, half of them struggling with the cannon that had been emplaced there. The rest squatted against the walls.

"Where are the others?" Feversham asked Bones.

Gridley, with the men around the cannon, saw Warren and came to join them. He had been up all night, his face unshaven, his eyes bloodshot.

"Ah, they got shit in their blood," Bones said. "Carter has a call to duty in Roxbury. He showed me orders. The bastard wrote them himself." Carter was one of the absent doctors.

"Why aren't we shooting back?" Warren asked Gridley, pointing to the cannon.

"Because the balls don't fit. These are ten-pound guns. The balls they brought up here are sixteen pounds. God knows whether we could hit anything if we had the balls. We can load with grape if we can find the proper angle."

"You know they're attacking today?" Warren asked.

"We got word. Look down there." He mounted the firing step, followed by Warren and Feversham, who tried to control his reflexes as the crash of guns sounded and the balls thudded into the redoubt and the hillside. Below them and to the right were the rooftops of Charlestown village, and directly beneath them, marked off with stone or wooden fences, were sheep pens and fields of wheat and ryegrass stretching north along the shore and over the gentle slope to the mouth of the Mystic River. A fleet of small barges and ships' boats was embarking British troops from the Boston docks and ferrying them across the half-mile-wide Charles River and onto the meadows, where they had just begun to disembark.

"God give me a gun and a real crew of gunners," Gridley moaned. "I could blow those bastards out of the water right there in the river. That shithead bookseller Knox claims he knows artillery. He read a book on artillery. And he sends up ammuniton that won't fit the guns. God Almighty, he ought to be skewered and reamed!"

Awe in his voice, Warren said, "Colonel, do they mean to attack face on, up the hill?"

"So they do, Doctor. So they do." He raised his spyglass and peered through it.

"Why don't we have men in those empty houses?" Feversham wondered. "They're within rifle shot."

"We do, maybe a dozen. We just don't have enough riflemen. Look there." He offered his glass to Warren, who pushed it aside. "I see it." What he saw was two men in the British ranks who suddenly collapsed. "Marines," Gridley said.

The marines responded with a blast of fire into the empty houses.

"They'll burn them now. You were right, Feversham."

"What about the other doctors?" Feversham asked Bones. "God help us if it comes down to you and me, with our men spread out from here to Bunker Hill."

"Forget about them," Bones said.

Prescott appeared, riding his horse up to the redoubt, standing in his stirrups. "Gridley," he yelled, "what in hell are those men sitting around for?"

"They're exhausted. They've been at it all night."

"We're all exhausted. The trench has to be dug. All of you!"

Warren climbed out of the redoubt. "Colonel," he said to Prescott, "there's so much a man can do."

Prescott, dismounting, said quietly, "So help me God, Doctor, the way things are now, we'll be slaughtered. The only men who are holding their line are Johnny Stark's riflemen and two hundred Connecticut men with Knowlton. You see that stone wall and the stretch of the ridge over to Bunker Hill. I had a thousand men there last night, and now I have a handful."

Gridley and Feversham joined them. "Where are the others?" Gridley asked.

"They ran away," Prescott said disgustedly. "We have over twelve thousand men in Roxbury and Dorchester and less than a thousand up here on the hills. I pleaded with Ward. He has two thousand good Massachusetts men sitting on their butts over by Cobble Hill. The old man has no guts."

"He's sick," Warren said. "He's in too much pain. I'll ride down and talk to him. I give you my word, Prescott. I'll bring the men back with me. They're good men. They won't run away."

"Ward's frightened," Gridley said. "I spoke to him last night. He can't believe that the British will attack the hills. He says it makes no sense, but he's wrong. If they wipe us out, they hold the high ground. They can drag their big eighteen-pounders up here, and that gives them the Charlestown neck. Did you tell him what Johnny Lovell said?"

"I told him. He doesn't want to believe it, because if he does, he has to give us the Massachusetts men."

"I'll get you the Massachusetts men," Warren said. "I'll have them up on the hills before noon."

Feversham walked with Warren to where Warren's horse was tethered. "Let me go with you," Feversham said. "You're a sick man, Warren."

"No, no, don't worry about me. Better if I'm alone." He climbed onto the horse with difficulty and rode off.

Prescott, leading his horse, joined Feversham and said, "How sick is he, Doctor?"

"He should be in bed," Feversham said shortly. He walked with Prescott along the line of trenches that were being dug from the redoubt to a stone wall. The men in the trenches dug slowly and tiredly. "The ground's all stone," Prescott said miserably. He took out his watch and stared at it. "Half-past nine. I'm a miser for minutes. If they attack an hour from now, we're finished. There'll be a slaughter up here that I don't want to think about. Those redcoat bastards love their bayonets. They won't take prisoners. They have to wipe out what happened on the road back from Concord."

Staring at the meadows below, less than a mile away, where the British troops were landing, Feversham said, "They hardly have more than a corporal's guard on shore. Maybe a hundred marines. And your rifles got another one. It'll be hours before they land the army."

Prescott pressed him. "How can you be sure?"

"Because I've seen them do it in Europe."

"It looks like they got every boat in the fleet in the water."

"They got three thousand men and better to take across the river," Feversham said. "Up north in the bay, Colonel, they're disembarking from the ships. They couldn't quarter the whole army in Boston. I'd guess they have half of them aboard the ships. If what Johnny Lovell told you is fact they're putting their whole army down there in the meadows, and you will talk about stupidity. They take lessons in stupidity. If you had a mind to, you could take Boston with a thousand men, and we got better than five thousand in Roxbury and Dorchester. I can't believe what they're doing. Can you mount an attack on Boston?"

Prescott sighed and shook his head. "No, God help us, it's too late. We're not a real army, Feversham. Every damn militia commander has his own ideas, and I told you what I think of Artemus Ward. The man's terrified. If I had three or four days to plead and threaten, then Putnam and I could put together a force to take Boston. Aside from Gridley here, and Johnny Stark and Tom Knowlton and old Putnam, we have no one who could lead and command and force Ward to fall in line. No, no, we have to defend the hills. So the question is, how much time do I have before they attack?"

Feversham replied, "There is no way on earth that they could be in a position to attack before one o'clock. On that I will stake my life. But if you want a reasonable guess, I would say closer to three o'clock in the afternoon. Maybe an hour later, maybe an hour earlier, but no way before one o'clock. That gives us three maybe four, maybe even five, hours."

"Three hours and we can do it." He mounted his horse and spurred away."

"He'll do it," Gridley said.

It was Sir William Howe, coming newly from Britain to the scene at Boston, who in a sense knighted Henry Clinton, dubbing him Sir Henry. Clinton's first reaction was displeasure. "I resent that, Sir William. It puts me down. It's a bad joke."

"It is no jape," Howe said earnestly. "My brother, Earl Richard, assured me that you were on the list and that the king would ennoble you any day. In fact, with all my heart, I believe it already done. Let me take the liberty. It helps us."

"How does it help me?"

"I want you to stand with me against Gage. The man's a fool."

Clinton had his own ideas about who was the fool. Born in Newfoundland, he could, better than any of his companion generals, put himself in the minds of the Continentals. He was well aware of the fact that they were not disciplined or trained. It took the positive threat of death, if he paused or retreated or turned his back, to make a British soldier walk to his positive extinction. Such an action was neither normal nor sensible, and if the Americans had no other virtue, they were eminently sensible. When the odds were overwhelmingly against them, they would turn around and run; nor would they stupidly walk to their deaths. They were neither enlisted nor paid, and their guns were their own, and they would accept a command if it made sense, and they would disobey it if it made no sense whatsoever.

But put them behind a stone wall or a redoubt or in a trench and they became a deadly opponent. He had seen that when the British regulars retreated from Concord to Boston. The farmers never stood against them, not even once, but from behind every stone wall along the way they maintained a withering, deadly fire that filled every bed the British had in the hospital they set up in Boston. When the redcoats turned to charge, the farmers ran like the very devil to take another position. It was a tactic they had learned from the woods Indians they had fought over the past hundred years.

He had tried to explain this behavior to Sir William, but Howe was too old to learn and was obsessed with the notion that he could wipe out the rebellion in one fell swoop and make for himself a place like Ireland, where he and Mrs. Loring could preside over a satrapy of their own. Indeed, Clinton in all his experience had never witnessed anything like this passion of a middle-aged man, a married man with a wife and children of his own, an honored member of the British peerage, ready to cast it all aside for a woman—a slattern, by Clinton's definition—with whom he had fallen madly in love. As Clinton had put it to General Gage, a man who understood the American mind, "I'm no saint, but this passes understanding."

It more than passed understanding as he stood with Sir William Howe on the shore facing Breed's Hill at eleven o'clock on the morning of the seventeenth. Clinton pointed to the slope that stretched up to the redoubt and the earthworks stretching away to the right. They could plainly see men digging, apparently undisturbed by the cannonballs that arched up from the warships and crashed into the redoubt.

"It's wasted," Clinton said sourly.

"It's a terrifying message," Howe said with satisfaction.

"It doesn't seem to terrify them."

"It will."

"You'll put the whole army ashore here? Every man we have?"

"Such is my intention."

"And Boston?"

"You will defend Boston," Howe said smugly.

"With what? Do I defend the city myself, alone?"

"I will give you a hundred marines."

"Good God, sir, they have seven, eight, thousand men in Roxbury and Dorchester."

"My dear Sir Henry, the Boston neck is two hundred paces across. There is no other approach to the city. We have four twenty-pounders and gunners to serve them at the Boston neck, and you have more than convinced me that the farmers will not attack a fortified position. If you cannot hold the neck with four guns and a hundred marines—"

"Did I say that?" Clinton replied angrily. "What is to keep them from pushing across from Dorchester? When the tide is out, you can almost walk across. What do I do with a hundred marines, put ten on the shore and ten on Beacon Hill and ten at the neck?"

"Dr. Church says that there is absolutely no chance that they will attack Boston. They are not an army, they are a mob. And by the way, I have made arrangements for Mrs. Loring to have a place on *Vindicator*, where she can watch the engagement. You will see that she has every comfort."

Clinton's retort died in his throat. He stared at his commanding officer for a long moment; then he nodded and walked away. He stood at the water's edge, watching the barges land the troops on Morton's Point. He saw the grenadiers stumbling under their great headgear and enormous packs, climb out of the barges and scramble up the rocky shore to the meadow, thinking that if there were a crew of gunners worth their salt up there in the redoubt, they could blow the barges out of the water, one by one, as deftly as a man shooting ducks from a blind. He could see the shape of the cannon in the embrasures of the redoubt, but for the life of him, he could not understand why they were silent. For a moment he fantasized himself up there at the redoubt with a company of trained artillerymen. That would give Sir William a thing or two to think about.

"And here I am, Evan Feversham," he said to himself, "and here's my medical staff." There they were, a tall, skinny, dark-eyed Jew and an aged, white-haired Welshman, the three of them apparently abandoned in a hodgepoge of confusion all around them. Warren had taken off, and so had Prescott, and Gridley was shouting at the men in the redoubt to get off their asses and start digging. Bones and Gonzales stared at Eversham. What do we do now?

Do something, he told himself. Say something.

At that moment, a cannonball took the head off one of the diggers. His body stood for a moment, headless; and the other men scrambled out of the shallow trench and began to run. It was the first casualty of the day.

Feversham found himself shouting at them, "Come back! Damn you all, come back!" He had never imagined himself in such voice, a veritable roar of command. Gridley leaped out of the redoubt and raced after the scattered men, waving a pistol wildly and yelling, "Stop, you lousy, cowardly bastards!" Another man, Captain Nutting by name, appeared from across the field, intercepting the flight and flourishing a sword. The only thing Feversham could think of at that moment was to climb up onto a pile of dirt and rocks and stand there, shouting, "Look at me! They can't hit me!"

"Heed me!" he shouted with all the voice he could muster. "I'm in full sight of them. They can't hit anything with those balls. They can't shoot grape at this distance." He waved his arms violently, and evidently the gunners below saw him and tried to train their guns on him. Two balls thudded into the pile of rocks and dirt, throwing up a shower of sand that covered him, and convincing him that he had made his point. He hopped down from the embankment, wiping the sand out of his hair and eyes. His action had its effect, and the men came walking back, shamefaced. They gathered around the headless man whose skull and brains were scattered across the ground behind the trench.

"What do we do with him?" someone asked.

"Bury him," Gridley said, putting his pistol back into its holster. Nutting came back and offered his hand to Feversham, whose own hand was shaking like a leaf.

"My name's Nutting, Captain Nutting. I'm with Knowlton. Who are you, sir?"

"Dr. Feversham."

"My word, that was certainly something."

The militiamen were staring at the corpse, still unwilling to touch it. Feversham motioned to Bones and Gonzales. "Give a hand with this."

"Dig a hole," Gridley growled to the men who had picked up their spades.

"Where, sir?"

"Anywhere. Over there."

They dug a grave quickly, furiously, to rid themselves of the headless corpse. Feversham and Bones and Gonzales picked up the body and put it in the shallow grave.

Feversham pointed to remains of the man's head. "Throw some dirt on that. It's not something we want to think about. What was the poor devil's name?"

"Simpkins, Doctor. He's from Marblehead."

"We ought to have some way to note the names," Feversham said to Gridley.

"I should have thought of that," Gridley said wearily. "I'll try to do something about it." He went back into the redoubt.

"You're doctors, all of you?" Nutting asked, pointing to the leather aprons Bones and Gonzales wore, the big pockets heavy with surgical tools. Feversham's equipment was in his saddlebag, his horse tethered to a rock in the shelter behind the redoubt.

"We're all there is at the moment," Feversham said ruefully. "Dr. Warren will be back. He's none too well, and he'll be in the redoubt. So there's three of us—Dr. Bones, Dr. Gonzales, and myself. Are you in command here?"

"Until Colonel Prescott returns."

"Then if you show us the line of defense, we'll be better able to position ourselves."

Prescott, whipping his horse down the road to the Charlestown neck, met up with Israel Putnam, who was leading a contingent of some 250 Connecticut militia.

"Thank God for small favors!" Prescott exclaimed. "You're the answer to my prayers. We're weakest at the barricade, from the redoubt to Knowlton's position."

"I'm not bound for Breed's Hill," Putnam replied.

"Then where the hell are you going?"

"We're fortifying Bunker Hill."

Prescott cried, "Why Bunker Hill? The attack is at Breed's Hill. There's no one there, do you understand me? A hundred men who've been digging all night and they can hardly stand on their feet and you're fortifying Bunker Hill!"

"General Ward says the attack will be on Bunker Hill," Putnam said, trying to restrain his hair-trigger temper. "And you will not address me in such voice, sir!"

"Ward doesn't know his ass from his elbow!"

"And you, sir, where the hell is your knowledge from?"

"From the eyes God gave me, General. Right at this minute the British are landing an army at the foot of Breed's Hill. Our intelligence says they're going to throw everything at us, the whole army, the whole three thousand of them, the light infantry, the grenadiers, the marines, everything, and you're fortifying Bunker Hill!"

"It's a ruse, Prescott!" Putnam snapped. "Not even Howe could be that stupid and order his men to climb Breed's Hill in a frontal attack. He'll turn your left flank and march on Bunker Hill."

"He won't turn our left flank. Johnny Stark's holding the flank with his riflemen. They know every move we make, and they know that we have nothing on Breed's Hill and nothing in the damn redoubt!"

"Fuck the redoubt," Putnam growled.

"To hell with you!" Prescott whipped his horse and raced past the file of Connecticut militia to the Charlestown neck. Across the neck, at the junction of the Cambridge Road, he saw the big brown tent that the Committee of Safety had raised for their command post. Dozens of men were milling around the tent. In the pasture beyond it, the Massachusetts militia were sprawled in the morning sunshine around their cook fires. A dozen horses were being watered at the Mill Pond, and still other troops were camped on the slope of Cobble Hill. Prescott felt sick at the sight. Back at Breed's Hill, Johnny Stark's few hundred New Hampshire men and Knowlton's few hundred Connecticut men and the hundred or so exhausted men around the redoubt waited for extinction, and here was a whole army lounging in the June sunshine.

"Is General Ward inside?" he asked as he dismounted.

"Yes, sir."

Prescott pushed through the cluster around the tent. Inside it was as crowded as outside, Ward sitting at a table, staring at a map. Three men whom Prescott recognized as members of the Committee of Safety were grouped around him, a clutch of militia officers argued hotly, and four men with muskets stood stiffly by the open flap. A large rent in the roof of the tent let in a shaft of sunlight.

Prescott, without so much as a by your leave, pushed the militia officers aside and leaned over the table, facing Ward, who looked up in surprise at the appearance of the colonel.

"Prescott? I thought you were at the redoubt?"

His voice as cold as ice, Prescott said, "Will you clear the tent, General? I must talk to you. Just the two of us, alone."

The two men were the same age, forty-eight years: Prescott a tall, broad-shouldered, powerful, and athletic man, Artemus Ward, small, paunchy, prematurely aged, with the precise, didactic manner of a schoolmaster.

"Why, sir?"

Prescott leaned over and whispered, "Concerning Johnny Lovell."

Troubled, Ward stared at him.

"Did he ever find you?" Prescott asked softly.

"When, sir? Do you mean today?"

"I mean today."

"No, not today."

"Then let me inform you of his intelligence," Prescott said coldly. "The entire British army of more than three thousand disciplined regulars is at this moment landing in the meadows at the foot of Breed's Hill. They will launch a frontal attack upon Breed's Hill and the redoubt within three or four hours from now. We cannot defend either the redoubt or the fortifications we have been trying to build between the redoubt and Johnny Stark's riflemen, who hold the left flank down to the Mystic River. The few men we have are exhausted."

Ward protested. "General Putnam says the attack will come on Bunker Hill."

"He's wrong."

"How do I know he's wrong?"

"General Ward," Prescott said deliberately, "you know me a little. Then believe me. I will not allow Johnny Stark and his riflemen and Tom Knowlton and his Connecticut men and the men who built the redoubt and are too tired to stand on their feet to die on that hill. And die they will unless you give me a thousand Massachusetts men to defend Breed's Hill. They're sitting on their asses outside this tent."

"They are here to defend the Charlestown neck."

"General, the British will not attack the neck. They have no men left to attack the neck. Their entire army is committed to the attack on Breed's Hill."

"So you say," Ward replied defensively. "Putnam says otherwise. If Johnny Lovell had this intelligence, why didn't he come here?"

"I don't know that," Prescott said, "and I don't give a tinker's fart for what Putnam said. The Committee of Safety gave me the command and the responsibility for the Charlestown peninsula. We have more damn generals and major generals than we know what to do with, but the command is mine, and I don't give a damn who calls himself a general."

"I sent four brigades to Bunker Hill. They are there right now, under the command of General Putnam." Ward's voice sank to a whimper.

"No, sir. I need a thousand men on Breed's Hill, and you will either order them to follow me now, immediately, or so help me God, I will put you under arrest and order them myself."

"You wouldn't dare."

Prescott put his hand on the butt of his pistol. "Don't try me, General Ward! Don't try me."

A long moment stretched itself between the two men, and then Ward bowed his head. "Very well, Colonel Prescott. Be it upon your head. You can have the men."

"Be it on my head, Prescott said.

June 17, 11:00 A.M.

*A*t eleven o'clock, on the morning of June 17th, 1775, Elizabeth Loring and Prudence Hallsbury stepped out of a lighter that had taken them to the side of *Vindicator*, a two-masted mail and supply ship attached to the British fleet in Boston Harbor. They were lifted to the deck very carefully, the winch under the direction of Lt. Horace Threadberry.

Lieutenant Threadberry, second in command of *Vindicator*, twenty-three years old, had been torn between his desire to enter *Vindicator* into the bombardment of Breed's Hill and his equally pressing desire to entertain the already notorious Mrs. Joshua Loring and the some-what less notorious Prudence Hallsbury. *Vindicator* carried ten guns, six-pounders, which might be of some use against a pirate but were of no consequence in this one-sided bombardment. Orders from Admiral Graves had advised Capt. Alex Woodly not to fire his guns and to take up a position between the frigate *Somerset* and the frigate *Falcon*, but at least three-quarters of a mile from the Charlestown shore, which would place it out of any possible cannon shot from the redoubt. Thus, *Vindicator* was in an excellent position from which to observe both the cannonading and the ascent of the hill which would follow. The ship was placed there in response to the pleading of

Mrs. Loring, who argued that she had never seen a battle. Since Sir William had assured her that this battle would end the rebellion, she would probably never have an opportunity to witness another one.

At this point in his romance, General Howe found it almost impossible to refuse any request of Mrs. Loring's, reasonable or unreasonable, and he instructed Admiral Graves to make *Vindicator* available.

Captain Woodly was a thin-lipped, moralistic man who had no tolerance for the loose and amiable ethics of the ruling class. He had worked and fought his way up from bosun to captain, a rare achievement in the British navy. He came from a Methodist background and a poor farm family. When he was handed Admiral Graves's instructions, he decided that he would remain in his cabin and have no intercourse with, as he thought of it, two notorious sluts. He handed the whole business over to Lieutenant Threadberry, much to the delight of the latter.

General Howe's infatuation with Mrs. Loring was already the delicious gossip of the fleet, and the opportunity of being with these two fascinating women was an answer to the lieutenant's own sexual fantasies. He had rigged an awning over a table and chairs on the stern deck of the ship and had warned the crew against any show of impertinence, whether by remarks or snickers. He had also provided tea and a tin box of sweets out of his own store, and he looked forward to being an enviable source of gossip on his return to London.

He welcomed the two women personally, in no way disappointed by their holiday costume and their beauty, deciding that neither Sir William nor General Clinton were to be faulted for their choice of companionship. He had assigned Midshipman Andrews, sixteen years old, to see to the service.

The ladies were seated with a clear view of the Charlestown docks, the long slope of Breed's Hill, and the redoubt and the entrenchments that stretched away on either side of the fortification. Lieutenant Threadberry then took it upon himself to explain the schematic of the battle:

"Those are the grenadiers. You can see them lining up on the shore, there with their tall hats." Indeed, the shore was no more than half a mile away. "General Howe's own command. He will lead them himself, from what I hear. They are just about the jolly best troops on earth, you know."

Mrs. Loring clapped her hands. "Hear! Hear!"

Gripped by the excitement of the moment, Prudence wondered whether she could bear to watch a real battle. "But some of them will die. Isn't that what happens?"

"Oh, some do, some do," Threadberry agreed. "It's in the nature of a battle. On the other hand, who knows? You see, my dear ladies, the grenadiers are very special. Each man is chosen for his height and bearing, and with their great shakos, they are seven feet tall. Oh, believe me, my dear ladies, there is nothing more fearsome than a charge of the grenadiers. Most likely, when the rebels see them coming, they will cut and run. From all I hear, the rebels dread our bayonets. And those others, over to the left, they are the light infantry, and still farther to the left, the marines. When they have all of them landed and formed their ranks, they will march up the hill, and that will be the end of these presumptuous colonials. With due apology, I recognize the difference between a loyalist and a rebel."

"Please, Lieutenant," Mrs. Loring said generously, "no apologies are necessary. Your own contempt for the rebels surely does not exceed mine."

"But there is no one up there to fight you," Prudence said.

Threadberry handed her his spyglass, and she peered through it. "Yes, I can see the fort they have built. You call it a redoubt, don't you?"

"Yes, my lady."

"But no one is there. Oh, yes; I see one man, and there's another." She handed the spyglass to Mrs. Loring. "Do look through it, Betsy. It makes one feel that one is up there. Isn't it wonderful how close we are!"

She turned to Threadberry. "I can't see anyone there on the hill. I'm sure they have all run away. I know I would, with those terrible grenadiers of Sir William ready to come and do such awful things."

Threadberry laughed tolerantly. "Oh, no, ma'am. I assure you, they have not run away. Not yet. But with our cannonading, they keep their heads down."

"I see three of them now, standing on the redoubt," Mrs. Loring said. "Why can't you hit them, with all those cannon thundering away? I can see where the shots land, all along the hill, and those men just stand there as if all your cannon don't bother them at all."

"Well, ma'am, you can't aim a cannon the way you aim a musket. We count on the guns to frighten more than to kill."

Mrs. Loring put down the spyglass and clapped her hands. "Splendid!" she cried. "That was right in front of them. They're gone now."

Midshipman Andrews arrived with the teapot, feasting his eyes on Mrs. Loring as he asked whether he might pour the tea? After he had done so and had dared to hold forth on the virtues of the sweets, he still lingered, unable to take his eyes from the abundant mounds of Mrs. Loring's bosom. Threadberry said, "That will be all, Anderson."

"What a darling lad," Prudence said. "How old is he?"

"About sixteen years, I suppose."

"Very manly for his age," Mrs. Loring observed, not unaware of Midshipman Andrews fairly salivating as he looked at her. A healthy, handsome young man like that, she thought. How much she could teach him!

Shortly after 11:00 A.M., Dr. Warren returned to the redoubt, bringing with him two pigskins of water attached to the pommel of his saddle and pen and ink and a sheaf of paper in a box behind his saddle. Gridley almost embraced him. "God bless you, Doctor. We were dying of our thirst." The forty-odd men who had been digging all morning under the burning sun saw the water bags and dropped their spades and ran toward Warren's horse. "Easy, easy," Gridley said. "There's enough for everyone, laddies. Make two lines, and I'll trust you to take one swig and give way. We have a long, hot day ahead of us."

"God's blessing on you, Doctor!" came from the men.

Feversham, Bones, and Gonzales joined the group, refusing water. "We'll wait our turn," Feversham said.

"It's all right," Warren told them. "Prescott's on his way, and he'll have a thousand Massachusetts militia. Good men. We squeezed that out of Ward. Putnam still believes the main attack will be at Bunker Hill."

"That's Putnam," Gridley said. "He's a stonehead. He makes up his mind, and that's the way it is. Did you tell him what's happening down there on the beach? Why doesn't he ride up and see? What on God's earth is wrong with him?"

"Born stubborn," Warren said. "Any more casualties?"

"Just one poor devil with his head blown off."

"Thank God."

"They keep their heads down now. Those ships in the bay have thrown at least five hundred balls at us. They mounted guns on Copp's Hill, and they're firing from there. They're as stubborn and brainless as Putnam."

"I think we'll find something that fits your cannon," Warren said. "They've been searching."

"We don't need it," Gridley said. "We've loaded the guns with pebbles. That's better than balls. If we get one round off when they attack, it will mean something."

Feversham drew Warren aside. "How do you feel?"

"Better."

Feversham touched his brow. "The fever's broken. It can happen that way. You put the body to it. I've seen that before."

Warren smiled. "I'm all right, Feversham. It was ridiculous making me the commander in chief. I brought my fowling piece, and I'll fight under Gridley. He has more knowledge of this business in his little finger than I have in my head. I also brought my writing box, if you want to make a letter to your wife?"

"I would like that," Feversham said. Warren handed him the box. "You don't want it now?"

"Later, perhaps," Warren said. "If we beat them off, I'll make notes. There ought to be a record of what happens here."

In the redoubt, Feversham spread a sheet of paper, using the box and the parapet as a desk and kneeling in front of it. The box contained an ink bottle and two wooden pens, fitted with copper points, a new departure from the quills commonly used.

"My dear and beloved Alice," he wrote.

A great deal has happened since I last wrote to you from the Hunt house in Watertown, and perhaps someone has already delivered my letter to Ridgefield. I shall keep this letter with me until today is over, and if I send it off to you tomorrow, you will know that I have lived through the worst that might befall me.

Now it is still before noon on the seventeenth of June, and I am writing this in the redoubt on Breed's Hill, across the Charles River from British-occupied Boston. I will attempt to be not too dismal about our situation here, since you frequently complain about my lack of humor. I say this not as criticism but as agreement, since a long life in the company of war and death turns a man moody or cynical. We have discussed this uprising of the Massachusetts people at length, and you helped to convince me that an opportunity for a sane society exists here in the colonies. However, if I chose humor, I could find ample substance for such an attitude, since we have no shortage of fools and clowns.

The other day, Dr. Joseph Warren, a wonderful and remarkable man, gathered together what doctors (*sic*, leeches and barbers included) are available for a move to defend the Charlestown peninsula. They were fourteen in number, but now they have shrunk to four—myself, Dr. Warren, and two others—one a Welshman, appropriately named Bones, and a Jew, Gonzales by name, out of Providence in Rhode Island, where I am told there is a considerable synagogue of Jews. He is, incidentally, the first Jew I have ever spoken to, a curious gentleman with the manners of a Spanish grandee. So now there are four of us to minister to an army of almost a thousand men who are waiting to engage in a battle with three times that number of the best British regulars that exist, among them the famous grenadiers of Gen. Sir William Howe. If that sounds utterly insane, it is no less insane than everything else about our situation here on Breed's Hill in Charlestown.

Let me attempt a small bit of humor. We have intelligence from an informant that General Howe, a person most honored and distinguished in British society and commander in chief of all the British forces here in Boston Harbor, has fallen madly in love with a woman, name of Mrs. Joshua Loring, a lady of exhuberant lust and small reputation. He has taken her into his home and heart as a constant companion, having bought off her husband with a commission in the British forces, while Gen. Henry Clinton dallies with the wife of a prominent Church of England priest. I know you enjoy a juicy bit of gossip, and I am sure this will provide entertainment for the ladies of Ridgefield.

For the past hour, the two excellent surgeons who have committed themselves and myself have been assembling bandages and dressings and tourniquets. We have been trying to enlist stretcher-bearers from among the thin line of men and boys who are at this line of defense. Since I wrote to you that perhaps thirteen or fourteen thousand men have formed an army surrounding Boston, you are probably puzzled as to why we face the British with a comparative handful. Well, there has been an ongoing argument among the leadership of our army, if one could call it that, on whether or not to defend Charlestown. No one is really sure who commands us. The Committee of Safety, who are supposed to be responsible for the conduct of the war, have appointed Dr. Warren as the supreme commander, a title he rejects, and he has stated forthrightly that he will fight as an ordinary under Col. Richard Gridley, who, along with Dr. Warren, is responsible for building, in a few hours, a remarkable earthworks fortification.

The nominal commander of our forces is a gentleman by the name of Artemus Ward, a person whose indecisiveness and ill health makes him as little fitted for his position as I would be. I thank God that we do have two most remarkable men who have taken over the fortification and defense of this high point of ground, which is central to our defense of Charlestown. One is Col. William Prescott, who has been charged with the defense of the high ground. He is an extraordinary man—tall, handsome, gentle in his orders—and as much as I could see, beloved by the men. The other is Colonel Gridley, who is in command of the redoubt, the fortification of which I spoke. Like Prescott, he is calmly in charge, soft-voiced, and not given to excitement. These two men have won my profound respect. I must add that perhaps a thousand paces behind our position here, there is another high point called Bunker Hill. That position is being held by Gen. Israel Putnam, who clings to the belief that the British will attack his position instead of ours—in spite of the fact that we can see the British forming for an attack upon our position even as I write. He is a stubborn man who smarts because Colonel Prescott rather than himself has been given command of the defense of Charlestown.

Let me explain that the peninsula which we are to defend is about a mile in length and somewhat less than a mile in width, shaped like a humpback whale, with the tail of the whale connecting it with the mainland. Charlestown itself is a tiny village of a few dozen houses at the foot of the hill where we are. If the British attack us head-on, which we think they mean to do, and if we are properly reinforced, we have a small chance of beating back their attack. I write this to you in detail because I must face the fact of my decision to be here. There is a very large possibility that I will be killed or captured, and I leave it to the honor of my captors to see that this letter reaches you. I try not to be pessimistic, but the situation here does not inspire confidence. At least half of the men here are not men at all, but boys of sixteen and seventeen years, wide-eyed, woefully innocent, and very afraid. Overnight, at least a third of them have disappeared, run away, gone home. Those still here are absolutely exhausted from building the redoubt and digging a barricade. Yesterday was a day of great confusion—"

A wild din of shouting interrupted Feversham's letter writing, and he ran with others in the redoubt to the gate on the backside, to see Prescott riding his horse at the head of a column of men marching four abreast, while the men in the redoubt and along the barricade waved their hats and shouted in excitement.

Feversham went back to his letter: "My dear Alice, suddenly, I am filled with hope. Colonel Prescott has just delivered to us a column of reinforcements. I leave you now, and I will finish this letter later, perhaps after this day is over. I must note, if the worst comes, that my wife, to whom I write, is Alice Feversham, in the village of Ridgefield in Connecticut, and I charge you who reads this to deliver it to her."

There was no shelter from the burning sun for the grenadiers, who were being landed in the meadow at Morton's Point. There were two well-leafed maple trees, but Howe felt it would be deleterious to the spirit of the men for them to huddle together in the shade; although he did order water to be given to them, as well as a ration of bread and cheese. Aside from their high shakos, the grenadiers carried full pack, consisting of cloak and canteen and powder and fifty extra balls of lead, made into cartridges. They were also in heavy uniform and leather boots, armed with musket and bayonet. They stood in the June sun, sweat running down their faces and soaking their underclothes. Whatever complaints they made were voiced in whispers.

It was Howe's plan to assemble his forces across the entire front of the half mile between Charlestown village and the mouth of the Mystic River and then, with the grenadiers in the forefront, to march calmly up Breed's Hill, take the redoubt by assault, and breach the entire line of defenses in one massive thrust. Laying out his plan to Burgoyne, he said, "My feeling is that they will cut and run, facing the grenadiers. Do you agree?"

"No question about it," Burgoyne assented. "We make a mistake if we consider them as soldiers. They are not soldiers, and they have no discipline whatsoever. Each does as he pleases. We saw that in April."

General Gage, aware that he was in the minority, his head aching from the heat, was less certain. "It's just that we don't know how many of them there are up there," he said, pointing to the top of the hill.

"I have a message from Church," Burgoyne said. "He writes that half of them assigned to the defenses deserted last night. They simply slip away. No punishment, no measures against them."

"Yes, I suppose some of them are afraid."

They were joined by Admiral Graves. His marines were landing on the extreme left, within rifle shot of the houses of abandoned Charleston.

"I've lost five men, and two more wounded," Graves told them angrily. "I can't ask them to stand there and be shot at."

"Why not?" Burgoyne quipped. "It's in the nature of their profession. It's what they're paid for."

"I don't appreciate that, General."

"If it came down to that," Burgoyne said as an aside to Gage, "I'd rather be shot at in what the marines are wearing than stand in this bleeding sun under a grenadier's shako."

"I don't appreciate that, either." Graves had caught a few words. "It's no joking matter."

"Can't we stand in the shade," Burgoyne asked, "and have this discussion out of the sun?"

"If you require your comfort, sir," Howe said, annoyed by Burgoyne's attempt at wit. As they moved into the shade of a tree, Sir William asked Graves what he proposed. "I must detail the men for the advance. Do you want the whole army huddled over here in the meadow?"

"Why must we endure those cursed riflemen?"

"What do you propose?"

"I'm willing to move into the village with the marines. We'll soon clean out that nest of vipers."

"And lose half a hundred of your men?"

"There's a clean and simple solution," Burgoyne observed.

"Is there? Enlighten us."

"Burn the filthy place."

"What!"

"Exactly."

"Clinton's up on Copp's Hill with the battery. He's out of it as far as the hill is concerned, out of range. Every shot he's fired falls short. Wasting ammunition. I like your notion, Johnny," Howe said to Burgoyne.

Gen. Robert Pigot of the grenadiers, second in command to Sir William, joined the group and informed Howe that in another hour or so the bulk of the army would be onshore.

Howe nodded with pleasure and turned to Admiral Graves. "Admiral, tell me, is the tide right to bring *Symmetry* and *Glasgow* up the Charles River and within cannon shot of the Charlestown neck?"

"The tide will be with us, but there's no wind to speak of, Sir William."

"You heard Pigot. In another hour, the army will be onshore. You could work the ships in with boats? Could you?"

"I guess we could. It might take a while."

"By two, three, o'clock?"

"Certainly by three o'clock."

"Oh, splendid!" Burgoyne cried. "They're rats in a trap. Cut them off at the Charlestown neck and we have them."

"And my marines?" Graves demanded.

"We'll solve that," Howe said. "We'll drop a few salvos of firebombs out of the siege mortars on Copp's Hill. That wretched village will go up like a bonfire."

"You can't be serious?" Gage said.

"I am very serious, General Gage, completely serious."

"Burn an entire village?"

"It's a stinking little village," Burgoyne said.

"We don't burn villages," Gage said. "My God, Sir William, we are not barbarians. There are rules of war."

"Tell me who are the barbarians, General Gage? They snipe at us from behind their damned stone walls. They hide in that abandoned village and murder our marines. There are no families left in Charlestown. No, let the world decide who are the barbarians. We'll burn that damned village to the ground!"

"Sir William," Gage said, "I beg your forbearance. Please, understand me. I know as well as you do the need to bring this wretched rebellion to an end. But we are fighting our own people. If we burn Charlestown, we will give them a source of rage and bitterness they will never forget. I know these people, and if you will forgive me, you do not. They are stiff-necked and determined beyond any of our folk at home. They are Puritans, and they believe they are God's chosen. They hacked a civilization out of the wilderness. They are not European peasants, and they are not Scottish gillies. We have them trapped on the peninsula, and we can destroy them in a fair fight. They will accept that because it will be a defeat with honor. But if we burn Charlestown, they will have a symbol that they will not forget."

"Oh, come on, sir," Burgoyne put in. "The houses are empty. The town is a spoil of war, a legitimate target."

"Am I to stand by and watch my marines murdered?" Graves demanded.

"You can assemble your marines out of rifle shot."

"Bloody nonsense!"

"I hear you, General Gage," Howe said, "but the command here is mine, and it is my responsibility to bring this wretched rebellion to an end." He signaled an end to the argument by turning to Burgoyne:

"Off with you, Johnny. Copp's Hill. Tell Clinton that he is to prepare firebombs and shell the village. Meanwhile," he said to Graves, "you may begin working *Symmetry* and *Glasgow* into the river to the range of the Charlestown neck. Once and for all, I intend to put a finish to what is up there on Breed's Hill and Bunker Hill. When the sun sets tonight, this rebellion will be done with."

On Breed's Hill, the officers' horses were tethered behind the redoubt. In the redoubt, Prescott sat on the firing step, facing the officers who would defend Breed's Hill. Feversham stood to one side, studying the faces and manner of the four men who would to one degree or another decide his own fate on Breed's Hill: Tom Knowlton, short, stocky, and amazingly relaxed; John Stark of New Hampshire, tall, brown as a berry, wearing a sleeveless waistcoat and fringed leggings, his pale blue eyes bloodshot from want of sleep; young Captain Nutting, nervous now, excited, rubbing his chin anxiously; and Gridley, three days' growth of red beard on his face, sunburned red on his bald head, chewing thoughtfully on a straw. Warren sprawled on the ground to one side, his bright, fanciful clothes stained and sweat-soaked. And on the opposite wall of the redoubt, crouched wearily on the firing step and taking advantage of the little shade the wall offered, were the thirty-two men who remained of the larger group that had built the redoubt. Feversham noticed, among them, two Negroes, both of them stripped to the waist and dressed in ragged pantaloons. They were barefoot, but so were others of the men in the redoubt. Probably, they were slaves, but whom they belonged to and what brought them to the redoubt, Feversham did not know.

"We are in good stead and good strength," Prescott said. "I come with five hundred and fifty-two men, and they're fine men and better rested than we are. I intend to station some of them here in the redoubt and to station the large part of the rest in a line from the redoubt to the first stone wall. That's about three hundred yards, which is easy firing position for four hundred men. Tom," he said, addressing Knowlton, "how many men have you?"

"Two hundred and twelve by last count."

"We'll anchor my left flank on the stone wall. You have a fieldstone wall along the whole slope of the hill. Put your men shoulder to shoulder, and that should take you to Stark's right flank."

He said to Stark, "Johnny, can you make your position tight enough to anchor your line to Tom's and yet prevent the British from flanking your left along the river?"

"I have three hundred riflemen," Stark replied. "There's a wooden fence, goes a ways, and a sort of stone wall. We been at it all morning, digging a little, stuffing the holes with hay, which won't stop a musket ball but might spoil their aim. If Knowlton here can hold my right and keep them from turning me, we can stop any damn thing on God's earth that comes at our front. We can not only stop it. We can send it to hell and gone."

Prescott turned to young Nutting, reminding him of a stone-and-log root cellar which made a sort of projecting knob between the entrenchments and Knowlton's position. "Could you find room for five men in there?" Prescott wanted to know.

"Maybe."

"The logs are rotten. See if you can knock one out and make a position."

"If they break our line," Knowlton said, "what's behind us?"

"Putnam's on Bunker Hill. He has three hundred men behind stone walls. I don't want any of you taken prisoner, but I don't want any of your men to run unless you give the order. I depend on you to measure things. We fire in volleys and under control. Don't leave it to the men. Put out stakes. I would say fifty feet for the first volley, and no one fires his gun before they cross the stakes."

The four officers sat in silence. A few moments went by, punctured only by the thunder of cannons from the bay.

"No questions?"

"We'll do our best," Stark said.

Gridley smiled and shrugged.

"I'd like to hear from the surgeons," Knowlton said, nodding at Warren and Feversham.

"I'll be in the redoubt," Warren said. "Dr. Feversham has walked through our line."

"Feversham?" Prescott said.

"Outside the redoubt, there are only three of us," Feversham told them. "We drew straws for position. I'll be with Colonel Prescott. Dr. Bones will be with Colonel Stark, and Dr. Gonzales, with Major Knowlton." Both men were standing at the entrance to the redoubt. Feversham nodded at them, and they acknowledged his introduction. "We'll do our best. Dr. Bones is an old hand at this. Dr. Gonzales is a physician in Providence, so he is new to this. I have confidence in him. I spoke to Colonel Stark about litters, but he holds that the lines are too thin to weaken by assigning men to litters. So be it. We have dressings and tourniquets. We can bind a wound and stop the bleeding, but where there is no rear and the battle is of itself, there is not much more that we can do. As Colonel Stark put it, we'll do our best."

"Thank you," Prescott said. "And now, gentlemen, God be with us. I thank you with all my heart. Go to your positions. I am going to send my horse off the peninsula. What is your will?"

"I think the horses will simply be an impediment," Knowlton said. The others nodded agreement. Feversham left the redoubt and unhooked his bag of instruments from his saddle. Stark and Knowlton strode along the ridge toward their lines of defense, and Nutting loped down the hill to the root cellar. He made a little dance of dodging two cannonballs that sent up their fountain of dirt on either side of him. Prescott climbed onto the embankment.

"Feversham!"

The doctor joined him, and Prescott handed him his spyglass. "Have a good look." In the meadow grass behind them, the Massachusetts militiamen that Prescott had brought to the hill were sprawled on the ground, their wide-rimmed hats tilted over their faces to shield them from the sun.

Feversham had a clear view of the landing troops. Two more barges were inching to the shore, both of them loaded with uniforms he recognized as light infantry, and toward Morton's Point he could make out the even ranks of the grenadiers. He tried to do a quick count, more of a guess than anything else. A mass of men in the uniforms of the light infantry were forming ranks.

He handed the glass to Prescott, who put it to his eye.

"About two thousand," Feversham said.

"They're warping two of the warships." The cannonading had suddenly stopped.

"Into the river," Feversham agreed, squinting.

"Oh, they're a canny lot, Doctor. They got it all worked out, every bit of it. Put the Charlestown neck under their guns. Trap us here, stick it to us with their cursed bayonets, and then back to England the conquering heroes go. How long do you suppose we have before they attack?"

Feversham shrugged. "An hour, perhaps. They're cooling their cannon. They'll blast away with everything before it starts."

"I must position my men," Prescott said, handing his spyglass to Feversham. "Keep a look on them, Doctor, if you would. Let me know when they decide to have a go at us."

"War can be boring," Prudence Hallsbury observed. "They just stand on the beach, and they don't do anything. They keep shooting those frightful cannon, and I do believe we'll lose our hearing. And it's so hot, even here on the water."

"When do you expect the battle to begin?" Mrs. Loring asked Lieutenant Threadberry, well aware of him standing behind her and enjoying her cleft.

"Well, ma'am, that's up to General Howe, isn't it? You can see some troopers being ferried over to Charlestown from the Boston docks. That's the Irish brigade, if I'm not mistaken. You can be sure Sir William will wait until he has all his troops on land. Then he'll move. Oh, you can be sure that he will. We have some wine in a net overside, excellent French Chardonnay that Sir William provided for us. Not to Captain Woodly's liking, but nothing French is."

"A net overside?" Mrs. Loring wondered.

"The day is hot, but the water's cold, Mrs. Loring. We put the bottles in a cord net and float them in the cold water."

Midshipman Andrews appeared with two bottles of Chardonnay, and Mrs. Loring asked Lieutenant Threadberry to join them in a toast.

"To victory?" Threadberry suggested.

Modestly, Mrs. Loring assented. It would only titillate the gossip if she suggested that they drink to Sir William. "Of course, he will lead the troops in the attack."

"Ma'am?"

"Sir William."

"No doubt about that."

In the years ahead, indeed for the rest of his life, Evan Feversham would recall and ponder the unreality of this day, this seventeenth of June in 1775. He was in place by courtesy of Prescott, who, seemingly unafraid, walked along the top of the earthen barricade, telling off the places of his men. "Just fall in—leave a foot of space between each man and keep your heads down—here, now, you want a bit of space to reload—and damn it, if the good Lord made a bullet for you, it will find you, so there's no worry about that—and you fire when I say fire, no sooner, no later. Knowlton!" he shouted suddenly.

At the far end of the embankment, Knowlton was spacing his Connecticut riflemen. "Colonel?"

"Tell off fifty of these men. I'm filling my line."

It was theater, Feversham thought. Here he stood, the whole American line visible to him, the redoubt, the line of earthen breast-works stretching away from the redoubt over a hundred yards to the stone wall that Knowlton had chosen for his position and for his Connecticut riflemen. Then, on the other side of a rutted cart trace, he saw Stark and his New Hampshire riflemen behind two fences and a stone wall, right down the slope to the Mystic River, a line of defense eight or nine hundred paces long and manned over its whole length by hardly many more than a thousand men. Certainly, they were betrayed, whether by design or not, facing more than double their number of the best-trained soldiers in the world, while an army of thirteen thousand of their compatriots were in Roxbury and Dorchester and Cambridge. Yet the incredible heart of it was, as Feversham considered, that those who were here had accepted so matter-of-factly the situation as it was, himself included. Were they as nervous, afraid, as he was, committed as he was out of shame and circumstances?

He tried to find an indication in their faces and manner, but with their lying behind the earthworks, there was no way to tell. Some of them appeared totally relaxed. Others fiddled with their muskets, wiping the flints so that there might be no spot of moisture from their perspiration. Still others lay back, hats tilted over their faces; some chatted softly. At the far end, a farmer-turned-rebel had a tin whistle and blew a plaintive melody.

Five or six hundred yards from where Feversham stood, the British troops were completing their landing, the last of the barges pushing off from the Long Wharf. Below him, giving him a sense of being in a vast theater on the top balcony, the marines and a regiment of light infantry stood in ranks. Two of their officers had spyglasses to their eyes and were obviously pointing at him. Across the river, in Boston, Feversham could make out clusters of people on the rooftops, perched in place to watch the destruction of the Americans and the end of the rebellion.

Meanwhile, Prescott, followed by a young man with a bundle of pointed sticks, was laying out a line of the sticks about thirty paces in front of the breastworks; and along the ridge, Knowlton was doing the same thing. "Mark these sticks!" Prescott shouted. "No one fires until they reach the sticks. That gives you a measure. That tells you when to shoot."

He left the young man to pound in the sticks and joined Feversham. "Well, Doctor, what do you see?"

"They're still bringing troops across the river. There's a boat pushing off now."

"Anything else?"

"There's something doing on Copp's Hill. They have a battery of mortars on the hill. There's a fire going." He handed the spyglass to Prescott, who peered through it.

"They're heating firebombs. You were right, Feversham. They're going to burn Charlestown."

It was not to Gen. Henry Clinton's liking. "They build of wood here," he said to Burgoyne, trying to explain his thinking and feeling that Burgoyne, if anyone, should understand how he felt. Burgoyne came to this curious spot and even more curious war loaded with honors, a hero of the Seven Years' War, a member of Parliament once, and a playwright as well. At thirty-six, Clinton was Burgoyne's junior in years as well as in military experience. For all that, he felt that Burgoyne was ill fitted for this action in America, not only unable to comprehend the nature of their adversaries but unwilling to grant them any character different from a European peasant. "Everything is wood, and they craft a house with a kind of reverence. You burn their homes and it's like burning their children."

"That is a romantic notion," Burgoyne countered. "Believe me, Sir Henry"—giving him the title that Howe had bestowed upon him and managing the put-down that went with a title not yet properly his— "who puts his body at risk and his honor at risk of necessity puts his home at risk. I see no difference. Tomorrow, when this battle is won, and it will be won, the question will be who to hang, not whose house to burn."

"No battle is won until it is won."

"Well put. But our orders are to burn the place, and burn it we must."

"There's another hour before the shot is hot. The situation could change."

"Oh? How could it change in another hour?"

"They might surrender," Clinton said.

Burgoyne regarded him strangely. "You really think so?"

Clinton pointed to where the two British warships were being warped into the Charles River. "When those ships are in position, we command the Charlestown neck. They can see the ships as well as we can, and they must know it is hopeless. They can never leave the peninsula, and if the war is to be over, well, good God, what do we gain by burning the town?"

"We teach them a lesson, and lessons come hard. "When I was in school, they beat me, and I learned."

"When does Sir William plan to attack?"

"No later than a half hour past two."

As Prescott and Feversham stood on the breastworks, studying the preparations on Copp's Hill and on the beach at Morton's Point, Gen. Israel Putnam rode up to the earthworks and sat on his horse, scowling as he contemplated Colonel Prescott's preparations. He was soaked with sweat, and his long gray hair was in a wild tangle around his head. He spurred his horse down the length of Prescott's line and along the walls that shielded Knowlton's men.

"He's angry," Feversham said.

"That son of a bitch is always angry," Prescott said. "It's his normal state of mind."

Putnam rode back to where they were and said sourly, "Do you realize that half your men are asleep, Colonel?"

"Those men raised the breastworks and built the redoubt. They've been working all night. Why shouldn't they sleep?"

Putnam thought about that for a long moment, and then he said, "I was right. The attack will be here."

Gridley joined them. "You're always right, General."

The militiamen within earshot burst out laughing.

"Thank you!" Putnam snapped. "How many men do you have in the redoubt?"

"A few dozen."

"Damn it, don't you have a count?"

Climbing out of the redoubt and joining them, Dr. Warren said quietly, "Forty-three men, General Putnam, counting Colonel Gridley and myself."

"That's not enough."

"Sir," Gridley said, trying to contain his anger, "the facing wall of the redoubt is thirty-eight feet long. In that space, eighteen men can use their muskets efficiently. Eighteen others will take their places while they reload."

"I'll thank you not to teach me tactics, Colonel Gridley," placing the accent on the word "Colonel."

"Then will you teach me tactics, General," Gridley snapped. "Give me a lesson in your tactics, and General Ward's tactics. We're on this cursed hill facing the whole British army with a few hundred men and boys while a whole fuckin' army of twelve thousand sit on their asses in Roxbury and Dorchester!"

"Oh, hold on, Richard," Warren said. "We can't fight among ourselves. Israel was all for more men. It's Ward who denied us the reinforcements."

"Ward and the damn Committee of Safety," Prescott said.

Silence for a few moments while the four men faced each other. Then, from Putnam: "I'll try to forget what you said, Colonel."

"I don't give a shit whether you forget it or not," Gridley replied. He dropped his voice, went close to Putnam, who still sat his horse, and speaking with hardly controlled rage, said, "As sure as there's a God in heaven, if I live through this day, I'll have satisfaction for this. We have been betrayed, sir, and you know that as well as I do. The men in this redoubt and behind that barricade are ready to lay down their lives and you come here and sneer at us!"

"I am not sneering," Putnam hissed. "Control yourself, Richard. I pleaded for more men. Give me that."

Warren took Gridley's arm and drew him away, whispering, "Please, Richard, let the old man be."

His face set in anger, Putnam turned his horse as if to ride away and then pulled back on his reins. "Colonel Prescott?"

"Yes, sir."

Putnam pointed to a pile of spades and pickaxes. "What are you doing with those tools?"

"Nothing," Prescott said shortly.

"What do you mean, nothing?"

"I mean nothing. We used them, and there they are."

"You mean to let them fall into the hands of the British?"

"If it comes to that."

"Those tools belong to the Committee of Safety. They must be returned to the army before hostilities begin."

Prescott stared at Putnam in disbelief. It appeared to Feversham that Prescott would literally spring at Putnam and tear him from his saddle. Somehow the big man controlled himself. He spoke slowly and evenly. "I am in command of these men and of this defense. My duty is to my country, not to a pile of rusty tools. If you want them, sir, take them with you. I don't give a damn."

It was like a dream, Feversham felt, both improbable and unbelievable.

"There are at least a hundred spades and axes in that pile," Putnam said. "They are an invaluable asset to the defense of our army around

Boston. I want you to assign a company of men to carry them away. This is an order."

"You can go to hell, General," Prescott said calmly.

Feversham watched Putnam ride off.

"I don't believe it," Prescott said to Feversham. "Tell me, Doctor, did you hear what I heard?"

Feversham nodded hopelessly.

"The man's under a terrible strain," Warren said to Prescott. "Give him that. We all are. He has tremendous respect for you, believe me. When this command was given to you, he was your most firm advocate."

After a moment of silence, Prescott said, "What time is it, Dr. Warren?"

Warren took his watch out of his waistcoat pocket. It was a large gold pocket watch with a caduceus bas-relief on its cover. He snapped it open. "Two o'clock, Colonel."

Prescott said to Feversham, "A very good estimate, Dr. Feversham. I think, now, the gates of hell are about to open."

June 17, 2:00 P.M.

No more than fifteen minutes after he had ridden away in a fury, Gen. Israel Putnam returned on foot, leading a motley crowd of some fifty men. He was carrying a musket, and he stalked up to Prescott and said, "Colonel Prescott, I am here to offer my service as a soldier in your ranks. I found these men in retreat, and I turned them around."

Open-mouthed, Prescott was without words. Then he offered his hand, and Putnam took it, and for a moment, the two men faced each other, hands locked. Then Prescott took a long breath and said, "I thank you, sir." He pointed along the ridge to where Knowlton's men were still piling rocks for their defense. "Take your men, sir, and join Major Knowlton. His line is too thin, and he'll be happy to receive you.

"What are my orders?" Putnam asked, making a final obeisance.

"To stop the British."

Putnam nodded, waved at his men, and yelled, "Follow me!"

Gridley and Warren leaped out of the redoubt. "What was that all about?"

Prescott told them, adding that if he had not seen it with his own eyes, he would not have believed it. "Thank God," Gridley said. "He's a wild old devil, but I'd rather have him with me than a dozen men. We were together in the French war with Rogers Rangers."

"Colonel!" Feversham called from the parapet. "They're ranking up. I think it's the beginning."

Prescott joined him and took the spyglass. "So they are. So they are." A young man, his armband marking him as an officer, came running up from Knowlton's position. "What's the word, sir?"

"It's close. Every man is to keep his head down. Let the officers watch it coming. I want heads down."

For the past half hour, the guns of the fleet had been silent. Now, from the water's edge, came the sound of drums, and then on top of that, a roar of cannons. All along the half mile of the American defenses, cannonballs thudded into the ground, sending up showers of dirt that fell like dry rain on the crouching men.

"Why did the cannons stop?" Prudence asked Lieutenant Threadberry. "How do they expect to drive those dreadful people out of Charlestown if they don't shoot at them?"

"Ah, now, ma'am, I expect it was to let the guns cool and give the gunners a bit of a rest. You'll soon hear enough of a thunder to make us deaf. Don't forget, the gun crews have been at it since early this morning. They want a spell of rest and a drink of water. It's hot here, but in the gun decks, it's just as hot as hell, if you will forgive the expression."

"They're going to attack now, are they not?" Mrs. Loring asked.

"Oh, soon enough, you may be sure. See how the general has put his men into parade position. It's a great army we're looking at. Starting there on the left, you have the marines, and then the light infantry, and right there in the center, Sir William's grenadiers, with their great bearskin shakos. Just the sight of them will make a brave man shudder."

"Will General Howe lead them?" Mrs. Loring wondered.

"You can be sure of that. They're his own."

"And won't that place him in awful jeopardy?"

"He won't be thinking of that." The lieutenant ventured to lay his hand on hers, reassuringly. "You're not to think of harm coming to him, Mrs. Loring. My own thought is that they will cut and run before he's ever in musket range. Ah, see—" He pointed down the deck to where Captain Woodly had appeared. "It's a high moment, and the captain has come on deck to watch.

All the rest of the crew were at the rail, their eyes fixed on the army drawn up at the foot of Breed's Hill. Both midshipmen had scrambled up the rigging, the better to see the drama that was to unfold before their eyes.

"When will it begin?" Prudence asked nervously. "Are we in any danger here?"

"Bless you, ma'am, here on this ship you're as safe as if you were at home in bed."

"I'm frightened."

"Nothing to be frightened of, nothing at all." He stroked Mrs. Hallsbury's arm reassuringly. "You're square in the center of the British navy. Safest place in the world. Not that I wouldn't give a pretty penny to be a part of this great encounter. But my place is here."

On Copp's Hill, General Clinton and General Burgoyne stood with the battery of mortars, watching the iron fireballs glow red hot as the gunners pumped the bellows. Sir Henry Clinton sighed and admitted that the Americans had not surrendered.

"I hardly expected them to do so," Burgoyne said.

"Give me your glass," Clinton said. "Somerset is signaling."

Burgoyne handed him a spyglass. "What do you make?"

"Commence firing."

"Commence firing," Burgoyne relayed the command to the gun crew.

"So we burn a village," Clinton said softly. "Where every prospect pleases and only man is vile."

The gunners packed the mortars with bags of gunpowder. Then they lifted the red-hot iron balls with tongs. No fuse or trigger was necessary. When the hot cannonballs touched the gunpowder, the mortars fired, and the flaming iron balls arched over the river into Charlestown. The effect was immediate. Where the fireballs crashed into the tinder-dry roof shingles, the resulting fire was almost instantaneous. Within minutes, a dozen houses were in flames. On the rooftops of Boston, hundreds of men, women, and children watched the act of pitiless destruction. Some of them cheered. Others, whose hearts were with the Americans, who had relatives and friends who had once lived in Charlestown, wept or cursed the British.

On Breed's Hill, the militiamen peered through the cracks and crevices in their fortifications and cursed impotently. Standing on the barricade, Feversham and Prescott and Warren watched in bitter silence, and when Warren asked Feversham, "Why? Why? You're an Englishman, Feversham. Tell me why?"

Coldly and thoughtfully, Prescott said, "It makes sense only if they considered that the smoke would cover them."

"When all the rest is senseless." Warren sighed.

That had also been in General Howe's mind, and his grand plan for the burning of the village, as he said afterward, was that the pall of smoke would cover their advance. But even as the fireballs began to fall, the wind shifted, and the thickening column of smoke drifted over the Charles River and away from the redoubt.

"There's a stinking piece of luck," Sir William said to General Pigot, and Pigot laughed, then shrugged and observed that wind was an uneasy ally.

"We're all in good order and ready," Pigot told Howe. Pigot commanded the light infantry and the marines, all of them drawn up rank upon rank in the tall grass of the fields that stretched from Morton's Point to the edge of the burning Charlestown village. "But damned if I see anything up there to oppose us?" He trained his spyglass on the hill.

"Who are those three men standing there?"

"One of them, I think, is Prescott. The big man. Shall we be advancing, sir?"

Major Wilkens of the marines joined them. "If I may offer an opinion, sir," he said to Howe, "I think we should go at them. My men are hot for it."

"All in due time, young fellow," Sir William agreed. "I'll have a word with the drummer boys. I lost my whistle somewhere. Can you spare your whistle, Wilkens?"

"Gladly, General. Where you go, we follow. I don't expect to whistle a retreat."

There were twenty-two drummer boys ranged in front of the waiting ranks of men. It was in the tradition of the British army that the drummers should be young and in their teens. Sir William had gone to the trouble of memorizing the names of half a dozen of them, holding that nothing a leader could do pleased their troops more than the ability to single them out with their family names. Sir William was good at names, and now he reviewed his men and named the drummer boys. "Haskins. Stout heart?"

"Yes, sir."

"Smith?"

Smith, skinny, fourteen years old, saluted sharply.

"Kermit?"

"Ready, sir. Very ready." He had long, straw-colored hair, gathered in a ponytail.

"Jackson?"

It was good for the morale of the men to see their commander aware of and interested in the drummer boys. As he went down the line, the men broke into cheers, a great shout that echoed over the cannonading.

On Breed's Hill, the militiamen listened to the cheers in sullen silence, and Gridley observed to Warren, "It's their worst mistake, burning the town. The men are raging. Whatever they felt before, now it's pure and simple hatred."

A gray-haired man on the firing step of the redoubt said to Gridley, "I lived there. I'm watching my house burn. I built the house with my papa. It took six years. I grew up building it."

Standing with Knowlton behind the stone wall that sheltered Knowlton's Connecticut riflemen, Putnam roared, "For every damn house, you will burn in hell!"

Still standing on the parapet with Feversham, Prescott remarked on the growling anger of his men. "The damn fools to burn the town and give me a gift of it. They give us what we need, hate and the will to fight. I don't think any of them will run away now."

At 2:15 P.M., on the seventeenth of June, Gen. Sir William Howe gave the final orders for the advance to his staff officers. He stood in front of his grenadiers, surrounded by eight men, and he pointedly reviewed the maneuver they had discussed on and off for the past hour. "General Pigot," he said, "you will take the Fifty-second, the Forty-seventh, the Fifth, the Thirty-eighth, and the Forty-third of the light infantry and go against the redoubt. You will destroy it frontily and enfilade both sides. Major Atkins, you will lead the rest of the light infantry around the right flank, and when you have taken whatever defense they have there, you will continue to advance against Bunker Hill, occupy it, and fortify your position. Major Wilkens, you will support General Pigot's left flank, circle the redoubt, and continue with your marines down the road to the Charlestown neck, according to our maps a distance of about a mile. You will take a position at the neck and prevent a retreat of the colonials.

"I shall advance against the center with my grenadiers and continue to advance until we have taken the high ground at Bunker Hill. Then I will join you with my Grenadiers at the Charlestown neck. We are not certain of how much effort they will give to the defense of Breed's Hill, but it should not be troublesome. I calculate that in two hours we shall be in total possession of the peninsula. Tell off parties for the prisoners. Any man who hesitates or retreats without orders faces death on the field. Now go to your regiments, gentlemen, and God be with you."

At a half hour past two o'clock, Gen. William Howe blew three short notes on the whistle he had borrowed from Major Wilkens, as a signal to the drummer boys, and they began to beat the alert. With a calm precision that caused Sir William's heart to swell with pleasure, the various regiments marched off and took their battle positions in a line that stretched from Morton's Point almost to the herb gardens of burning Charlestown. The Connecticut riflemen who had been concealed in the Charlestown houses had fled as the first firebombs fell. The marines on the extreme left were now in no danger from hidden snipers. Sir William, at the head of his grenadiers, raised his arm and let it fall, and the drums changed their tempo into the quick chatter of the advance. The long line of troops, twenty-three hundred British regulars, in their bright uniforms, knapsacks of food, and water and blankets on their backs—for this was a commitment to take and hold a position— marched forward to Breed's Hill.

Feversham's memory of the battle was like a patchwork quilt. The last volley of cannon fire from the warships made a lucky hit on one of Prescott's militiamen who would not keep his head down, searing his arm and almost ripping it from his body. Feversham applied a tourniquet, sutured the wound as best he could, bound it, and gave the man a mouthful of rum. He was aware that the cannonading had stopped. He stood up to see the long British line, a third of a mile in length, advancing up the hill, the young drummers leading the way with their rolling rhythm.

In the redoubt, the Americans knelt on the firing step, their muskets ready. Prescott loped back and forth along the line of trenches and breastworks, telling his men to hold their fire. He kept repeating it, although it was plain that the British were well out of musket range; indeed, out of rifle range as well. In the center, where Howe led his grenadiers, there were a number of small farm holdings, each with a stone wall. The grenadiers had to climb the walls and re-form. Prescott watched this slow progress with amazement. In each instance, the marines and the light infantry halted and waited for the grenadiers to form a parade line once again.

But off to Howe's right, the light infantry continued to advance, their progress unimpeded, General Pigot evidently convinced that there would be no resistance, and thus the advancing line bent into a bow shape. It was Pigot's intent to circle around and cut off any retreat from the redoubt.

Aside from the head of a man here and there, the British commanders had no knowledge of what might await them. They knew that the redoubt was manned, and they knew that earthen breastworks had been thrown up for a hundred paces, from the front of the redoubt and off to the British right. But for all the information that Dr. Church had been able to bring them, they had no clear picture of any real defense. They simply accepted the fact that the Americans would be foolish to allow any considerable number of men to be trapped on the peninsula, that the men in the redoubt were heroic fools, and that there would be no significant opposition.

On the British right, where the land sloped down to the shore of the Mystic River, a place of rocks and boulders, John Stark and his New

Hampshire riflemen had taken a position from the rock-strewn river edge to the sharp slope of Breed's Hill, connecting them with Knowlton's Connecticut militia, who in turn held a position up the ridge to Prescott's earthen embankment. But except for the embankment and the redoubt, none of this was visible to the British. Stark's riflemen were crouched behind a stone wall and a wooden rail fence, which they had stuffed with baled hay, with Stark's cold promise to "kill any stupid bastard who shows his head." Knowlton's Connecticut men were equally well hidden behind a stone wall. Both Knowlton and Stark had planted stakes of wood about fifty feet in front of their lines. Stark had with him Jimmy Grass, a New Hampshire farmer who had learned to beat a tattoo on a drum he had picked up during the French war. Jimmy, seventy years old, was not much good for anything else, but he had talked Johnny Stark into taking him along as a drummer. The stakes of wood were Stark's measure for the range.

When General Pigot's light infantrymen were within a hundred feet of the fence that hid Stark's riflemen, already in front of the rest of the British line, the general felt that he had done the trick, and he shouted for double time, sending his men into a race that would allow them to swing around the ridge. Stark stood up, and as they passed the stakes, signaled to Jimmy Grass, who beat out his tattoo. The New Hampshire riflemen raised up on their knees and fired at forty feet. A solid sheet of flame roared across their front, ripping into the light infantry like a fiery saw's edge, tearing the British soldiers to pieces.

The junior officers wore crossed white bands on their chests. "Target the officers," Stark had told them. Pigot saw every officer crumple and fall, his entire front line a bloody mass of dead and wounded, men screaming in pain and rage. The riflemen, each of whom had a second weapon, passed their rifles back to loaders and fired again. Now the whole slope in front of them was covered with light infantry, dying and wounded men who were trying to crawl away from the horror of it. Pigot was not unused to war, but he had never seen a slaughter like this, and he shouted to his troops to rally. Only one British drummer boy was still alive, and he played his drum valiantly. The light infantry managed a volley and then began to fall back. Stark's riflemen were shouting at the top of their lungs, and in the heat of the slaughter they had done, they started to climb over the fence in pursuit of the British. Stark yelled, "Come back, you damn fools!"

Two of the riflemen were dead. Three others had been wounded, and Bones worked desperately to stop their bleeding and dress their wounds.

General Pigot, standing unhurt, with his officers dead all around him, ordered his light infantry to fall back, leaving the tall grass littered with corpses, while the wounded light infantrymen, moaning with pain, tried to crawl away from the horror of the unending fire of the New Hampshire riflemen, who continued to load and fire as long as the light infantrymen were in range of the long Pennsylvania rifles.

Then, suddenly aware of the horror they had caused, the New Hampshire men stopped firing and shouting and knelt behind their barricade.

A tangle of brush and thicket prevented Howe from seeing the catastrophe that had overtaken his right wing, and as he heard the roar of gunfire and the screaming of the men in the engagement, he halted his own advance, still two hundred yards short of Knowlton's Connecticut men. His grenadiers, burdened by their heavy packs, had to pause again and again to climb the wooden fences. He sent one of his aides, young Lieutenant Freeman, to advise Wilkens, leading the left wing, to hold back until the grenadiers were in formation and ready to attack.

Panting, covered with blood, Pigot joined him and told him of the situation. "Major Watkins is alive," Pigot said, panting. "All my other officers are dead."

"How many men have you lost?"

"God knows. Over a hundred."

"Then goddamn it, reform and we'll attack again."

"Where are the cannon?"

It was in their overall plan to drag cannon up the hill and blast through, but the cannon were still mired in mud at the base of the hill.

"Fuck the cannon!" Howe roared. "Bring your men around to support the marines. I'll cut the whole thing open with my grenadiers."

On the deck of *Vindicator*, lying a few hundred yards off the Charlestown shore, close enough to feel the heat of the burning village, Mrs. Loring

watched the ranks of brightly uniformed British troops marching slowly, in precise order, as they mounted Breed's Hill. She clapped her
hands in pleasure.

"What a sight!" Mrs. Loring cried. "I do wonder whether it was ever
given to people to be so fortunate, to sit here in safety and watch those
gallant men go to battle. Oh, I have heard and read of such things, but
to see it before one's eyes!"

"But some of them will die," Prudence said. "I don't know whether
I can bear to watch."

"Ah, but war is war," Lieutenant Threadberry said. "It is in the
nature of it. Some live and some die. We must accept that. There's the
glory that built the empire."

"How well put," Mrs. Loring exclaimed, reaching out and taking
the lieutenant's hand. "But I'm only a woman, sir, and it's hard for me
to think as a man thinks."

"Of course," he said, daring to allow his other hand to brush Mrs.
Loring's breast, as if by accident.

She picked up the spyglass and peered through it. "They are so close.
But where is Sir William?"

"Leading his troops, ma'am. Leading the grenadiers. You can't see
him because he's in front of his men."

For the first time the cold thought touched Mrs. Loring that General
Howe might die in the battle. Where would all her dreams of a marriage and a conquest of fashionable London go? Where indeed?

Threadberry saw the tear on her cheek. "My dear lady, you must not
weep. This will be a great victory, I assure you."

On Copp's Hill, Burgoyne and Clinton, watching the advance of
Breed's Hill, heard the crescendo of rifle and musket fire from the
encounter with Stark's riflemen, although the encounter itself was out
of their range of vision.

Burgoyne cried, "I can't stay here and watch it happening over
there."

"Absolutely," Clinton agreed.

"We're no damn use here at all."

"None."

There were twenty-two men in their mortar crew and twelve light infantrymen assigned as guards. "Weapons, all of you," Burgoyne called out.

Leading the thirty-four men, Clinton and Burgoyne raced down Copp's Hill to the wharf, where they piled into one of the barges that had been used to take the army across the river.

Little Isaac Hampton, fourteen years old, came racing over to Major Knowlton to tell him what had happened at Stark's barricade and then, hardly pausing to catch his breath, ran on to Prescott's position. Knowlton turned to Putnam. "Can you believe it? Stark stopped them, and they ran."

The men behind the stone wall heard him and began to cheer.

"This is crazy," Knowlton said, pointing to where the grenadiers were forming up, less than two hundred paces down the hill, standing calmly, as if on parade. "What are they up to?"

"There's the light infantry, crossing behind them. That's General Howe, the big man with the white wig," Putnam exclaimed excitedly.

The two drummer boys at the front of the grenadiers began to beat a quick tattoo, while at least half of the light infantrymen who had survived the attack on Stark ran past their rear to join the regiments that extended from the grenadier's left to face Prescott's entrenchments and the redoubt.

"My God," Knowlton whispered.

"Lord God of Hosts, be with us," Putnam thundered.

At the redoubt, little Isaac Hampton gasped out his news to Prescott, Gridley, Warren, and Feversham.

"You say Stark beat them back?" Prescott demanded.

"They were dead all over the place, hundreds of them."

"It's our turn," Gridley said. And to Prescott: "We'll hold the redoubt as best we can. God be with you, Colonel." All the British drums were beating now, from the grenadiers to the reinforced light infantry facing Prescott to the marines on the extreme left.

Israel Putnam scorned the shelter of the stone wall. As he put it once, "The great Jehovah has my life in his hands for the twopence it's worth." Short, stocky, his barrel body on two gnarled legs, he stood with a musket in his hands. It was his intent, as he said later, to put a bullet in General Howe's red rosette.

Major Knowlton walked along the stone wall behind his men, calling out, "Heads down, children, heads down and trust me. Listen for my whistle. Let them shoot their loads away."

The grenadiers were in four columns of eight men, their front of thirty-two men a hundred feet wide, General Howe leading at their right flank, Major Canby, a distant relative of Howe's, on their left flank. Since they had been enlisted for height, with their great bearskin shakos, they were close to seven feet tall, their packs and blanket rolls making them even more menacing. They were veritable giants in comparison to the tiny drummer boys who led the advance, in keeping with the British conviction that age did not put any loyal subject of the Crown out of harm's way.

They had fixed their bayonets, making a glistening ripple of steel along their front. What was not visible was the perspiration that soaked their heavy uniforms, never designed for a New England summer. The perspiration ran down from under their shakos into their eyes, cruel sweat which could in no way be dried or wiped away. Along with that impediment, the afternoon sun shone in their eyes. For all of that, they were a terrifying sight, and Major Knowlton was thankful that he had stormed at his men and threatened to kill anyone who dared to raise his head and look over the wall before the signal was given.

When he called a halt to his grenadiers at sixty yards, Sir William was puzzled. He had instructed General Pigot, who had crossed over, to take command of the main body of light infantry and marines. These soldiers would storm the redoubt and the entrenchments to concert his attack with the attack of the grenadiers. Now, as he stood facing the long stone wall, he still had no idea of what was behind it. Was the only real force on this right flank the riflemen who had sent the light infantry reeling back? What faced him? Only two men were visible: General Putnam, whom he recognized from the wild tangle of gray hair, and Knowlton, whom he did not recognize. Nevertheless, convinced of the power of his grenadiers, he ordered a volley, and the thirty-two-man front of the grenadiers turned into a sheet of fire. The roar was picked up by volleys from the light infantry and the marines to his left.

Then General Howe ordered an advance at marching pace to close quarters with bayonets.

Neither Putnam nor Knowlton had been hit by the volley. A ball lifted Knowlton's tricorner hat, sending it sailing off, and a shot tore through Putnam's sleeve. At fifty paces, the grenadiers reached the stakes that Knowlton had placed to mark the distance, and Knowlton put his two pinkies in his mouth and blew a piercing whistle. The 220 Connecticut men behind the stone wall stood up and discharged their muskets and rifles at point-blank range into the grenadiers. It was a sight, as Knowlton said later, too terrible to take any joy in. The entire front rank of the grenadiers, thirty-two men and the drummer boys and three junior officers and Major Canby, were killed instantly, as well as a dozen others in the second rank. One moment, there was the proudest regiment in the British army in full parade, and a moment later the meadow grass in front of the stone wall was covered with dying men and the screaming wounded.

Gonzales was crouched to the rear of the wall, his instruments laid out and ready. He realized that no American had even been wounded.

Miraculously, Howe was untouched, for all of Israel Putnam's determination, and he roared for the advance to continue. Slipping on the blood and stumbling over the dead of the front rank, the grenadiers tried to advance.

Meanwhile, the loaders were passing fresh guns, and those Connecticut men who were not backed by loaders reloaded desperately. The grenadiers were only yards from the wall when Knowlton's whistle brought a second storm of fire, and once again the entire front of the four columns of grenadiers went down in a tangle of dying men.

Still Howe urged them on, laying about him with the flat of his sword, but now the Connecticut men were firing as fast as they could reload, and in spite of themselves, the grenadiers gave back, firing their muskets as they retreated, leaving the ground between their shattered ranks and the stone wall covered with blood and bodies.

This time, the Connecticut men paid a price. Six of them were dead, and nine others had been wounded, two with shattered arms that called for amputation. Dr. Gonzales had never been in a battle before, and in his lifetime of practice, he had only three times dealt with bullet wounds, all of them hunting accidents. He did what he could, forcing the wounded men to submit to the pain of raw rum, bandaging and suturing while the men cursed him for a damned sadistic Spaniard.

Feversham was one of that strange group of humans who are destined to be outsiders and thus observe everything differently than the majority of the human race. In all of his encounters with war, he had been a surgeon, thereby watching the horror that brought him his practice as a theatergoer might watch a play that menaced him without including him. A bullet in his thigh, which still caused him to walk with a slight limp, had proved that there were hazards to his profession, and in his time he had seen other surgeons killed at their work. He had come to Boston for two reasons, firstly because he had married an American woman, whom he loved dearly, which made his presence as a Catholic—even a fallen Catholic—and an Englishman in the bigoted white Protestant town of Ridgefield difficult, to put it mildly, and secondly, because for the first time in his life he felt that he had found some principles worth believing in.

He had joined the huge, loosely organized mob around Boston that called itself an army with a good deal of cynicism, yet he found himself accepted without prejudice and with open arms. And in the few hours he had been with this handful of men who were willing to face the best soldiers in the world with simple decision and without vainglory, he had forged a very real attachment to them. He was not the kind of man who indulged dramatics, who might say to himself, I believe in what these men are willing to die for, and I have decided to stay with them and offer whatever comfort I can, even if it should result in my own death, as it probably will. Yet that was the case, and he knew perhaps better than anyone on Breed's Hill how hopeless their situation was, even if they should manage to slow the attack with their handful of men.

Feversham was filled with admiration for Warren and Prescott and Gridley. He had never really known such men before—their easy comradeship with the volunteers they led, their lack of pretension, Warren's willingness to laugh off the fact that he had been made a general by the witless Committee of Safety, Prescott's flexibility with old Putnam, Gridley's rocklike patience and fortitude. Feversham felt strongly that they were as convinced as he was that somewhere along the line they had been betrayed, left on this little peninsula with a comparative handful of men. Yet they accused no one and never even entertained the notion of retreat.

When the drums first sounded from the beach below, he had found himself a slightly sheltered spot, a small hollow about ten paces behind the entrenchment. There he had meticulously laid out his instruments—his needles, strung with catgut, his tourniquets, tied and ready for use, his dressings and bandages, his jug of water and quart flask of rum, his shears and bone saw and probes and forceps. He had in his jacket pocket a piece of linen, about a yard square, upon which his wife, Alice, had embroidered the word SURGEON. It might help if he were trapped with wounded in a retreat. But in spite of his commitment to what he was supposed to do, he could not remain there as the sound of drums came closer, and when the crash of rifle fire exploded from Stark's position, he joined Prescott on the parapet.

"You shouldn't be here, Doctor."

"Forgive me. My teacher swore I was born to be hanged."

"Then look and tell me what on earth they're waiting for. Stark beat them back. The kid said they took terrible losses."

"Now," Feversham said as the drummers beat their furious tattoo and the line of light infantry began their advance, even as Howe ordered his grenadiers forward against Major Knowlton's Connecticut militia. Both men leaped off the parapet, and Prescott raced along his line of defense, pleading, "Don't shoot. Don't shoot. Keep your heads down. Wait till you see the white's of their eyes. Wait! Wait!"

At sixty yards, the light infantry and the marines paused and fired. As with the grenadiers, they were in columns of eight, with the marines, ten columns, an advancing front of eight men, two hundred feet across, the marines facing the redoubt, the light infantry facing Prescott's long earthworks, the long front bursting into a sheet of flame. Feversham felt the wind of bullets inches from his face, and still he stood erect, gripped with a fascination stronger than fear. Then the whole front of the British, the ten columns of men, egged on by their shouting officers, bayonets fixed, surged forward at the barricade.

At forty feet, Prescott shouted at the top of his lungs, "Now! Now!" And the Massachusetts farmers stood up and emptied two hundred muskets and rifles at point-blank range, even as the men in the redoubt fired.

As with the grenadiers, the whole front of the British force buckled, as if some flaming scythe had ripped the eight men into shreds of torn flesh. The ranks behind them pulled back, stunned by the execution of their entire front, staring for a long moment at the carpet of broken bodies, while Prescott dashed back and forth shouting: "Reload! Reload and stay down! Reload!"

They had less than fifty second guns, and the loaders passed them forward. The single British officer who remained on his feet screamed for his men to follow him and raced for the embankment. As he mounted it, Prescott killed him with his pistol. In front of the redoubt, General Pigot staggered away with a bullet in his thigh. As the light infantry swayed back and forth, caught between the desire to run and the training that urged them to advance, the Massachusetts farmers loaded and shot methodically.

In the redoubt as at the embankment, the rush of flame from the American muskets had sent the marines reeling back, but they formed again in better order than the light infantry and charged the redoubt once more. Prescott waved his reserve loaders into the redoubt, and a wild hand-to-hand struggle raged on the firing step until the marines were beaten back. Eight of the defenders of the redoubt were killed, and Gridley had a bayonet thrust in his arm.

Bit by bit, the light infantry and the marines gave back, even as the grenadiers had given back, the whole British force retreating down the slope of Breed's Hill, leaving the grassy slope red with blood and carpeted with their dead.

Feversham had torn himself away from the awful struggle, and now he was at work, surrounded by bleeding men. There was no time to be careful, to take pains. Stop the bleeding. Suture where he had to. No time to probe for bullets. Use dressings, bandages, tourniquets. He was being overwhelmed, and he shouted, "Warren! Warren, can you help me?" He had no idea of what had happened in the redoubt.

Gridley appeared and said, "Warren has all he can handle." He was holding the cut in his arm. "We're out of bandages. Can you spare something for my arm?" He was trying to stanch the flow of blood with his other hand.

"Let me," Feversham said, cursing the lack of foresightedness. He needed more of everything. He applied a tourniquet. "I'll suture it later."

"Yes, of course, it's nothing," Gridley said, wincing, as Feversham sprinkled rum on the raw wound.

Some of Prescott's men leaped the barricade and picked up muskets from the dead light infantry. They wanted the bayonets. Prescott roared at them to get back behind the earthworks. Feversham glanced up and saw Gonzales. "I can help," Gonzales said, and told Gridley, "Tear up shirts for bandages." Knowlton's Connecticut men had few wounded.

Panting, Stark appeared, reported to Prescott, and then loped back across the rise to his own position. He saw his son standing behind the barricade, unharmed, and he broke into tears. He had been told that his son had been killed, and stifling his sobs, he resisted an impulse to embrace the boy, but instead raced back to his position. Knowlton, shaking, informed Prescott that the grenadiers had been destroyed.

Ninety percent of Howe's beloved grenadiers had been killed or wounded. The sloping meadow in front of Knowlton's position was covered with their bodies. Weeping tears of rage and frustration, Sir William stormed at the light infantry and marines, commanding them to stand and fight. He looked for the junior officers, but only two were on their feet, Lieutenant Fredericks and Captain Ford. "Form the men!" he shouted to them. "Form ranks!" Limping and bleeding, Pigot joined him.

Out of rifle shot, the British retreat halted. Marine major Sutherman, calm and reassuring, managed to control his troops and whip them into order. General Howe took a center position, sword in hand, and pointed to the earthworks that stretched off to the right of the redoubt. Pitcairn, another marine major, only slightly wounded, joined Howe and spoke a single word, "Again?"

Only one of the drummer boys was still alive. "Beat the advance!" Howe said sharply. The drumbeat began, and Howe, Pitcairn beside him, moved forward deliberately, Sir William with sword in hand. A

British soldier, carrying the blue banner of the grenadiers, which he had rescued from among the dead, ran forward and took his place beside Howe. As the three men began to climb the hill once again, the light infantry and the marines burst out cheering and surged forward. At one hundred yards, a rifleman killed Major Sutherman, but Howe marched on, seemingly invulnerable.

Behind the barricade, Prescott talked to his men. "Easy, my braves, easy my darlings, easy now. Don't fire. Hold your fire. Hold your fire."

Feversham and Gonzales, working with the wounded, heard Prescott's voice as background. Occasionally, Feversham glanced at Gonzales, wondering what was in the man's mind. Here they were trapped; here they must stay. Under the pressure of what he did, he could lose his fear and awareness of himself in jeopardy. He had lived this awful scene before. But what of Gonzales? Who was this tall, painfully thin man with his long, dark Spanish face?

"Bones is dead," Gonzales said suddenly. "Shot through the head." He worked meticulously and did not stop suturing a torn shoulder as he spoke.

With the death of Sutherman, the heart went out of the British. Yet the light infantry and the marines continued to advance. Their formation was ragged, and they began to fire at sixty yards. At thirty-five yards, with no answering fire from Prescott's men, they surged forward, and the men behind the earthworks, backed up now by Knowlton's Connecticut men, stood up and released a sheet of fire that literally flung the British back, as if some giant hand had reached out and swept them away. There was no holding them now. The British line collapsed, and the light infantry and the marines broke into full retreat, running, stumbling, falling, as they fled down Breed's Hill, with a forlorn Sir William Howe, sword in hand, disdaining to run and marching majestically behind them.

"Give the stupid bastard his due," Burgoyne said to Clinton later. "He doesn't know the meaning of fear."

The Americans shouted and cheered and waved their guns and danced wildly. There were sixteen dead who did not dance, and another thirty wounded, crowding around Feversham and Gonzales and

Warren, the latter out of bandages and using what was left of the supplies that Feversham had brought with him. As the enthusiasm calmed
down, the loaders as well as the marksmen began to complain about
powder. Some had no powder left to them, and others had only a charge
or two.

The attack had been directed at the redoubt and at Prescott's breastworks. Stark had led his men in a half circle. The New Hampshire
riflemen, in loose order, continued to fire at the retreating light infantry
with their long Pennsylvania rifles, and then, seeing the British out of
range as they retreated down to Morton's Point, he called his men back
and led them to join Prescott behind the barricade. "We're almost out
of powder," he told Prescott.

Prescott, pulling himself away from the unbelievable sight of a
British army in full retreat, called out to Feversham, "Doctor, spare me
a moment."

His face grim, Feversham went on with his ministrations to the
groaning, bleeding militiamen. Prescott went to him. "Can you take a
moment to look?"

"No," Feversham said shortly.

"They're in full retreat, all of them."

"Yes."

"You know them. What will they do now?"

"How many men have they lost?"

"Five, six hundred. Maybe more. How the hell do I know?"

"They still have two thousand." He paused, a needle in his hand.
Head to foot, he was covered with blood, exhausted for want of sleep.
Putnam and Johnny Stark joined them.

"We're almost out of powder," Putnam said.

"God help me," Feversham exploded. "I don't understand your people. What in hell goes on here? You have twelve thousand men around
Boston sitting on their bloody asses. Why don't you ask for reinforcements? With a few thousand fresh troops, you could go down the hill
and sweep the British into the sea. What are we? Some kind of stupid
sacrifice?"

Controlling himself, Prescott said quietly, "I sent messengers five times.
I sent runners to plead for reinforcement. There are no reinforcements."

"That bastard Ward," Putnam said bitterly. "He's a coward or a traitor."

"I don't want that kind of talk," Prescott said. "We're here, and there's no hope of reinforcement."

"I can't hold my position," Stark said. "I have three hundred men, and half of them are out of powder. They can't use the British cartridges, and even if they break them open, they won't rob the dead, and even if they take those guns, they can't fight with bayonets. It's not their way. They won't give up their rifles."

"Feversham," Prescott said, "you were in the British army. You spent years with them. You know how they think. What will they do?"

"They will attack again. They must," Feversham said tiredly. "Their position down at the water's edge is untenable. A British army was half-destroyed by a handful of Continentals. Every officer in the army faces court-martial and disgrace. If they go back to Boston, they carry a badge of shame forever. That's how they think, and that's how they come to a decision. So what is their choice?" As he spoke, in fits and starts, he sutured a hole in a militiaman's side, aware that the ribs under his fingers were shattered, knowing that the wounded man would die.

"What is their choice?" Prescott insisted.

"They will attack," Feversham muttered. "That is all they can do."

Knowlton, Stark, Putnam, and Gridley held council together on what the next hour might bring them. Since Putnam had been instrumental in preparing a line of defense on Bunker Hill, arguing that the attack would be there rather than on Breed's Hill, the others questioned him about the possibility of falling back to that position and surrendering both the breastworks and the redoubt.

"There were over a hundred men on Bunker Hill when I left," Putnam said.

Gridley laughed painfully and declared that he would eat his hat if a dozen of them remained.

"I won't surrender this position," Prescott said. "We tore them to pieces when they came at us before. We can do it again."

"Not without ammunition."

"We can use the British powder bottles. They don't all carry cartridges."

"We'll find little there," Knowlton. "My men searched."

Stark said, "The point is, we don't have the powder. You can't brush that away."

"Can't we spread it?" Prescott wondered. "Have we enough for two volleys?"

"Hardly," Gridley said.

"I never agreed with this redoubt," Putnam said. "I went along with it for Warren's sake, but it's wrong. Without Stark's riflemen, they turn our flank. We can fall back to Bunker Hill, and if we hold Bunker Hill, we can keep the neck open."

"On the other hand," Prescott argued, "if we can hold the redoubt and the line of entrenchments and send those bloody bastards down the hill one more time, then it's a victory plain and simple, and the war's done."

"Not so simple," Putnam said slowly. "Wars aren't done that way."

They were interrupted by a rattle of drums from Morton's Point, and the men at the barricade crowded the embankment to see what was happening below. The light infantry, the marines, and another brigade of troops Prescott did not recognize were being formed into ranks.

"By God," Prescott whispered, "Feversham was right. They're going to attack." He swung around to the four officers who shared his command. "What do you say, gentlemen?"

"We fight," Stark said. "I won't show those red-jacket bastards my heels."

"We fight," Knowlton agreed.

Gridley nodded.

Putnam shrugged. "What the hell, fuck the lot of them. At my age, what difference does it make?"

Knowlton said that men whose powder was either gone or down to the last shot were slipping away.

"Let them go," Prescott said. "We have more than enough to man the barricade." Stark's riflemen had joined the Massachusetts farmers behind the barricade, as had Knowlton's Connecticut men. Prescott walked over to where Feversham and Gonzales were still treating the wounded.

"Doctor?"

Feversham looked at him without expression.

"I'm sending the wounded across the neck."

"How?"

"Let those who can walk do so. There are men—" He paused, unwilling to say that his men were beginning to desert. "Some of them have no powder. They won't fight against bayonets. They don't know how. We'll send them to you and let them carry the wounded down to the neck."

"Some of these men can't be moved."

"Then the British will finish their work," Prescott snapped. "Don't argue with me, Feversham. You assured me that the British will attack. We have ten, fifteen, minutes, and I have work to do. Do you want to go with them?"

Feversham shook his head. "I'll stay," he said bleakly.

Prescott had forgotten Gonzales's name. "You, Doctor Spaniard, or whatever. Do you want to leave with the wounded?"

"I'll stay with Dr. Feversham," Gonzales replied without looking up.

"As you wish."

"The doctor with Stark—where is he?"

"Dead. Shot through the head," Gonzales said.

"I'm sorry. Feversham, do you want a gun?"

Feversham managed a hollow laugh.

"You find humor, sir?"

"If I do, it's a poor joke, isn't it? No, Colonel, I don't want a gun. I'm a surgeon. What would I do with a gun?"

"I'm sorry," Prescott said. "Today is not good for any of us, is it, Doctor?"

"No, Colonel." Feversham rose. "Try to walk," he said to the man whose leg he had just bandaged.

Prescott took Feversham aside. "Doctor," he said, "you're English, and you have a British army record. They'll hear it in your speech, and as sure as God, they'll hang you."

"Only if they defeat you." Feversham smiled and rubbed his bloodshot eyes. "I'm tired and cranky, Colonel, but I'm filled with admiration for you and your demented farmers."

"And who is more sane? Those bastards who have left their dead like a carpet on the hillside? Go with the wounded, Doctor."

Feversham shook his head. "It would set a poor example for that man," he said softly, nodding at Gonzales and smiling bitterly. "He's a Jew out of Providence. Would you have a Christian gentleman take off, where he is willing to stay? Only one favor from you, Colonel, and I know the burden you carry. I have a wife in Ridgefield in Connecticut, and I have a letter to her in my pocket. If you live and I die, will you see that it reaches her?"

"That I will."

Prescott strode off, eager to get away from the moans and whimpers of the wounded. But he had no feeling that he would live through this day, and he passed Feversham's letter on to Dr. Warren.

June 17, 4:00 P.M.

A lighter, pulling alongside *Vindicator*, informed
Captain Woodly that Sir William's grenadier guardsmen had been
practically wiped out. An officer on the lighter commandeered the eight
marines stationed on board Captain Woodly's ship for reinforcements
onshore. It fell to Lieutenant Threadberry to bring the news to Mrs.
Loring.

The two women, Elizabeth Loring and Prudence Hallsbury, had
been watching the battle on Breed's Hill with interest and mounting
excitement. The view from their place on board *Vindicator* was interrupted only by the clouds of smoke from the gunfire, the smoke from
burning Charlestown blowing away from the battleground and toward
the Charles River. At this distance, the lines of soldiers, in their bright
red uniforms, were quite unreal. The encounter of the light infantry,
which attacked the American left flank, defended by the New
Hampshire riflemen, was hidden from their view by a fold of ground.
The charge of the grenadiers was hidden in part by brush and gunsmoke
from the riflemen. The main attack against the redoubt and the breastworks held by Colonel Prescott and his militiamen was in full view. The
ladies cheered and clapped and toasted the exciting toylike soldiers until
the attack was sent reeling back, after which both women became silent.

However, Mrs. Loring's faith in the prowess of Sir William was unshaken until Lieutenant Threadberry appeared with the bitter news. She asked him why they were taking away the eight marines.

"Well, ma'am," he said uneasily, "they be wanting all the reinforcement they can find."

"Are we losing the battle, then?"

"Oh, good heavens, no. The battle's only begun."

"And what of Sir William? What news do they bring of him?"

"Well, ma'am—"

"Well, ma'am, well, ma'am. I asked you a question!"

"Not easily answered, ma'am."

"And what does that mean?"

"It's hard to say."

"Please say it!" she snapped.

"Well, ma'am, the grenadiers have suffered. Yes, they've suffered deplorably—"

"Go on."

Threadberry sighed and shook his head. "They've been wiped out, more or less."

"Wiped out?"

"Killed and wounded," Threadberry replied unhappily.

"And Sir William?"

"We don't know—"

Mrs. Loring did what was expected of a woman in such circumstances. She fainted, but slowly enough for Lieutenant Threadberry to catch her and ease her abundant body onto the deck. Prudence immediately searched in her bag for smelling salts, and the lieutenant, taking advantage of his position and the emergency, allowed one hand to cover her breast, the better to hold her as he lowered her. Her eyes fluttered, but she did not ask him to remove his hand. Prudence came to her aid with the smelling salts, and Threadberry had quick visions of what the future might hold if the commander in chief passed out of the picture.

"I am all right now," Mrs. Loring whispered. "Please help me up."

Lieutenant Threadberry helped her back to her chair, nor did she chide him for his loose hands.

"You must find out," she begged him. "I will die a thousand deaths if you don't find out."

"Well, ma'am, unless a boat comes from shore— Well, I don't know how."

"You have signal flags."

"But that's an odd one to signal. I don't really know how to put it into flags, but I'll try."

Burgoyne and Clinton had picked up over a hundred men by the time they reached the mass of retreating light infantry and marines from the burning houses of Charlestown to Morton's Point. Their broken ranks were spotted with wounded men in bloodstained uniforms, men on the ground, groaning and weeping with pain, men trying to stanch the flow of blood. In all his years of war in Europe, Burgoyne had never witnessed a scene like this one, an army smashed and disorganized so quickly. And there was Howe, alive, unhurt—and ready to embrace Burgoyne.

"We must go back," Howe shouted. "Now! We must attack again."

Burgoyne grabbed him by both arms. "Steady, sir. Steady. Of course, we must go back."

Major Pitcairn joined them. "We lost most of our officers. The bastards picked them off. If we are to attack again, General Burgoyne, you and Sir Henry must lead us. There's Captain Freddy with the Irish Guards and Templeton with the marines. Maybe half a dozen other officers."

"Good man," Howe said generously. "Good thinking, Pitcairn. Go with the marines. Henry, you command the light infantry. I'll lead."

"What's our point?" Pitcairn asked, quivering with excitement.

"The redoubt, left and right flank," Howe said. "Sir Henry, you agree?"

The question gave Clinton leadership, and he did not hesitate to accept it. "Absolutely. The redoubt and that damn barricade. Now, these are the orders. All men are to drop their packs. We go in with bayonets. No stopping to reload. We go up in four columns, four abreast, no pause, no mercy, no quarter. We mount the hill slowly, save our strength. We'll each of us head a column. No turning back." He turned to Admiral Graves, who had just appeared. "Admiral, I want every gun you can give us on the Charleston neck!" He took out his watch. It was four o'clock. "An hour from now, gentlemen, we'll have this cursed peninsula, and this rebellion will be over."

There were no more bandages or dressings. The catgut was gone. The rum and water had been used up. Gonzales and Feversham had treated thirty-two wounded men as best as they could. The dead and those wounded who could not walk were on their way to the Charlestown neck. Two mule-drawn carts had appeared. One was loaded with dead bodies; the other, with the badly wounded. Feversham had put his bloody instruments in his bag.

From the waterside, at the foot of the hill, the British drumbeat began. The guns on the ships in the Charles River stopped firing as they began the process of being warped toward Charlestown Neck. In the strange silence that ensued, the tattoo sounded clear and sharp. Overhead, the afternoon sun was hidden behind one of the fluffy white clouds that sailed slowly through the burnished blue sky, and a cool shadow covered the men behind the barricade. The fire in Charlestown village, which had eagerly consumed the dry wooden houses like an angry, ravishing dragon, began to die down.

"If they hold," Gonzales said to Feversham, "we can help. But if the British break through—"

"Which is why I say you should go."

"I understand that, Dr. Feversham."

"Damn it," Feversham said, "I don't know why I'm here. Chances are we'll both be dead before this day is out. What's your stake here?"

"My great-grandfather, Dr. Feversham, was driven out of Cuba by the Inquisition. He came to Providence a hundred years ago, and I am the third generation in this land. That's my stake here. And now I think the attack is beginning."

Gonzales rose and walked to the barricade. Feversham walked with him. Even with the addition of Stark's New Hampshire men and the few hundred Connecticut volunteers who had been with Knowlton, Prescott's line was no thicker than it was before the first attack. At least two hundred men were missing, slipped away for want of powder or excess of fear—or wounded or dead.

There was no need now to pretend that the barricade was undefended. The line of militia and riflemen watched in silence as the four columns of light infantry, royal marines, and even a small cluster of the surviving grenadiers, in their big bearskin shakos, began their slow, deliberate approach up Breed's Hill.

"My God," Knowlton said to Prescott. "Give the bastards their due."

"That's Burgoyne leading them," Prescott said.

Walking along the position his riflemen had taken, John Stark said quietly, "If you have powder, start picking them off at two hundred yards."

The sun glinted from the bayonets of the advancing soldiers.

Here and there, along the American line, men turned and ran. Prescott ignored them. From the redoubt, Gridley shouted to Prescott, "Colonel, can you spare us a few men?"

"Any volunteers for the redoubt?" Prescott called.

The bleakness of it struck Feversham. Why had they ever built that cursed redoubt? It was a death trap.

Half a dozen men left the line, walked to the redoubt, and climbed over the entry port.

Feversham thought, More courage than I can understand. He tried to comprehend them—Prescott and Gridley and Stark and Warren and Putnam and the hundreds of men crouching behind the barricade.

Prescott paused by Feversham. "We have two shots, Doctor. Will they run again?"

"No. They'll come in with their bayonets."

Now the New Hampshire riflemen were beginning to fire, a ragged shooting, and here and there, a British soldier collapsed, but the pace of the advance neither slowed nor quickened. Clinton led one column; Burgoyne, another. Sir William Howe and Pitcairn marched before the marines. At fifty paces, they surged into a run, screaming at the top of their lungs, and the farmers and riflemen behind the barricade and in the redoubt fired their volley. The front ranks of the four columns went down, but those behind them leaped over their bodies and swarmed over the barricade and into the redoubt. The Americans clubbed their guns and swung savagely. Some of them beat back the light infantrymen, and others were skewered with bayonets, stabbed again and again by the hated and fear-crazed British soldiers, and over all a screaming, wailing sound of pain and terror.

Feversham saw a bayonet coming at him. He had no memory of the man who held it or how he was able to dodge the blade, but suddenly, he was on the ground, struggling with the British soldier for his weapon, and then a militiaman swung his musket against the soldier's throat. With all the sound, Feversham heard the man's neck snap, and he scrambled to his feet, dazed as the battle surged around him. He saw Prescott, standing on the barricade, swinging his sword, and all along the barricade, the same wild struggle.

Later, dressing Gridley's wounds, Feversham heard the story of the fight in the redoubt. A young fellow from Amesbury, name of Currier, took command with Gridley after Dr. Warren was killed, shot through the head as the first marines leaped over the wall, led by Major Pitcairn. The Negro slave—Gridley knew him only by the name of Robert— shot Pitcairn and killed him, a sort of grim justice, since Pitcairn had been in command of the troops that shot down the minutemen at Lexington two months before. Gridley had laid about him with his sword, and three other marines were either killed or wounded, which halted the attack on the redoubt long enough for the rest of the men there to leap over the rear wall, giving up the redoubt and running down the road to Bunker Hill.

Prescott saw this pell-mell retreat from the redoubt. Knowing that now his right flank was undefended, he realized that the less than two hundred men fighting the bayonets of the light infantry on the barricade were getting the worst of it. He shouted for them to retreat.

Putnam, amazingly calm, yelled, "Follow me!" Along with Knowlton, he led the wild scramble down behind the redoubt toward Bunker Hill, while Stark's New Hampshire men formed a sort of line, facing the British, their long rifles presented, Stark at one end of the line, Prescott at the other end. About a dozen of the New Hampshire men, their rifles still loaded, fired at the light infantry, and six of the British soldiers fell. The British paused, and the New Hampshire men, in an incredible display of calm and discipline, moved backward, their rifles still presented. The ground between them and the barricade was littered with the dead Connecticut and Massachusetts militiamen.

General Howe, standing on the wall of the redoubt, screamed, "Onward! Onward! Charge the fuckin' bastards!"

Still, the British held back.

Then Burgoyne and Clinton burst through to the barricade, waving their swords wildly, and Prescott yelled, "Run! Run!"

The riflemen poured down the slope behind Breed's Hill, the light infantry after them. Feversham, who had witnessed this scene from a dozen paces behind the riflemen, ran with them, desperately fighting not to stumble and fall. One of the riflemen fell, and British bayonets stabbed into his back.

The distance between the base of Breed's Hill and the barricade Putnam had ordered built that morning on the slope of Bunker Hill was no more than 150 paces. As he ran down the hill behind the redoubt, Feversham saw, to his amazement, a line of sixty-five men, standing in open order, facing the oncoming British. They stood like rocks, allowing the men racing away from the British to pass through their line and forcing the oncoming mass of light infantry and marines to halt their pursuit. The men running down from Breed's Hill slowed, stopped, and turned. The calm, stolid courage of these sixty-five men had an electric effect on the militiamen who had been driven off Breed's Hill and out of the redoubt. The riflemen who had powder left reloaded with desperate speed, as did those of the militia who had powder for their muskets, in all perhaps two dozen of the Americans. They moved up Bunker Hill, walking slowly backward. Another hundred or so men, who had been waiting as a second line of defense on Bunker Hill, took courage and left their stone wall and advanced down the hillside.

Feversham realized that the British had only their bayonets now. They had never stopped to reload. The sixty-five men, he would learn later, were a well-drilled, well-trained little company from the town of Ipswich. It was a demonic, incredible display of courage and madness on both sides. Already almost half of the entire British army had been killed or wounded, and Breed's Hill was littered with bodies of the American dead. Now a few hundred Americans, most of them without ammunition, still presented so terrifying a face that the British hesitated to advance.

Yet they did advance, Howe and Clinton leading them with utter indifference to the burst of flame from the Ipswich guns. Then the combat was hand to hand as the Americans retreated up to Bunker Hill and the stone walls Putnam had fortified earlier in the day.

There was a pause now. Halfway up the slope of Bunker Hill, the British stopped to reorganize, just out of musket range. The riflemen were out of ammunition, and almost half of the Ipswich contingent had died under the British bayonets, along with at least twenty of the militia and riflemen.

Panting, bloodstained, and exhausted, Prescott conferred with Gridley and Putnam and Knowlton. It was up to Prescott, and he said flatly that it was over. "We did what we could do, and we have no ammunition, and we can't fight bayonets with clubs. Tell me, General Putnam, tell me why that bastard, Artemus Ward, left us here to die. Why didn't he send ammunition? Why didn't he reinforce us?"

Gray-faced, so exhausted that he could hardly speak, old Putnam only shook his head.

Colonel Little, who led the Ipswich men, said, "The neck is still open. The British ships are warping back with the tide. We can still get across."

Prescott called to Feversham, who, with Gonzales, was tying wounds with strips of torn shirts. "Feversham, leave off! We'll carry those who can't walk. We're going to run for the Charlestown neck."

The orders were passed along. As the British prepared to renew their assault, what was left of the American force that had defended Breed's Hill and the redoubt formed ranks and marched down Bunker Hill, carrying their dead and wounded across the Charlestown neck.

June 17, 5:00 P.M.

At five o'clock, in the early evening of June 17th, in the year 1775, Sir William Howe, supreme commander of His Majesty George III's troops in America, stood on Bunker Hill, on the Charlestown peninsula, and watched the last of the American defenders cross the Charlestown neck.

He said to Clinton, quietly, "Henry, put what is left of the Thirty-eighth and the Fifth on guard across the Charlestown neck. Have the rest of the light infantry fortify the top of this hill. Take two field guns down to the neck and load with grape, just in case those bastards have a notion to return."

Too tired to stand, Howe sat down on the stone wall. The sky in the west turned pink as the sun began to sink behind a cluster of cumulus clouds. A cool breeze broke the heat of the day.

"Major Wilkens," he called out to the only marine officer left unwounded.

"Sir?"

"Have the marines pick up the wounded and take them down to the ferry landing. The surgeons from Somerset are waiting at the dock. I want a burying detail."

"The American dead, sir?"

"Bury them."

"And our dead?"

"Shroud them and dig a pit at Morton's Point. Tell Hallsbury we shall want a service tomorrow. For the officers."

General Pigot appeared. "We have thirty-one prisoners, most of them wounded."

"Put them in Boston jail."

"They're almost all of them wounded, some badly. Can we spare a surgeon?"

"Leave that to Captain Loring. The little swine's our jailer now, and if he can find a surgeon in Boston, let him tend them. We can't spare a surgeon. What is our toll, Pigot? Do you have any kind of a count?"

"Not yet. I'll make a guess. Almost three hundred dead and perhaps a thousand wounded, most badly. You don't live with a bullet in the gut. We've taken almost fifty percent casualties."

Howe closed his eyes for a moment and shook his head. "The grenadiers?" he whispered.

"Seven of them survived unwounded."

"I wonder," Howe said, almost to himself, "has there ever been a battle like this?"

"It's a victory," Clinton said flatly.

Burgoyne joined them and said, "I'll write the report. They don't count the dead in London. They'll have torchlight parades." And to Clinton, half-mockingly: "Sir Henry, you'll be Lord Henry before your knighthood arrives."

"Go to hell," Clinton said.

"Get on with it," Sir William told them harshly. "I want the wounded out of here before dark."

Colonel Prescott and General Putnam organized a defense line across the Charlestown neck, about two hundred yards from the British line. Like the British, Prescott ordered the single cannon available to be loaded with grape to face the enemy. But on neither side was there any plan or desire to attack. The battle was over. The British held Charlestown peninsula, and Prescott's feeling was: Good riddance and be damned!

Prescott's body cried out for sleep and rest, but he had one more task before this day was over. He found his horse, thanked the young militiaman who had taken the responsibility for the officers' horses, and rode to Clement House on Willis Creek, where, he had been told, the Committee of Safety was meeting. Prescott stormed into the holding room of Clement House, where he found Artemus Ward seated at a table with Dr. Benjamin Church and Thomas Gardner, maps spread out in front of them, and a young clerk at the end of the table.

They all looked up in astonishment at the appearance of Prescott, the big man covered with blood and dirt, his shirt hanging in shreds, three days' growth of beard on his face. He stalked over to the table, leaned across it, grabbed Artemus Ward by his jabot, and snarled, "You filthy, scabrous bastard. I ought to kill you."

"Let go of me, sir." Ward's voice was a squeak of anger mixed with fear. "How dare you."

Prescott flung Ward back in his seat.

"What is the meaning of this?" Gardner cried. "Have you lost your senses, Colonel Prescott?"

"Come to them, come to them!" And to Ward: "Why did you do it, you lousy wretch? Who paid you? What price did you get for our blood? Three hundred of the best men in this army—men whose boots you're not fit to lick—are dead on Breed's Hill. We pleaded for help, and you let us die."

"Get hold of yourself, sir," Dr. Church said. "You are talking to your commanding general."

"You fuckin' little toad!" Prescott snarled, turning on Church. "Sitting here on your ass while my men bleed to death! Get out of here and do your duty before I kill you. Out!" He dragged Church from his chair and flung him across the room. Church fought for his footing and then fled through the door.

"Oh, this is unseemly, sir," Gardner cried.

"I had to think of my army," Ward pleaded, cowed now. "My army came first. Supposed the British had attacked us at Roxbury? What then?"

"You dare to say that to me. The whole damned British army was there on Breed's Hill. And you dare to plead the defense of Roxbury.

Well, sir, I am not finished with you. Be thankful that I don't draw my pistol and kill you where you sit. More will be said on this subject."

"I am your superior officer," Ward wailed.

"You are shit, sir," Prescott told him, and then Prescott turned on his heel and left.

"We must find you a horse," Feversham said to Gonzales as the wounded were being laid, as gently as possible, in carts that had been brought to the Charlestown neck. Two houses in Cambridge had been converted into hospitals, and Feversham had been told that there were eight doctors already present and waiting to help.

"Yes," Feversham told Gonzales, "just as there were twelve thousand militia waiting for a few hundred men to hold the British. It's an interesting world, Doctor." They walked down the road to where a group of boys had tended to the officers' horses. Feversham found his horse and explained the situation.

"Lieutenant Berry from Marblehead, he's dead," one of the boys said. "We'll be sending his horse back home, but if the doctor here needs a horse, he can have it and deliver it to Marblehead when he's finished with it. Jack Berry. They'll know him there."

"We'll get it to Marblehead," Feversham assured him.

Both Feversham and Gonzales were stripped to the waist, having torn their shirts into bandages. Head to foot, they were covered with blood and dirt, both of them with their instrument bags hanging from their shoulders. In the milling crowd of militiamen who had crossed the Charlestown neck, sweating, most of them naked to the waist, they brought a worshiping respect from the boys. Women were present with bottles of water and pots of coffee. News and details of the battle had already spread through the area around Boston. The tired, limping Americans were the heroes of the moment, and as the sun began to set, people with torches lit up the area around Willis Creek, talking excitedly, asking questions.

Major Knowlton sought out the two doctors and shook Gonzales's hand warmly. "We'll be making an army out of this, Doctor," he said. "This is no time for details, but if I have a command, I want you with me."

Gonzales nodded. Evidently the thought of a regular army had never occurred to him. After he mounted Jack Berry's horse and rode alongside of Feversham on the road to Cambridge, he spoke of the offer to Feversham. "What do you think?" he asked Feversham. "Will they make an army?"

"Who knows? They don't appear to have any leader who knows what to do now."

"Prescott?"

Feversham shrugged. He had trouble keeping his eyes open, and a moment or two later, he dozed off. Their horses didn't need guidance. They moved along with the crowd of carts and men on foot headed toward Cambridge. As night fell, men with torches joined the procession, lighting the way. The summer night air was warm and benign, so neither man suffered from his nakedness.

Awakened from his doze, Feversham gave into the man's need to speak.

"You were sleeping," Gonzales apologized.

"I could fall off my horse. It's happened to me."

"No. You ride too well. Feversham, I never saw a man killed before. I never saw a battle."

"The first time is hard."

"You've seen battles?"

"Yes."

"Like this one?"

Feversham thought about it before he replied. "No. Not like this one."

"Someone wins, someone loses."

"So they say."

"Feversham, who won and who lost?" And when Feversham rode on without replying, Gonzales said, "Did they win?"

"I don't know."

"I stood behind Major Knowlton's line when the men with the great hats attacked."

"The grenadiers."

"I couldn't take my eyes away. They marched up to us, and we shot them down. Then the next rank stepped forward, and we shot them down. Then they walked over the bodies of the dead, and we shot them down. Then the whole place in front of us was covered with their bodies, and they walked over the bodies of their own men, and we shot them down."

Feversham could think of nothing to say.

"I have been trying to understand," Gonzales said, almost plaintively.

"There's no understanding," Feversham said.

"When our men were frightened and ran, Prescott let them run."

"Yes."

"But the grenadiers. They didn't."

"No, Doctor," Feversham said tiredly, "if the grenadiers had turned their backs on us, they would have been shot by their own men."

Israel Putnam walked slowly along the Cambridge Road, leading his horse and debating with himself whether it would be reasonable to strangle Artemus Ward with his naked hands. He didn't climb into the saddle, for he was convinced that if he tried to ride, he would fall asleep and fall out of the saddle and break his neck. The adulation of the militiamen who recognized him in the darkness was pleasant, but he would have preferred at this time to be left alone. He knew that he should be doing something to pull the Connecticut volunteers together into some kind of order, but he couldn't bring himself to take any positive action. He was naked to the waist, his shirt having gone the way of other shirts, and the night air was cool. Finally, he tethered his horse to one hand, took his field blanket from the saddle, wrapped himself in it, and stretched out on the roadside. In a few moments, he was asleep.

Gridley found Elizabeth Warren, Dr. Warren's wife, at the Palmers' house. She was a good-looking woman of thirty years, with bright blue eyes and a head of soft, honey-colored hair. She and her husband had a house in Boston, now occupied by the British. She pleaded with Gridley for a shred of hope.

"It's no use to hope, Mrs. Warren," Gridley told her. "I was there beside him."

"And you saw it?"

"Yes."

"Then tell me. I must know."

"Isn't it enough to know that he died?"

She shook her head. She whispered, "Why was he there when he was so sick?"

"He had to be there."

"I must know, Colonel Gridley."

Gridley, tired, weak from loss of blood, said unhappily, "He was shot in the head. I killed the man who killed him. He died without pain."

"But where is his body?"

"In the redoubt, ma'am, where he fell."

"You left him there?"

"We were overwhelmed. They poured into the redoubt, and it was either get out or be killed. We had shot away our ammunition, and they came at us with their bayonets. We were only a handful."

"But how can I bury him?"

"We'll try to take that up with General Gage. I trust someone will, tomorrow."

Jacob Bother, fifteen years old, and Levi Goodson, fourteen, were both Boston boys, distantly related to Dr. Warren. At ten o'clock on the night of the seventeenth, they took an old rowboat that was beached on the Mystic River and quietly paddled to the shore of the Charlestown peninsula, landing on the rocky ledge where John Stark and his New Hampshire riflemen had made their line of defense. Their intention, as they afterward confessed, was to find the body of Joseph Warren and bring it back for burial. Since they were well aware that their mission would have been forbidden, they told no one of their intention.

After landing and anchoring their boat with a rock, they made their way up Breed's Hill toward the redoubt. As they climbed the hill, they saw the flaming torches of the British soldiers, who were still looking for their own dead. They advanced carefully, crawling sometimes. Once they lay absolutely still as a couple of British soldiers passed within a few feet of them. Finally, they reached the redoubt.

There were four dead bodies lying in the redoubt, one of them a black man. Now the moonlight, which had been blocked by clouds, was sufficient for them to recognize the body of Dr. Warren. He lay naked, stripped of all his clothes, his body stained with blood and dirt.

By now the boys, who had started their mission with a high sense of excitement and purpose, were thoroughly frightened. Crouched in the redoubt, they saw torches all around them, and for at least an hour they were trapped where they were, not daring to leave the redoubt. They were gagging and vomiting at the sight of one of the dead militiamen, whose chest and stomach had been ripped wide open. To make matters worse, rats were scampering about, eating the flesh of the dead. They crouched quietly and prayed that no soldier would enter the redoubt.

When the torches finally moved away, they tried to lift the body of Dr. Warren over the port entry. For all of his apparent slenderness, Dr. Warren had been over six feet in height, with wide shoulders and large bones. Rigor mortis had already set in. As much as they struggled, they only managed to lift the body to the firing step when they saw torches approaching up the hill. At that point, their courage failed them, and they tumbled out of the redoubt and ran down the hillside to where their boat was tethered. They pushed off the shore and paddled back up the Mystic River.

Fame, fortune, and the fulfillment of a dream come to people along various avenues, and Joshua Loring was not the first to achieve his ambition through a marriage to a woman who despised him but cherished his wealth. Not only could he boast of his rank as captain in His Majesty's armed forces, but here he was wearing the red coat, the white britches, and the high black boots of a British officer, not to mention a dress sword by his side. Along with his uniform, a detachment of six British marines was his to command, as well as Sergeant Perkins to relay his orders to the ordinary enlisted men.

At seven o'clock, on the seventeenth of June, Capt. Joshua Loring received thirty-one American prisoners of war on a dock in Boston, brought there by lighter from Breed's Hill. All of them were wounded, some so badly they could hardly walk. When Sergeant Perkins suggested that litters might be found for the most sorely wounded, Capt. Loring replied that they had come to the battle on foot and they would damn well walk to jail. One of the prisoners, Caleb Johnson, was supporting Col. Moses Parker, who had been seriously wounded with a musket ball that shattered his kneecap in the struggle in the redoubt. Each step was agony for him. Johnson, who had kept a chicken farm in Dorchester, had often sold fresh eggs to the Loring household. He had a nodding acquaintance with Joshua Loring. Now he pleaded, "For God's sake, Mr. Loring, this man can't walk. Show some mercy."

Loring specified his rank with a blow across Johnson's face. "*Captain* Loring, you rebellious son of a bitch!"

Then he led his contingent of thirty-one wounded men through the streets of Boston to the jail, a trail of blood marking their passage.

At eleven o'clock, on the night of the seventeenth of June, Sir William Howe was cleansing himself of dirt and perspiration in the anteroom of his commodious bedroom. His personal orderly, Dick Higbe, had filled the tub with hot water and then had been sent packing by Mrs. Loring, with instructions that they were not to be disturbed for any reason whatsoever before ten o'clock on the morning of the following day.

General Howe was a large man, and the tub, typical of the time, was rather small, so he sat in it with his knees drawn up while Betsy Loring soaped him and gently sponged the various parts of his abundant body.

"Not even a scratch anywhere on your dear body," she observed. "Here I died a thousand deaths and you not even one."

"Oh, say not so."

"True, true. And when they brought the news that your wonderful grenadiers had suffered so, I fell into a faint. I cried out for death to overtake me."

"Forgive me for causing you such pain, my darling, and if you continue to wash that part of me, we shall waste what has been waiting for you all this terrible day."

"What strength," she said admiringly. "What wonderful strength and fortitude!"

"You give it to me, my love," he replied gallantly.

"You were in God's hands."

"I find no other explanation. A thousand men took aim at me. Every gallant officer in my grenadiers fell, and I was unharmed. There are ten rents in my clothes where the musket balls tore through, yet my skin—"

"You have the skin of a young man."

"What have I done to deserve God's favor?"

"Something noble," Mrs. Loring assured him. "You were a mountain of courage. God rewards courage."

"My darling Betsy," he said gently, lifting her hand away, "don't deprive me of what we should share."

"How very well said, Sir William. I have always been of the opinion that a proper man makes love with his speech as well as his hands—"

"Hands?"

"Would you want me to speak less delicately?"

"Say what you will, in prose or poesy."

"If all the world and love were young," she said softly, "and truth in every shepherd's tongue, / these pretty pleasures might me move, / to live with thee and be thy love."

"You quote me Raleigh," he said, surprised.

"You thought me no more than an ignorant wench, Sir William" she replied, feigning hurt.

"Never!"

"And ignorant of the finer things."

"Never, my dear Betsy. Enough, now. Help me out of this miserable little tub."

He stood up, and she folded the towels around him.

"And now to bed," she said. "Give me a moment and I will be with you."

At midnight, Feversham and Gonzales were still at work in the big holding room of Rev. Samuel Cook. Mrs. Cook had found them clean shirts. Almost three hundred of the militia had been wounded, and the men lay on the floor in the holding room, the adjoining parlor, and the dining room. Three doctors and two leeches were already at work when Feversham and Gonzales arrived, all five of them part of the group Feversham had spoken to earlier. They were full of explanation as to why they had not appeared in Charlestown. They were reluctant to probe for bullets, and only two of them had ever sewn with catgut.

By midnight, Feversham's hands were shaking with fatigue. He had come to the end of his strength. Feversham said to Mrs. Cook, "I don't think Dr. Gonzales and I can do anymore. We must rest."

"Poor man, of course," Mrs. Cook agreed.

"The worst are taken care of, and these doctors can do for the others. If there's a place where we can lie down . . ."

A comfortable, motherly woman, she clucked with sympathetic sounds and offered to feed them. They shook their heads. "Only sleep, please, Mrs. Cook."

She led them upstairs to a tiny room where a small boy lay on a trundle bed. "Every other place is taken. Can you sleep on the floor here? There is a chamber pot, if you need it."

"The child?" Feversham wondered.

"You won't wake him." She spread a quilt on the floor. "It's a warm night. Will you want a blanket?"

Feversham shook his head.

She left them, and the two men pulled off their boots and lay down on the quilt. Feversham fell asleep almost instantly, but for the next hour, Gonzales stared into the darkness. Then he, too, slept.

June 18, 8:00 A.M.

*E*van Feversham awakened in response to a gentle pressure on his shoulder and a soft whisper in his ear. He opened his eyes to a room lit by diffused morning light and saw Mrs. Cook bending over him. "Forgive me, Dr. Feversham," she said softly, "for waking you when you need your rest so much, but Abraham Watson is downstairs and says he must see you."

Gonzales, sprawled facedown on the floor, still slept. Feversham struggled to his feet, every muscle in his body aching. He told Mrs. Cook that he would be downstairs in a moment or two, wondering who Abraham Watson might be. She whispered in his ear that Mr. Watson was a member of the Committee of Safety. This information puzzled Feversham, since the day before, on Breed's Hill, he had not heard a good word spoken about the Committee of Safety.

He came downstairs a few minutes later, rubbing his beard and wondering where he might shave and from whom he might borrow a razor, or did he have one in his saddlebags? He was met by a tall, gray-haired man of middle age whom Mrs. Cook introduced as Mr. Watson. They went through the holding room, still crowded with wounded men, some asleep, some awake and in pain, to a table in the yard outside. There they found a crowd of men, women and boys, relatives of wounded and missing men, as well as militiamen, with their muskets slung over their shoulders, women desperate to find their husbands, boys and girls who should have been in school but were a part of the general disruption.

Watson motioned to the bench at the table, and Mrs. Watson brought them two steaming mugs of coffee.

"I have heard good things about you, Feversham," Watson told him. "Prescott says you are not a fearful man."

Feversham gathered that this was praise in spite of Watson's misuse of the term. "If you mean that I am courageous, let me disabuse you."

"I like a man who will not speak well of himself. Let me get to the point. They have taken a round number of our men prisoner, exactly how many we don't know, but the indication is that most of them were wounded. The committee chose me to go to Boston with a white flag and to plead a doctor's attendance to our men who are their prisoners. I am told that you are the best surgeon we have and that you have years of experience with military wounds. Will you come with me?"

Feversham felt a cold chill in his heart, and he took a long moment before he said, "I am British, you know."

"I know that," Watson said. "Do you think you might be recognized?"

"I don't know. I have never met any of the officers whose names I heard spoken, and it is full seven years since I left the British army."

"If you refuse, I shall understand."

"The trouble is," Feversham said ruefully, "if I refuse, will I understand?"

"Sir?"

"I would want to shave," he said, rubbing his beard, "and find my horse and my instruments. It will be best if you do the talking. I feel a proper fool when I try to cover my accent. I'll want a jug of rum and a couple of skins of fresh water."

"Then you'll come with me?"

Feversham said, "I don't feel hopeful about it, but I'll come with you."

An hour later, Feversham, shaved and with a clean waistcoat, rode with Watson down the Boston turnpike, through Roxbury to the Boston neck. They led a third horse, loaded with water skins and jugs of rum. Where the land narrowed, at the edge of Roxbury, the American fortifications had been set up, a stone and dirt wall, with embrasures for five cannons, eight-pounder field pieces. The cannons were loaded with grapeshot, gun crews in attendance. In a field nearby, a large force of militia, at least two thousand men, were encamped. Feversham reflected that a hundred men could have defended the position. The sight of this army sitting around their cook fires or lounging in the shade of the trees evoked bitter memories of the day before. He felt a surge of anger at the thought of Ward's plea that he needed his army of twelve thousand men to keep the British bottled up in Boston, while less than a thousand fought to the death on Breed's Hill.

Captain Appleton, in command of the fortification, welcomed them without enthusiasm. "God's will that the bastards don't shoot you down. The gossip is that they've a raging hate for the damage done yesterday. Were you there, sir?"

"Dr. Feversham was on the hill," Watson said.

Captain Appleton voiced his admiration. Watson took a staff from the packhorse. A white banner was attached to the staff. Watson anchored the pole in his stirrup, and the two men rode through the opening in the wall, on across the Boston neck. For a quarter of a mile there was nothing but marsh grass and sea gulls, and then, suddenly, the British fortification came into view, a few hundred yards down the road, rock and sand and cannons, houses beyond the wall, and the cross of St. George flapping in the breeze. They walked their horses slowly, coming into view, and drew up forty or fifty feet from the fortification. They could see the faces of soldiers now and the place in the wall where a gate had been constructed.

They sat on their horses and waited.

"What now?" Watson wondered. He was a calm man, Abraham Watson, not an easy thing when there was a reasonable chance that the British might decide to blow them out of existence. "Will they let us sit here and ignore us?"

"Or kill us."

"Do you think so, Doctor? I have heard that they abide by the rules of engagement. We come under a white flag."

Still, they sat and waited.

"I think," Feversham said, "that a captain or possibly a lieutenant would be in command here at the gate. He'd probably decide that it's not his to judge, and he would send someone back for a higher rank. They'll guess that we're here for the prisoners, and there would be some talk on that score." He took out his watch and looked at it. "If only we had something to bargain with."

"They have a sense of decency."

"What makes you think so?" Feversham asked. "It comes down to class, doesn't it? A gentleman deals with a gentleman. It's their credo. We don't have a knight, a lord, or a duke among us."

"I consider myself a gentleman," Watson said. "I consider you a gentleman."

"That's generous of you," Feversham replied.

And still they sat and waited.

"Should we ride up to the gate?" Watson wondered.

"I don't think so. They might consider that a provocation."

"Or dismount?"

"No!" Feversham said sharply. "Please, sir, do not think of those bastards as men of honor. If they should take it into their heads to shoot us down, we have a chance on horse." He looked at his watch again. "Ten minutes."

"Can they ignore us?"

"I don't think so. Plain curiosity will bring them out sooner or later. For all they know, we come to surrender the whole army."

"Really, Doctor?"

"It would not be inconceivable. Mr. Watson, when you introduce us, would you call me Dr. Smith? It's a long chance, but someone might recognize my name."

"Of course. I should have thought of that. If they did recognize you, what then?"

"They'd take me and hang me," Feversham said simply.

"God willing, they won't."

Looking at his watch, Feversham said, "Twenty minutes."

The gate opened, and two men on horseback rode through, walked their horses up to a point a few feet from Feversham and Watson, but made no move to dismount. They wore the red coats and cocked hats of the light infantry. From the insignia, Feversham recognized one as a major and the other as a captain.

"I am Major Butler," the senior officer said coldly. "This is Captain Selkirk. What business do you have with us? Have you come to surrender?"

Feversham's lips twitched in spite of himself.

"I am Abraham Watson, member of the Committee of Safety, and this is Dr. Smith."

"We recognize no Committee of Safety, Mr. Watson."

"Nevertheless," Watson said evenly, "I represent the patriot army which holds Boston in siege."

"I know of no patriot army, as you call it. A mob of lawless men hold this neck of land until we see fit to sweep them aside."

"Will you allow me to state my case, Major?"

"If you wish. Tell me why you have come here under a flag of surrender?"

"It is a flag of truce, sir."

"Whatever," Major Butler said.

"Would you be kind enough to tell me how many Americans you hold as prisoners?"

Major Butler took a few moments before he answered. "Thirty-one," he said.

"Many of them, I presume, are wounded?"

No reply.

"Major Butler," Watson said, "I speak not of war now but of human suffering and Christian mercy."

"A mob that resisted the lawful progress of British troops on British soil can hardly speak of mercy."

"I will not argue legalities, sir," Watson said softly. "I ask only that you allow Dr. Smith here and myself to give medical aid to brave soldiers who fought under the rule and orders of the Continental Congress, which is convened in Philadelphia and was duly elected by the American people. Like the soldiers of the king, they are enlisted and did their duty."

"I recognize no Continental Congress," Major Butler said shortly.

"Will you allow Dr. Smith to attend their wounds?"

"That is impossible."

Watson took a deep breath. Watching him, Feversham had new respect for his restraint and courage.

"Major Butler," Watson said, "there are rules and practices of civilized warfare."

"Warfare, Mr. Watson? A mob of criminal bandits resisted arrest and fired upon the king's troops. If you wish to render medical aid, you can surrender yourselves and join these criminals in Boston jail."

"Is that you last word, sir?"

"It is."

Watson turned to Feversham. "Come, Doctor. There is no more to say to these men."

They drew their reins and turned their horses. After a few paces, Feversham said, "Slowly, sir. Don't let those bastards see us run."

They rode along the Boston neck, back to the American barricade.

In the early evening of that day, having found himself a bed and shelter in the home of Rev. Gideon Cooper, at Cambridge, and having completed his rounds of the wounded, Dr. Evan Feversham sat down to write to his wife. Reverend Cooper was kind enough to offer the use of his desk and his study. Feversham, shaved and bathed and moderately rested, was able to contemplate, more or less objectively, what he had been through during the past few days.

"My dear and beloved Alice," he wrote.

I have written to you a few days ago—it seems like months— but I am afraid the letter is lost. In any case, now, on the evening of the eighteenth, I am well and whole, unwounded by the grace of God, although what I have done to deserve such fortune, I do not know. If God is love, as my mother used to tell me, then perhaps my love for you defended me, although in all truth I struggle mightily for any belief.

When I came to Boston and to this army of militia that surrounds it, I was taken into the trust and confidence of a wise and thoughtful man, Joseph Warren by name, a physician, who won

me immediately not only by his grace and courage but by agree-
ing with me that raw liquor poured into a wound, in spite of the
pain it causes at the moment, will prevent festering, but you know
my arguments on that score. In the few hours I knew Dr. Warren,
we became close, a kind of closeness that binds men in battle. He
is so loved by the Boston folk and the people hereabout that they
made him a sort of honorary commander of the army, but he went
into the redoubt built here on Breed's Hill as an ordinary soldier
and surgeon, and there he died. Two brave boys who climbed the
hill, slipping past the British, found his body, stripped naked, and
it lies in some nameless grave, tossed there by our enemies.

I speak of Warren thus because I recall how often you would
accuse me of being cynical and disbelieving, in God as well as
other things, but all I know at this moment is that I have been witness to such nobility and courage on the part of plain people as I
have never known and also witness to a terrible display of the
madness we call war.

The town of Boston here is a peninsula, and alongside of it,
separated by half a mile of water, is another peninsula called
Charlestown. Of course, you have heard of both these places, but
they were new to me. The British had occupied this peninsula, a
hilly piece of land a half a mile wide and about a mile long, which
overlooks Boston town, and then for some reason, they abandoned it, and the Committee of Safety decided to occupy it and
mount guns on the hills, which would have made Boston town
untenable for the British.

But instead of placing a significant part of their militia army on
the hills of Charlestown, they sent a few hundred men to build a
redoubt and hold the main hill, Breed's Hill, as it is called, while
the main American army, perhaps thirteen thousand men or more,
remained camped around Boston. There are at least eighteen surgeons and leeches with the militia, but only four, including
myself, were willing to join the defenders of Breed's Hill. Two of
them, Dr. Warren and a brave Welshman named Bones, died in
the fight on the hill. The other surgeon, Gonzales, who comes
from Providence, survived. How I survived without even a
scratch, I do not know. Perhaps God took mercy on a disbeliever
and answered your prayers. Gonzales, who is a Jew, did his duty
with quiet courage. I must say that he is highly regarded here, so

different from the hatred directed against those people in Europe. The British, who, I am told, have some three thousand men in Boston, used almost their entire army in the attack upon the few hundred men who held the peninsula, and in spite of all the pleading of Colonel Prescott, who led the defense, and Gen. Israel Putnam from Connecticut, Artemus Ward, the commander of the militia, refused to reinforce them, an act of either filthy treachery or monumental stupidity. The battle for the hills, which lasted only a few hours, was the bloodiest and most awful conflict I have ever witnessed. The British lost fully half of their army in dead and wounded, and the militia losses were equally awful, an agony which makes me shudder even as I write. It was a battle with no victor, only death and suffering, as terrible and senseless as war ever is. The position and expectations of the militia army are no better or worse than before the battle took place. The leaders of the few hundred men who defended the hills, a Col. William Prescott, a man named John Stark from New Hampshire, Maj. Thomas Knowlton, an engineer by the name of Richard Gridley, and old Putnam fought with the kind of cool courage that defies description, putting me to shame with my own fears and doubts.

I have always hated war, feeling that the settlement of a dispute by killing those who disagree makes us little better than animals. Our presumed Christianity is washed away in the insanity of our decisions, and precious reason and compassion, which are all that makes us human, are cast aside. This morning, I was persuaded by a member of the Committee of Safety, one Abraham Watson, to go with him to the British lines in Boston and plead with the British to allow me to attend the wounds of the thirty-one prisoners they have taken. It was a piece of gross stupidity for me to allow myself to be persuaded, for the British would have surely hanged me had I been recognized as a onetime surgeon under British orders and oath, but shame and pride made me go with him. The British officers we met sneered at our request and damned us as a band of outlaws. So much for Christian compassion.

Forgive me, my dear, my bitterness. In time I will wake up from this nightmare and be my old self. I trust I will return to Ridgefield and be with you within the fortnight. I must, for the

time being, stay with our wounded. There are a great many of
them, and they desperately need what crude care I can offer. After
that, we shall see what the future brings out of this strange rebellion. Meanwhile, I reassure you that my health is good and my
love for you is undiminished.

    I remain, your loving husband,
      Evan Feversham

Afterword

While this account of what has come to be remembered as the Battle of Bunker Hill is cast in dramatic form and while I have taken certain dramatic license, I have attempted to hew as closely to the known facts as possible. As with any event of this kind, there are many contradictory accounts, and one must simply choose that which appears most likely. I have come to this view with a lifetime of colonial study and writing behind me, and in all cases I have tried to strike a balance between what would be archaic and what would be modern. I have used modern spelling for the convenience of the reader, as for instance, spelling gaol as jail. To avoid confusion, I omitted the names of many minor characters in this drama.

For those readers who are curious as to the subsequent role of the major characters, I submit the following:

Col. William Prescott continued as a leading officer of General Washington's army through the Revolution. A solid, loyal, unshakable man, he was valued and honored.

Col. John Stark and his New Hampshire riflemen became the stuff of legend. Again and again, they held a lost field, and Stark emerged from the war with honor.

Maj. Thomas Knowlton gained an enviable reputation for cool thinking under fire. Washington increasingly depended upon him, and when Knowlton was killed in the battle for New York, Washington wept. His death was a great loss to the American struggle.

Richard Gridley was promoted to major general, called upon again and again for problems of engineering. He was with the army through the war.

Artemus Ward is little remembered. After the battle at Breed's Hill, he was removed from his command. He had a curious background, the son of a man who became wealthy in the slave trade (not at all uncommon among New Englanders) and a man old and sick in his middle years. Along with Samuel Adams, he was a radical leader in Boston. He bore much of the blame for the tragedy at Breed's Hill.

Joshua Loring had the distinction of becoming the most hated and vilified man in the British forces. His corruption defies description. When the British decided to evacuate Boston and make their base in New York, he asked for and received the privilege of auctioning the valuables taken from American homes. He was put in command of the notorious Brison prison ships in New York harbor, and it is said that he was responsible for more American deaths in his prison ships than were killed in battle. At the end of the war, he went to England, where he disappeared from history.

Loring's wife, Elizabeth Loring, stayed with Gen. William Howe until he was recalled to England and then went with him as his mistress. We are told that Howe never flagged in his adoration of her. Howe was so utterly absorbed by his affair with Elizabeth Loring that he became indifferent to the pursuit of the war. By the spring of 1778, his affair had become an international disgrace and he was recalled to England, to be replaced by Sir Henry Clinton. It was said that he never fully recovered from the slaughter of his grenadiers on Breed's Hill.

Gen. Thomas Gage was recalled to London after the battle. It was said that without his insensitivity and intransigence, the war might have been avoided. He was held responsible for the raid on Concord and the battle on Breed's Hill.

General Burgoyne—Gentleman Johnny—was trapped by General Gates at Saratoga in 1777 and surrendered his army of fifty-seven hundred men to the Americans. He decidedly revised his opinion of the military qualities of the Yankees.

Dr. Benjamin Church was tried for treason before the Massachusetts general court. He was found guilty of treason and sent to jail. Attempts were made to break into the jail and lynch him. Eventually, he was exiled to the West Indies. The schooner which carried him in that direction went down in a storm. So ended his life and his career.

Dr. Joseph Warren's body was found by a British burial party the day after the battle. He was buried in an unmarked grave.

Papers found in the redoubt by the British incriminated John Lovell, who had brought the information about the battle to Prescott. He was jailed by the British. Eventually, he was exchanged for a British prisoner. The influence of his father, one of the most important Tories, saved him from hanging.

All of these events occurred even as the Continental Congress formally and legally created an American army, appointing George Washington as its commander in chief. But this battle at Breed's Hill and Bunker Hill took place before the news came to Boston.

As for the British occupation of Boston, after a halfhearted attempt to break the American encirclement with the badly battered remaining British troops, both General Gage and General Howe concluded that the Americans were serious in their uprising, that a vastly larger force was required, and that the central embarkation point should be New York rather than Boston. In March 1776, the British fleet sailed out of the Boston Harbor. Four months later, the British had assembled in New York harbor an army of more than thirty thousand men and the largest congregation of British warships ever brought together.

ABOUT THE AUTHOR

Howard Fast is the author of over seventy novels, including eight dealing with the American Revolution—among them the classic *Citizen Tom Paine* and *April Morning*—making him our preeminent novelist in this area. His other writings include children's books, short stories, plays, biographies, and, under the pseudonym E. V. Cunningham, detective and police novels. He lives in Greenwich, Connecticut.